T0266426

profound
and perfect
things

profound
and perfect
things

A NOVEL

MARIBEL GARCIA

She Writes Press, a BookSparks imprint
A Division of SparkPointStudio, LLC.

*Dedicated to everyone
whose "Plan A" did not work.*

Published 2019

Printed in the United States of America

ISBN: 978-1-63152-541-4
ISBN: 978-1-63152-542-1
Library of Congress Control Number: 2018962241

For information, address:
She Writes Press
1569 Solano Ave #546
Berkeley, CA 94707
She Writes Press is a division of SparkPoint Studio, LLC.

prologue

I didn't realize it then, but I started to hate Cristina immediately after it happened. She's my sister, I know. And I should have known better, but we are equally guilty. I know she feels ugly about what we did, but hands down, I am the one who has suffered the most. For years, I have been polite, circumspect, and professional like the lawyer I am. I have been forced to keep my distance. Physically and emotionally.

It's taken me years to come to this decision. I have thought about it long and hard, but the truth must be told. Empathy, sympathy, family ties, and obligation. Always putting others' needs before my own. No more. Tonight, after Mom and Dad's big anniversary party, I am going to talk to them. I am going to talk to Mom and Cristina. Dad will eventually find out. I cannot continue to harbor these feelings toward my only sister. It's not right, and I don't like it. I want us to be a family again. Maybe among the three of us, we can figure it out. Because I can't live with this any longer. I just can't.

PART ONE

chapter 1–Cristina

Rio Chico, TX
2003

Grief demands an answer, but sometimes there isn't one. The more Cristina looked for answers, the more questions she had—without them, she couldn't heal. Her mother disagreed. "*Sabes que, hija?*" You know what? "You are not going to find any. *El chiste es saber como vivir sin ellos.*" The trick to getting on with life is learning how to live without answers.

∼

After weeks of trying to gently coax her anguished daughter out of her self-imposed exile, Beatriz had decided to intervene. She used her key, barged into her daughter's home, and marched straight into her bedroom. She yanked the covers off her grown daughter's head and flung them across the room. If she wanted them back, she would have to get up. She threw the dark curtains open and watched her daughter turn away from the harsh light of day. Beatriz's voice was both stern and gravelly. "Get up. Get dressed. Eat something! Do something, anything!" Cristina went from startled to indignant in seconds. "*Ama?* What are you doing?"

"I can't just let you lie there."

"*Ama*, you have no idea."

"*Hija*, no one is saying that it doesn't hurt. It's called suffering, and I can't make it right. Trust me, if I could trade places with you, *criatura*, I would. Anything to ease your pain."

"I can't live like this."

"Yes you can and you will. It's happened. This is part of who you are now."

"So what do I do?" Cristina had said through her sobbing.

"You join the living, that's what you do. You start by making something to eat, washing your plate, and then putting it away. Then you do it again. You do the little things a hundred times until it hurts less. It's the only way human beings can protect themselves from themselves."

❧

Fortunately even the most insurmountable problems don't stay problems for long. They go away. Months had now passed since her mother's intervention. Cristina was healing from the loss, no longer paralyzed by it. She was buoyed by the new life inside her. It was a significant risk, but it had happened without them even trying. Their first two babies hadn't made it, and when she stopped asking why, the answer had come. Bad things just happen. She still felt the loss, but grief was now punctuated by intense emotions so profound and perfect that they were not to be questioned, just felt. Her pregnancy was the only thing that mattered now.

Having gone through too many periods of self-neglect during the months when she was deeply depressed, Cristina had sometimes spent whole days in stained clothing and unwashed hair. She was a new person now; she had slowly fallen back into her old routine, the daily ritual that involved, in addition to her regular ablutions, "*prettifying*" herself. It was the word her husband always used. She needed to get back into the custom of not walking out of the house until she looked in the mirror and liked what she saw, because if she wanted to return to the old Cristina, feeling good meant looking perfect, and that usually involved makeup and thoughtfully styled hair.

With her mother in tow, Cristina circled the parking lot for the second time. Gripping the wheel tightly and scanning the lot for a space, she quietly reminded herself to be appreciative. Of all things. What did her favorite blogger always write about? Gratitude. Having been unable to muster gratitude when she needed it, she was making it a habit now. She was grateful for hot water in her morning shower and coffee pots with automatic timers. She was thankful that the only problems she had right now were confined to minor issues, like her inability to find a parking space, and the excessive South Texas heat.

She was ready to face the world, and in Rio Chico, the hub of that world lay on the outskirts of their small border town. It was the Walmart Super Center where townspeople could enjoy both leisurely shopping and socializing. It was where you went to see and be seen, and if you were a local, you could probably play the Kevin Bacon game and find that you were linked by six or fewer acquaintances with anyone in the store.

On the third try, Cristina and her mother finally found a spot. Unfortunately, it was on the outside perimeter of the parking lot, far enough that they could see what appeared to be pools of water some distance ahead, asphalt mirages brought on by the crushing heat. Beads of perspiration pooled on their foreheads, and Cristina could feel the makeup melting off and her freshly blow-dried hair frizzing up. She trudged slowly to the store to look at clothes for her baby—the one Cristina hoped would live—while impatiently urging her mother to move faster.

⋰

When Cristina was younger, she had struggled to keep up with her mother on account of Beatriz being disturbingly tall.

It wasn't every day that you saw five-foot-eleven-inch Mexican women. Today, however, her mother's thick, long legs were slower than usual. The heat was slowing her down. And maybe it was just Cristina's imagination, but she also seemed to be putting on more weight. It seemed like an eternity before they reached the store's heavy automated doors and were swallowed up by the store's blast of icy, cool air. The frigid climate inside made up for the apocalyptic, triple-digit temperatures outside. Looking out into a sea of every product known to man, the women could not resist its allure. They both wiped down their sweaty brows, grabbed a cart, and feeling invigorated, followed the glossy, white tiled paths before them.

To their immediate right was a display of "As Seen on TV" products. Next to a pyramid of items stood a clear glass bowl with a display board claiming that the Sham Wow could soak up spills and hold up to twenty times its weight in moisture. Neither of them could resist, so they both tried it out. Two minutes later, when their initial excitement had subsided, Cristina leaned on the cart and pushed it forward, already bored with the aisles of familiar mass-produced products.

The harsh bright lights of the store made her mother's skin look worn. She was in her sixties, and her sixties were by no means "the new forties." Unlike her father's dark skin, Beatriz's pale complexion had withered and hardened in the relentless South Texas sun. Beatriz was tall and had always carried her weight well, but these days, against everyone's advice, she was carrying way too much weight. On bad days, the diabetic sore that she swears is just a scratch bothers her and reminds her of her own mortality. It's a lifetime of honey buns, a dozen honey-glazed donuts (for less than the price of a yellow bell pepper), and jugs of generic grape soda. Anytime Cristina reminds her of her poor eating habits, Beatriz's response is always the same. *"Ay mija,* I'm too old to do anything about it. At this point in my life, what difference will it make to substitute a carrot for a cream-filled donut from Sotero's Bakery?"

Mateo, Cristina's father, wasn't any help either. The man had eaten the same meal for years and never gained a pound. Every morning, for as long as anyone could remember: *huevos rancheros*, beans, and leftover rice, always accompanied by three tortillas, a side of his own homemade salsa, coffee, and half a banana. Always half a banana.

Cristina could see her mother's worry wrinkles as they followed each other down aisle after aisle of discount "designer-style" outfits—enough to outfit a small village in the Yucatán. Beatriz had something on her mind; she was worried about her daughter, unsure whether this baby would be viable. Still, Cristina had warned her on the way out to the store, this was a positive trip. This baby, unlike the others, was going to live. Cristina just knew it; she felt it with her entire being.

She was going to someday hold a baby in her arms. This baby.

Ignoring the look on her mother's face, Cristina pulled a nice cream-colored cardigan from the rack. It was perfect for work. South Texas might be hot as hell, but inside most businesses, the AC always felt like the inside of an industrial-sized freezer.

Cristina wasn't yet showing, but it didn't stop her from making her way over to the small maternity-wear island, two lonely racks wedged between the baby section and the plus-sized wear. She wanted to look at clothing but didn't want to tempt fate. She was trying to decide whether to sort through the maternity T-shirts or move on when she was spotted by someone she did not want to see. It was Aidé, the daughter of her mother's second cousin Zoraida.

"Cristina! *Comó estás?*" called out Aidé, as she hugged and kissed Cristina's cheek, while simultaneously looking her up and down.

"*Bien, bien. Y tú?*" Cristina responded, not very enthusiastically, but self-consciously making a mental inventory of what
she was wearing. Aidé and her mother had recently moved in
with relatives in Rio Chico. Back home, across the border in
their native México, this mother-and-daughter duo had been
well-off. For years their family had looked down on Cristina
and her mother's family. They had been able to stay in Mexico
and live rather comfortably. They didn't have to scurry north
to eke out a living like common "wetbacks." But when their
drug-dealing patriarch was locked away in a Mexico City jail
and later accused of snitching, scurry they did. They left their
fancy homes and multiple cars to seek refuge from their enemies in the US.

Now the two were living with relatives in Rio Chico, but
instead of being humbled, they were as arrogant and preten-
tious as ever. Cristina was convinced that Aidé's mother had
always resented their carefree lifestyle. She had married a drug
dealer and inherited all of the problems that go with the lifestyle. She envied people who were free to come and go and who
were guilty of nothing. Cristina also suspected that it was due
to the way that her mother had always carried herself, proudly
and confidently. She wore her poor, working-class status like
a badge of honor. Still, it was Aidé and Zoraida's overly prying nature that always made her uneasy, that and their sidelong
glances of envy.

"Do you still live in El Valle Dorado?" asked Aidé.

"Yes, we are still there," answered Cristina, resisting the
urge to invite her out of obligation. In the past, none of Zoraida's
grown children who lived in Rio Chico had ever extended an
invitation, but when Zoraida's clan found out that Cristina
lived in a well-to-do neighborhood they were suddenly "close
kin" and not just distantly related.

Fortunately, Beatriz managed to exchange pleasantries

without feeling obligated to stay and chat. She quickly set a tone and expectation: their interaction would be brief. Beatriz politely exchanged a few words and then expertly maneuvered both of them out of the maternity section and over to a different part of the store, where they could still feel Aidé's gaze, looking them over, mulling over the details. The two were probably making a mental note of the brand names that Cristina wore or didn't wear, the quality of her makeup, while also noting that Beatriz's taste hadn't changed much. Still wearing one of her many faded knit pant sets, Beatriz had never felt the need to impress anyone and Cristina had, over the years, tried not to care about what people thought of her mother, but she did.

⚓

Then, almost as if she had been reading her daughter's mind, Beatriz led her over to the baby section. Together they pulled out one adorable baby outfit after another. From questionably themed leopard-print onesies with matching booties to pale blue cashmere-like sweaters for little boys, which featured Walmart's generic equivalent of the Polo logo. Together, Cristina and Beatriz moved from rack to rack, checking out outfits for every occasion, each more darling than the last. When they reached the shoes, Cristina couldn't resist. She reached out for a pair of size-zero knockoff Converse high tops in bright red and held them up.

"*Amá, mirá?* Can these shoes be any cuter?"

"*Ay, que cosas.* What will they think of next?"

"*Amá*—look at these!" Cristina exclaimed while holding up a similar pair of shoes in pink.

"Let's buy something."

Cristina had meant to purchase something on this trip: a new set of hand towels for the bathroom, toiletries. She'd even considered looking at a new shower curtain, but she had not, even for a minute, given any *real* consideration to getting something for the baby. It was one thing to think it, another to do it. Noting that Cristina was in over-thinking mode, Beatriz intervened.

"Don't even think about it, Cristina. What did you tell me back at the house? To think positively. If you keep thinking you are going to lose this child, you will. This baby needs all the encouragement and positive energy you can muster."

Cristina relaxed and thanked God for her mother. She may not have trusted her with her choice of food (or clothing), but she was wise on every other topic. Beatriz had given birth to both Cristina and her sister Isa after the age of thirty, a little over a year after being married. No one back in her native town in Mexico had ever expected to see her wed, much less become a mother. Relatives had dismissed this scenario on account of both her age and unusual height. She was Beatriz, plain and tall—and old, to boot. Mateo had come along and changed everything.

Beatriz knew what it was like to lose all hope. She had been down this road before. Cristina placed the shoes back on the shelf and selected a baby bluebird made out of soft, almost velvety plush. She caressed it against her cheek and pictured it in her child's hand. Her mother was right. She couldn't afford negativity.

Beatriz was the only person who truly believed that Cristina could be a mother. Cristina felt like everyone else had given up on her. Even her husband. Perhaps, sensing her daughter's thoughts, Beatriz asked, "How can any baby do well when their own mother doesn't believe they can?" And that was it. It was all that Cristina needed to brush all of her worries aside. *For the moment.*

ᴗ◢

Cristina had found their shopping expedition uplifting, and she carried the optimistic feeling around for days. She was full of energy, and even though no one else could see it, she could feel her belly growing. Leo, on the other hand, had misgivings. He tried to be happy for his wife, but he wasn't very convincing, and one day, a week after the shopping trip, the couple had a big fight in the kitchen.

"Would it kill you to be happy?" Cristina asked.

"I am happy."

"No. It's like you're just waiting."

"Waiting?" He turned around and stopped. Cristina could see her husband's muscular arms tense up as he leaned against the kitchen island. The man she married was good-looking, taller than she, and had always been sympathetic—but Cristina's obsession with having a baby had worn him out.

There was a time in their relationship when just the two of them was enough, and Cristina felt like the luckiest woman on the block. Their mutual friends had grown up and in less than a decade lost their waistlines, their hair, and their vigor for life. Leo and Cristina, on the other hand, still went out to the movies, held hands in public, and on the rare occasion, even stared longingly into each other's eyes. Cristina felt especially fortunate because when they met, Leo was a popular high school athlete. She was attractive, pretty with potential, but not popular.

In high school, Leo stood out because he had been the center of their small hometown's attention for one whole semester. He had broken the state's track record and was headed to Nationals, but two days before traveling to the big meet, he'd had his right calf sliced open by another runner's metal cleats. His story had made the local paper, and after making a few calls, his coach convinced some guy from *Sports Illustrated* to interview him.

The story was never published, but all the hype had made him a local celebrity. Everyone, girls especially, wanted to carry his books and help him with his crutches. Cristina thought he was really cute, but she was in no way brazen enough to talk to him. At some point, Leo interpreted her disinterest as playing hard to get and asked her out. They started dating, and before long they were a couple. Unlike Leo, Cristina had no ambitions. She barely tolerated school and wasn't the least bit interested in going to college.

Now Leo is a teacher in the same school district where they both grew up, and there isn't a single person who doesn't compliment him on how well he has aged. Or not aged. The scattering of premature gray hairs at his temples makes him look alluring and sophisticated. Those from his high school clique greet him at school events and public events in town, but Cristina always feels that their enthusiasm towards her is disingenuous.

Like Leo, Cristina had also improved with age. She's the woman every other woman admires while waiting in line at the bank, the slender beauty who looks ten years younger than her real age. Still, Cristina remains insecure among her husband's colleagues. And her jealousy is neither subtle nor kind. To her knowledge, Leo has never cheated on her, but women are drawn to him, and he can be quite charming. And despite the fact that he is always telling his wife that she is too beautiful to be insecure, he never adds "too smart." Cristina detests that the women who are drawn to him are intelligent, professional women. They are female teachers and school administrators who can relate to him on a different level. They share the common language of college grads, working for the same school district and attending similar professional conferences.

The first time Cristina dared to admit the source of her insecurities to Leo, he suggested that she go back to school. He told her that he would support her and help her get started as a part-time student. Cristina had taken it as an insult. Irrevocable proof that she wasn't good enough as she was. It's not like

Cristina hadn't tried. All through junior high and her freshman year of high school, Cristina had tried to be a good student. Like her sister, she had stayed up nights reading and rereading difficult passages out of the classics but retaining nothing. Her math skills were even worse. And when she tried to get interested in current events, she realized she didn't care much for politics.

It was Cristina's older sister, Isa, who was the smart one. Unlike Cristina, Isa was neither charming nor Rio Chico beauty-queen material. She had inherited her father's dark skin and her mother's indifference about what others thought of her, but there wasn't a math problem she couldn't solve or a paper she couldn't write. No one had to drill her with multiplication tables or struggle to teach her how to tell time. When Cristina was a freshman in high school, she had asked her high school counselor if she could take the classes that her older sister had taken—even though she realized that keeping up with Isa would be difficult. Despite not having the grades to qualify, she was allowed to, but halfway through the year, Cristina was close to failing half her classes.

When it became clear to Cristina that her best was just a bit below average, she started to pretend that she didn't care. And sadly, she accepted the role as the "pretty one." The one who didn't care for school. As an adult, Cristina hated herself for quitting. It took her years to realize how much she did like to learn, reading everything she could get her hands on. She just hadn't been interested back in high school. This is the one thing that she was actually thinking of doing if things didn't work out. Just last week, she'd had a conversation with Leo.

"I think I might go back to school."

"What?"

"If I lose the baby, I'm going back to school."

Leo had put the knife down and looked at her sadly. He

could sense that she was giving up, again. And it was his fault for not having been more supportive. For a minute, Cristina thought that her husband would come and hold her, but he turned around and went back to his work.

"Leo, don't you want to have a child with me?"

"Do I want to have a child with you? Are you really asking me that?"

"I don't know; maybe you don't want that kind of responsibility yet."

"Cristina, don't start."

"Do you wish you had married someone else? She would be a teacher, like you, and given you a house full of children."

Leo slowly turned away from Cristina and walked out of the house. Cristina had gone too far. She had used her insecurities to gain his attention but had overstepped, ultimately defeating the purpose of getting closer. Now Leo was hurt and offended. Cristina felt like she had been stupid again and cried herself to sleep. This was supposed to be a happy time for them. She slept right through dinner. When she woke up, the late afternoon sun filled the bedroom with the orange evening glow that she always found so gloomy and depressing. The day was ending, and the dusk reminded her of everything she hadn't accomplished.

She had messed things up. And she didn't know how to fix them. And now she was ravenous. She was suddenly craving thick slices of avocado with the tart and tangy taste of *pico de gallo*. Hunger was quickly interrupted by anxiety when she realized how abrasive she had been. Why was she always trying to drive him away?

Getting out of bed was pointless. It was Friday, and there wasn't anything fresh in the fridge—no ripe avocadoes, and definitely no ingredients for *pico de gallo*. Cristina turned over and buried herself under the covers. Sleep came quickly. Not long after falling back to sleep, however, she heard the bedroom door open and sprang up. She had never been so happy to see her husband. Gesturing for her to move over, Leo held a white, grease-stained bag behind his back.

"Okay, sleeping beauty, scooch."

"Babe, I'm sorry, I should never have said that."

"No worries, leave it. We were both hungry."

"It smells delicious, what is it?" she asked.

"I don't know what you're talking about," he said, laughing.

Cristina sat upright in bed and arranged the pillows so her husband could do the same.

"It's a Deluxe Combo Number Nine from Chucho's for milady."

Neither of them spoke. They didn't have to. Cristina tore into her burger and stuffed lukewarm fries into her mouth, while Leo watched and smiled.

"Did you eat?" Cristina asked, with food in her mouth.

"Did I eat? Yes, I sat at Chucho's and had a Number Three Combo and a large side of onion rings. I'm stuffed." After pulling a handful of cheap restaurant napkins out of his pocket, Leo stood up, reached out, and offered Cristina his hand. He pulled her out of bed and led her to the empty room they were hoping to turn into a nursery.

Formerly a half-office, half-guest bedroom, the medium-sized room had been emptied of all its contents. The only things left were some outdated curtains and a beige carpet faded by the sun and stained by Cristina's various craft projects. That evening, however, there was a mysterious extra-large gift bag sitting in the center of the room.

"What is it?" Cristina asked.

"Beats me."

"Where did you find such a big gift bag?"

"Same place where I bought the tissue paper."

Cristina didn't even care what was inside. She threw her arms around his neck and hugged him tightly.

"I wanted to bring home a crib or a rocking chair, but I figured you would kill me."

"Oh, Leo!"

This was the man that she had fallen in love with. The person in her life who knew how to make everything better. Leo was what she had always wanted in a man. He had an honest face. A slightly crooked, but becoming nose and sumptuous lips. *Lady lips*, Cristina always joked. Good looking, but not too self-absorbed.

Cristina knelt down on the carpet and gently pulled out the tissue paper. It was a fancy diaper pail. "Guaranteed to seal the worst baby poop," he said mockingly. Cristina looked up at her husband with tear-stained eyes and swollen lids, while he stood there, hands in his two front pockets, looking proud.

～ﾑ

Two weeks later, they were both picking out baby furniture and bedding. They had refused to buy anything the first two times; now they were going to do things differently. She had wrestled with the decision to look for furniture when it was still too risky, but in the end, Leo had urged her to just do it. Cristina wanted the nursery painted, and she chose a pale yellow to mimic the warmth of the summer sun. Mateo helped Leo change the old carpet. They both threw themselves into the project, even adding a light green trim and painting the baseboards white.

After work, both Cristina and Leo would change out of their clothes and get to work on their nesting projects. They installed shelves in the baby's closet, added crown molding, and even replaced the windows in the room. Working together, they would lose themselves in the world of what would come next. Neither of them ever spoke about the dreadful reality. Together, they were hopeful.

As Cristina's belly grew, so did their confidence. They picked out a nursing chair, bought baby bottles and pacifiers. They found lovely white wicker baskets and filled them with newborn baby diapers, baby shampoo, and bath towels. They were determined to live every day like there wasn't a possibility of anything going wrong.

The day after the baby furniture arrived, they both took the day off from work for a doctor's appointment. This was Cristina's seventeenth-week appointment. They had missed her fourteenth week because Leo was out of town. Leo suggested that they honor the occasion with a special lunch, so he took her to the Jalapa Grill, one of their favorite restaurants, and in the doctor's office they acted like newlyweds, joking about the goofy socks on the metal stirrups. They exchanged knowing glances while the surly ultrasound technician with yellow teeth and squeaky white sneakers shuffled in and out of the room.

Leo was in the middle of some silly joke when someone knocked on the door. They thought it was the technician, but it was their doctor.

"How are you feeling?" asked Dr. Morin, as he walked in, shook Leo's hand, and patted Cristina's shoulder.

"Excellent," Cristina blurted, with a big smile.

"Looks like we're getting VIP treatment," Leo joked.

"Well, we saw something in the last ultrasound that concerned us, but we weren't a hundred percent."

Dr. Morin prepped Cristina's belly again with the gooey, cold blue gel. Leo looked calm, but Cristina grew more and more anxious with every circular motion of the ultrasound transducer. When Dr. Morin had examined the image sufficiently, his fear was confirmed.

"Mrs. Alvarez, Mr. Alvarez—this doesn't look good. I'm sorry, but I am afraid I have bad news."

chapter 2–Isa

Georgetown University Law School
Washington, DC, 2003

Isa put the phone down and surveyed her surroundings. She had been dialing Cristina all morning without any luck. She looked out the window of graduate student housing and watched as a group of undergraduates chased each other. She was twenty-nine and felt like the oldest law student in history. Thank God it was her last year. She didn't regret her circuitous route. Unlike many of her peers, she knew what to expect, and she was doing just fine. Her eyes were wide open. The only thing she did regret was leaving her circle of friends back in Notre Dame and living so far from her best friend from college, Aisha. After working at an Immigrant Legal Resource Center for three years, Isa decided to get a law degree and see where it would take her. She was one of the few people in her class who didn't expect to save the world.

She had done time as a victim's advocate and was over it. Over the idea that helping those in need would solve all of the social injustice in the world and make her feel instantaneously better. "It's a long, drawn-out process. Nothing gets fixed overnight." These were the words that her supervisor, Tamra, liked to repeat. When it came to social justice, she had learned more from Tamra than from any of her undergraduate professors. Isa had started out as a passionate college graduate, eager to support victims of domestic violence. She took pride in her training and offered the best emotional support she could. She helped victims navigate the judicial process and helped them restore their lives after a crisis. She hung in there when, time after time, women returned to their abusers. When she had internalized too much of her clients' traumas, she would manage her stress and set reasonable limits, but it had been her supervisor's idea that she go back to school. "Isa, you're smart. Why not study and come back to us as a lawyer?"

Isa didn't want to admit it, but she decided to try law school because she was emotionally burned out and tired of living from paycheck to paycheck. She knew she had to walk away when she started blaming the victims and finding herself angry with them. She knew, in both her mind and her heart, that she no longer had the energy to be on the front lines. And she wondered if perhaps, with this newfound cynicism, she could help victims in a different way—a more detached and methodical way. Tamra was right; nothing was going to get resolved overnight. She might as well learn the law and figure out an alternative strategy. If she was going to hate it, she would soon find out. Naysayers kept telling her she would loathe the profession, but as far as she could see, everything the critics saw as a negative, she found quite seductive. She didn't mind working long hours. When warned about the toll the profession took on women with children, Isa couldn't help but laugh. Children never had and never would figure into her plans. If there was work to be done, bring it on; that was her motto.

⤝

Isa lifted a pile of binders and heavy books off the couch. She had a lot of studying to do, but she could no longer ignore the big stain on the couch where she had accidently fallen asleep on a slice of pizza. In addition to scrubbing the couch, she wasn't looking forward to tackling the rest of her chores. Laundry meant a trip to the laundromat, and food shopping meant that she couldn't meet with her study group. That just wasn't going to happen. Thinking of the mundane things on her to-do list, Isa felt a major jab of guilt. In comparison with her sister, Cristina, everything in her life suddenly seemed so trivial. Sometimes, it was easier to take care of others. Fixing their problems had brought Isa a satisfaction that allayed her need for order.

The past six years had been fairly traumatic for Cristina. She had struggled with infertility for many years, and when she finally did become pregnant, she'd experienced two miscarriages. Before her sister's string of misfortunes, Isa used to envy her. Not because of what she had, but because of how simple and uncomplicated her life seemed. She didn't live with the fear of everyone discovering her big secret—the one thing that held her back from feeling truly free. Not to mention all the challenges of trying to get out of Dodge, which for Isa meant endless graduation course requirements, getting shining letters of recommendation, signing up for standardized tests, and writing more than her fair share of college application essays and résumé drafts. She had sacrificed things like proms, parties, and beach weekend getaways in order to put herself in the best position for school scholarships. Cristina had done the exact opposite.

When Isa took her first psychology class in college, her professor had talked about the Pollyanna principle. Described as a subconscious bias towards the positive, this theory seemed to best describe her younger sister. As far as Isa knew, Cristina had benefited from the quintessential high school experience.

It was Cristina's inability to believe that there was bad in the world. But then again, she hadn't faced the kind of rejection that Isa had. Cristina didn't have to be wealthy or popular to be noticed. She wasn't just stunning, but charming and authentically sincere. People were drawn to her, and she was attracted to people. She didn't sweat the small stuff, and she certainly didn't worry about the big things. She looked forward to the kind of events that made Isa cringe. Cristina had made the most of her experiences in high school and cherished them. Her thick, not to mention gaudy, high school scrapbooks and kitschy high school keepsakes were a testament to that.

Cristina had also met her husband in high school. She had spent the first couple of years after graduation planning her dream wedding, and as soon as they had saved enough, they had settled in a beautiful neighborhood. Growing up, Cristina was the golden child. Literally and figuratively. In addition to being the "dark-skinned" sister, Isa had been the older sister with the nonexistent social life, because of her bookish ways and her inability to blend in with the crowd. Isa's younger sister was everything she wasn't, a light-skinned, green-eyed beauty who took after their fair-skinned mother. She was the gregarious one with the light-hearted aura. Isa, on the other hand, was all Mateo. She was, like her father, a loner, but also what Mexicans call *prieta*, the dark one.

"You two look nothing alike!" People's everyday comments were code. A polite way of calling attention to their differences. Isa could be standing right next to her sister, and relatives would hone in on Cristina to compliment her green eyes or fair skin. This would happen all the time, and people were so used to it that no one ever noticed how blatantly bigoted they were being.

Isa had never blamed Cristina or resented her. She couldn't. Cristina was one of the kindest people Isa knew, the only one who would notice her discomfort with these remarks and change the conversation. Growing up, it was clear that Cristina loved and respected her sister. When Isa's high school counselor tried to discourage her from applying to out-of-state colleges, even though she was at the top of her class, it was Cristina who pointed out how small-minded people in their town could be. It was also Cristina who reminded her of the size of her dreams and that everything was possible.

In return, Isa had always been protective of her little sister. Since their parents had never really learned English, it was Isa who cut up cereal boxes and used the backs to make multiplication flash cards. When Cristina wasn't having any luck learning to read in first grade, it was Isa who had asked her fourth-grade teacher for help. Isa had been the one leading her mother through the maze of open houses and school conferences, acting as her younger sister's advocate, and helping the whole family navigate a completely foreign educational system.

And as far as comparisons went, Isa was also smart enough to know that people made a big fuss over Cristina's light skin because they were ignorant. She figured that people would come around and acknowledge how petty and hurtful their prejudices were. She knew who she was. She knew who she wanted to be, and she had faith that once people saw her the way she saw herself, the whole "light-skinned" bias would get old. It wasn't, of course, until many years later that Isa realized that being "lighter" would never go out of style. She would have to be the one to adapt.

Fortunately, Isa had always been able to see the big picture. When she was as young as thirteen, she had been blessed with a self-awareness that other kids her age didn't possess. She could look around the school cafeteria or scan the large gym at Gloria Anzaldua Middle School and know how the story would unfold for most girls. She predicted that Marcie Rivera wouldn't make it past junior year. Sadly, the judge's daughter would lose her virginity in her parents' pool house and drop out of school on account of an unplanned pregnancy. She could pick out the girls who demanded that their parents live beyond their means so they could wear the "right" shoes and all the name brands sanctioned by their peers. She rarely met anyone, male or female, who inspired her to want to get to know them. Nobody had goals and aspirations similar to hers.

Unlike some of her peers, Isa was curious and hungry for success. She was okay with small-town-pariah status, because the best was yet to come. She pitied the popular girls. She knew, sadly, that their luck would run its course. She had watched enough television and read enough books to know how the narrative arc of their lives would eventually play out. So in this regard, Isa was optimistic about her future. She made plans, checked off lists, and imagined a brighter future for herself. Rio Chico was her home, for now. In time, it would be a launching pad for a better life.

～

Eventually, it became clear to Isa that Cristina didn't need her. When Isa had sat Cristina down and urged her to think about her future, Cristina had protested. "Isa," she had said, quite exasperated, "you need to back off. I'm not missing out on life, you are. Can't you see it? You are always running, and you can't make memories like that." Cristina had always thought that Isa was in a hurry to get absolutely nowhere.

～

Instead of reading wisdom into her words, Isa had always dismissed Cristina as naïve. One of Isa's biggest failures had been her inability to get her little sister to apply to college. Even technical schools were out of the question. Isa eventually gave up on the idea of turning Cristina into somebody she wasn't. Her sister had never measured herself by anyone else's yardstick.

She had always pursued her own dreams and not the dreams imposed by others.

Of course, that was before Cristina started experiencing repeated pregnancy losses. Now her sister was pregnant again, and everyone was worried. She had been warned against it. What if she miscarried again?

~&

Cristina's series of unfortunate events didn't start with her inability to have children; health issues played a big part. A year before her first miscarriage, Cristina had been struggling with a thyroid problem that had caused her to gain forty-five pounds. Isa's beautiful, once so slender younger sister was almost unrecognizable. When Isa was home visiting, she was appalled at the looks her sister would get. Relatives and neighbors would talk about her as if she had passed away. "She used to be so slim. So beautiful!" These comments had devastated Cristina. Her looks were a big part of her identity, so being overweight was crushing. Cristina eventually had thyroid surgery and regained her trim figure. She was her old self when she started having the pregnancy problems. And the changes and havoc of pregnancy and loss had been difficult on everyone. To Isa, Cristina's current life epitomized the saying, *Why do bad things happen to good people?* It had been hard to watch life knock Cristina down so much. For once, Cristina's problems made Isa's seem small, and that made Isa feel guilty. She was usually the one with the insuperable problems.

~&

All her life, Isa had compared the weight of her baggage with the burdens of others. And her woes always seemed to outdo everyone else's. If oppressions were to be tallied, she was the winner: dark-skinned in a light-skin-loving culture, plain-looking in one that valued "classic" features, and gay in a straight world. Isa was convinced that she was suffering more than most people her age and that her affliction was both biological and inoperable. As far as she was concerned, it was also something that she would take to her grave—no way on God's green earth was she coming out to her parents. Or her sister. Ever. Very few people knew her secret—Aisha, a handful of lovers and school acquaintances. Aisha was always begging her to come out, but Aisha had not had it as difficult as she had, despite being a woman of color born to immigrant parents. Aisha's parents were the absolute coolest. They had raised an only child, led an upper-middle-class existence, and even when she had come out, her parents embraced her wholeheartedly. Isa remembered the first time she'd met Aisha, at an Earth Day event at college; Aisha had assumed that Isa was South Asian as well. Still, they got along beautifully, even after Aisha realized that Isa was Mexican American. Isa, for her part, had never had a South Asian friend; her small Texas town was mostly Mexican American. Isa wanted to know all about Aisha's culture. What music did she like? Did she pray all of the time? Had she been to India? Turned out that Aisha was the only child of two very devout and much older Catholics who emigrated from India a couple of years before Aisha was born.

The girls bonded their freshman year and became inseparable. Practically the same height, they even looked like sisters. If Aisha's South Asian student organization had something interesting happening, Isa would come along and vice versa. But what sealed the deal on their friendship was the fact that they were both lesbians. Aisha had had grown up in Seattle and her high school had started one of the first LGBT student groups in the country, but she was cool with Isa's not being out. She always introduced Isa as one of her best "heterosexual" friends.

Aisha knew that she could have easily been the one in Isa's

shoes, had her circumstances not have been what they were. When Isa asked Aisha, "Your parents know?" Aisha proceeded to tell her all about the day she had come out.

"OK, so, how did you tell them?"

"Well. They sort of found out."

"What?"

"Well, during my junior year in high school our counselors held a workshop for parents of LGBT students."

"In high school?"

"It was Seattle, baby. While you ladies in Texas were still wearing butt bustles and suffering from the vapors, we had moved on."

"Wow, why can't Notre Dame get it together?"

"Duh, because we would all rot in hell."

"Oh, that, yeah . . . right, silly me. So, your parents just agreed to go?"

"No, I told them that it was a meeting for parents of gifted students and they had to go. Mom wore one of her best saris and they both left the house so proud. Their daughter was *gifted*."

"You did not?"

"Did too."

"You are freakin nuts!"

"There weren't many parents there. Maybe three families—and that included us. I remember the attendees clearly. It was Erin Dey and his single mother, and Terrence Hanes and both of his parents. You could tell that Erin and his mother were best friends, and Terrence's parents . . . well . . . they were a trip."

"Why? What were they like?"

"His father was African American and his mom was white. They were both social workers or something and really into diversity and all things progressive. I mean, no joke, when God was assigning open-minded parents, Terrence scored. The workshop had been their idea and they ended up doing most of the talking."

"And your parents, sounds like an ambush! That's cold."

"And awkward."

"You're nuts. No way could I ever do that to my folks."

"Well, as soon as my mom got over Mrs. Hanes's white-woman dreadlocks, she figured that with all of the conversation about changing times and the meaning of everything LGBT, we must have been in the wrong room. My mother kept trying to make eye contact with me. She later told me that she thought that maybe we were at the wrong meeting and she thought that I was just being polite and sticking around until it was over."

"Oh my God! Then what happened?"

"Well, at the end, the counselor said something to the tune of, 'It warms my heart that you are so supportive of your children. If all of our LGBT students had such supportive parents . . .' Then he said something about gay teens and high suicide rates."

"Your dad? What did he say?"

"He was quiet the whole time. Like, not too surprised."

"Then?"

"When we walked out of the classroom Mom said, 'Aisha, why didn't we leave? We missed your workshop. We were obviously at the wrong workshop.' My mother had actually sat through the whole session and thought that we were in the wrong place."

"That poor woman!"

"I looked at her and mumbled something about not being in the wrong place and her face just lost all of its color. She waited until she was in the car and then just burst out sobbing. And then my old man just said, 'We love you as you are, Aisha, even if you want to dress like boy. This is a man's world and if woman has to act like men, then the lady woman does what she needs to do.'

"My mother looked at my father, really angry and annoyed and yelled, 'Aisha does not want to dress like a man. She likes the lesbiany girls.'

"Dad just sat there. Looking out the window. He couldn't even look at me. Absorbing the information and letting it all sink in. In less than thirty seconds, his only child had turned into something worse than a tomboy. I hated the silence. I kind of didn't want them to speak, so I acted all indignant and started a fight. I got real mad."

"You? Got mad?"

"Oh, yeah, I went off. When I shouldn't have, really. My parents have always been so nice and understanding. I knew that they would never turn me away, but I still went all drama queen on them. I wasn't playing fair. I told them that they had to accept me as I was. And if they didn't like it I would be happy to leave their house. I would go and roam the streets with all of the other homeless teens—who were probably gay too. That if they didn't want me, they could go out and find someone 'perfect'."

"Wow."

"Then, I really overdid it."

"What did you do?"

"I started to get out of the car and I said, 'Or I could just kill myself'."

"Oh my God! Aisha! You did not!"

"I sure did."

"Then what happened?"

"Then my father did something that he had never done in my whole life."

"What? What did he do?"

"Raised his voice, actually, shouted."

"What did he say?"

"He yelled my name, reached out and grabbed my scrawny

arm, pulled me back into the car and ordered me to shut the car door."

"Then what?"

"Then he told me that I was to never, ever, speak of killing myself. Told me that they had always let me do whatever I wanted: listen to my crazy music, wear my weird clothes and shoes—even when my aunties told him that I was out of control and disrespectful. I had no right, absolutely no right to treat them that way.

"He reminded me how he had met my mother when they were both in their forties. That no one ever thought that either would get married. And after they were married, they were told that they were too old to have a baby. But one year and a half later, there I was. Their miracle. I was their whole world and have been since. That I meant more to them than their lives, more than a son-in-law, future grandchildren, more than religion."

"Unbelievable! More than religion, he said that?"

"I think he did, maybe I made that part up, whatever, anyway, there I was, bawling my eyes out. My mom was weeping and sniveling. Dad had said that they would always love me, no matter what I decided to be, but to never, ever talk about killing myself again."

"And then?"

"We were cool."

"Just like that?"

"Well, they didn't get on the phone and invite the relatives to a Gay Pride parade or anything, but they came around. Although sometimes I think that Mom thinks that I'll change my mind."

"What makes you think that?"

"She said that someone at church told her that boys who were gay were always gay, but women could always change back."

"Change back?"

"Yeah . . . isn't that hysterical?"

&

Isa wasn't born feeling anxious. Her life hadn't always been affected by concerns that were out of her control. The first eleven years of her life had been comparatively untroubled. Her thoughts and actions weren't regularly interrupted by the knowledge that she was different—so different that sometimes she wondered if she should bother to exist at all. The presence of this *condition* was so marked in her life that the way Isa divided time was before *It* and after *It*.

&

Isa remembered almost everything about the day she became aware of who she really was. She was home sick with a cold and a temperature. It was late January, and bitterly cold by South Texas standards. Her mother had plopped the family's old black and white portable television beside her bed. Cristina, her little sister, was upset about having to go to school when Isa was staying home. From the comforts of her grandmother's comfy wool *colchas*, Isa watched reruns of *Good Times* and *The Jeffersons*. In between napping and watching TV, she enjoyed her mother's delicious *caldito de pollo* and *té de manzanilla*.

At some point, Isa fell asleep. Maybe it was the cold medicine, but she was out and didn't wake up until the next morning. She woke to the sound of noisy clanking and clattering in the kitchen. She figured her mom was knocking around pots and pans for what she thought was dinner but turned out to be breakfast. She had slept all day and into the next. She had sat up and realized that her head no longer hurt when she moved. She felt rested and refreshed. Then she remembered. The dream! Everything had felt so good during it, but upon awakening, the weight of the dream's significance, what it said about her, was crushing. A realization that made her almost sick in her own mouth. It was all wrong, in its own all right way.

In the dream, Isa was at a birthday party at an unfamiliar house. Grownups were eating cake in the living room. She was upstairs, standing by pink-and-yellow curtains with a floral pattern. She wasn't alone. She was kissing a girl with long, brown hair, and the girl with the long, brown hair was kissing her back.

The feeling had been a good one; the sensation was intense and pleasurable. But it also had the unfortunate consequence of coloring both her mood and emotions—not just for days, but for the rest of her life. Everything about their contact had felt right. Until she woke up. No one had to tell Isa that liking a girl was wrong, the message was everywhere. Loud and clear.

She could be watching one of her mother's Spanish-language sitcoms and cringe when the laugh track played every time the flamboyantly effeminate hairdresser would swoon over an unsuspecting straight male. And when gays were not the brunt of others' jokes, they were demonized in the media. There was that one awful night when she happened to be watching the late-night news with her mother. The headline was, "When Unrequited Love Turns Deadly." She had to both translate the news and listen to her mother call "those" people "sick and twisted." This had been nothing in comparison to some of the dreadful news she had heard on one Spanish news magazine. One known for delivering atrocities from every corner of Latin America to their Spanish-speaking audience. If there was a man killing babies before breakfast in Peru, the scantily-clad reporters had their microphone shoved in the killer's ninety-year-old grandmother's face, asking her about it. So many evil deeds, some too terrible even to repeat, but one lesbian kills her neighbor, and her mother is ranting about the state of humanity.

After the dream, even small moments of pleasure—tearing

through birthday-present wrapping paper, or trying on a new pair of sneakers for the first time—were punctuated with a sick, uneasy feeling in the pit of her stomach. She hated feeling that there was something about her that made her bad, something that she had to keep secret. It wasn't something that she could run to tell her mom, like when a random man in the neighborhood asked her, while grabbing his urine-stained crotch, if she wanted to go back to his house and watch television with him. Her parents had been outraged. Her father, usually silent, started yelling obscenities and had gone out in the street to confront the pervert.

Isa's dream wasn't something her parents could protect her from. In her own perceptive way, Isa already knew that it was actually the other way around. She would have to protect them. Never let them know about it. Keep them sheltered from the realities of her truth. After all, if told, this wasn't just difficult news, it was a life-altering revelation. One that she would never be able to take back. And the fear, her worst nightmare, was rejection. How would she ever be able to reconcile that the woman who had raised her could eventually hate her?

By the time Isa was in middle school, she knew that no boy would ever hold the same attraction that a girl would. She also knew by then that there were names for her feelings, and the names were not good. Isa's dream needed to be kept secret, and this made her uneasy, all the time.

By the time she was in high school she had secretly named the feeling Kill Joy. Kill Joy liked to sneak up on her and remind her that true happiness would always be out of reach as long as she had those thoughts and feelings she wasn't supposed to have.

⚓

This is not to say that she didn't have any good days. There were days when she was oblivious to It. As an adult, she could get absorbed in a school- or work-related task and It didn't bother her. There were also those rare glimpses of progress when gays were praised or deemed important. She remembered at least two appearances by Liberace, whom Henry Silva, the know-it-all, had declared "gay as the day was long." It was his appearance on both an old *Batman* show and as a guest on *The Muppets* that had given her faith, assurance that people like her could both succeed and be accepted. Because as young as she was, she was aware that Liberace was two things: famous and not straight. And if he was that well-known, that meant he had been accepted, had made something of himself in spite of being gay.

Those moments, however, were short-lived. No sooner was she floating on the billows of such wistful optimism, when life would happen, like when Darío Montez, a boy in her sixth-grade class, had passed her a folded note and asked if she wanted to be his girlfriend. Sometimes it was so tempting to give in, to act against her nature and appear normal, but she could never bring herself to do it. Her acts of omitting the truth were not gross acts of prevarication, just dances with the untruth. When "vagueness" asked for her hand, she gladly accepted and extended hers, eventually filling her dance card with other skilled partners: avoidance, distraction, and omission.

It weighed on her again in the seventh grade, when she attended her first sleepover, and all the girls could yap about were the crushes that they had on boys. She told them that she was in love with Jerry Cruz. She lied. Isa kept a diary, but she didn't feel very comfortable disclosing sensitive information on scented, purple-lined paper. What if someone found it? Her reflections and ruminations included (among other things) a longing for a certain pair of jeans or sneakers, items that she could never get because they were too expensive. Other entries comprised details about epic fights between her and Cristina. But every once in a while, she felt bold and entered coded versions of the truth. Her parents couldn't even speak English, let alone read it, but she still confessed her feelings with trepidation. When she felt compelled to chronicle her feelings for a girl, her name was usually changed to that of a boy. But even salacious smoke-screens felt too daring, so she had really done this only once. It was the year she wrote about Elena. She had renamed her "Joey" and, buoyed by a quiet courage, written her a poem. It was as close as she was going to get. The idea of exposing herself to a bound set of papers—well, it was just too perilous. Totally and completely out of the question, as far as she was concerned.

◆

But now, it was Cristina facing the biggest of all uncertainties. Having a baby and starting a family was all Cristina had ever desired. Isa admired her for her ability to find satisfaction in a role that she simply could not identify with. Unlike Isa, who was always seeking *more*, Cristina knew how to live life in the moment. She could attend a barbeque or cook a meal while being present and feeling grateful for everything she had. Isa was always planning ahead and anticipating what was to come. Enjoying the everyday required a monumental effort on her part. Her life was one big to-do list, and she only exhaled when something was checked off—if it was ever checked off at all, because usually she fell into the trap of over-thinking every little problem until each item on the list had categories and subcategories. She was nothing like Cristina. Cristina, who after two miscarriages, had optimistically decided to try again.

◆

On her way to her study group, Isa was feeling heavy and burdened with her sister's problems. She didn't share her sis-ter's optimism for this third pregnancy; all she could see was another miscarriage in her sister's future and, inevitably, a life without children, despite her sister's certainty. But that wasn't the worst part. Isa was afraid that Cristina would regret not having a career or a hobby when all else failed.

Her sister had been working at a small insurance company as a general office-support assistant since graduating from high school. She was efficient and took great pride in her work. Isa feared that if Cristina were to leave, finding a similar position with just a high school diploma would be challenging.

⚜

When Isa arrived at the study group, one of the participants was bouncing a baby on her lap while trying to open her book to the correct page. The child looked so happy and content. Sucking on his pacifier, he explored his surroundings with his big, wide eyes. Isa was not a baby person, not in the least bit interested in ever becoming a parent, but Cristina and her mother would see this as a good omen—a premonition that her sister's pregnancy would be tremendously successful and she would be the doting aunt of a little guy (or girl) just like this one.

But Isa thought differently. Dana, the baby's mother, hadn't been able to find a sitter, that's all. Isa didn't believe in destiny. She saw coincidence, not providence. Her mother loved to say, "*Mientras hay vida, hay esperanza.*" While there is life, there is hope. And this is where faith as a concept was complicated for Isa. She could never truly discern between expectation—the assumption that something is going to happen—and hope, the wish for something to happen. Why was it that against all odds, people liked to hope? When the opposite of hope was far more certain.

Isa despised uncertainty; certainties were truer and thus real, as real as the ground beneath her feet.

chapter 3–Cristina

Rio Chico, Texas, 2003

Cristina braced herself for a troubling diagnosis. If her baby had Down syndrome, she didn't care. If he or she had more than ten toes, she still didn't care. She wasn't going to be one of those parents praying for the perfect child. She didn't care if her baby was not destined for greatness, just as long as he or she was destined to *be*.

"What's wrong?" asked Leo, looking at the ultrasound.

"Your baby seems to have a very serious congenital birth defect." The doctor started pointing to the ultrasound. Words escaped his mouth, but it took Cristina a long time to register them. The doctor spoke like he was lecturing a crowd of medical students and not two parents whose lives were being changed, again. Anencephaly . . . no brain . . . partial brain . . . missing cranium vault. Short life expectancy. Cristina hadn't even noticed that her hands had started shaking. She was focused on Dr. Morin's thin, colorless lips. His mechanical and unemotional delivery of this devastating news was shocking. At that moment she didn't know what was worse, how he was delivering the news, or the news itself.

"But this is just a possibility, right?" she asked.

"No, I'm afraid we are certain of the diagnosis."

Leo took Cristina's shaking hands in his. Cristina turned and saw his eyes well up with tears. Yet, she was still convinced that there was a possibility that this was all a big mistake. *Not her baby.* "Dr. Morin," she spoke, calmly, "I'm healthy, I feel good. The baby is growing just fine. This could be a false alarm, right?" No tears, no sobbing. Cristina just wanted the facts. She could cry later. Usually, at this point in her previous pregnancies, she had been given the news that her baby's heart had stopped. *But not today.* Today, her baby's heart was still beating. Their child was still alive, and she was still going to be a mother.

"I strongly advise that the pregnancy be terminated."

"Can Cristina die?" Leo interjected, alarmed.

"No, she will be fine."

"Dr. Morin, we are talking about a baby, a real child," Cristina interrupted.

"Cristina, the fact is that you will be carrying a baby that will not be . . ."

"Not be, what?" asked Cristina.

"Whole or equipped to live . . ."

"But I would be able to go to full term?" she interrupted.

"Mrs. Alvarez, the probability that your child will die is high. I'm sorry. We want to spare mothers and fathers the trauma. The closeness of the mother-infant bond during the pregnancy will only get stronger."

"I'm keeping this baby."

"As you wish," answered Dr. Morin as he stood, looked away, and impatiently thumbed through Cristina's file. He was suddenly in a hurry to get out and see his next patient. Dr. Morin gave a perfunctory nod and, straining to come off as compassionate, repeated, "Again, I am really sorry, but it is my duty to let you know about your options."

"Dr. Morin?" asked Cristina.

"Yes?"

"It is possible to carry the baby to term?"

"Cristina," Leo pleaded, "the baby won't live long after birth, is that correct, Dr. Morin?"

"How long will the baby live?" asked Cristina.

"Well, it could be hours, days, weeks and in very rare cases, a month. Most babies don't make it at all. Look, this is a lot of information to absorb in one sitting. You two should go home and talk about it, but remember, you shouldn't wait too long. I recommend that you come back within a week."

Dr. Morin closed the door behind him and left them alone. Leo stood against the wall, as if he were single-handedly holding it up himself, and Cristina just sat up and stared at the counter in front of her. She noticed the pamphlets stacked up neatly against an empty glass jar and a stack of manila folders with multi-color tabs. She mentally pictured herself sweeping her arm across the counter and sending it all across the room. She didn't want to deal with any of this. She wanted to make it all go away.

"Cristina, please," Leo urged, "Please don't do this to yourself. To us."

Cristina's eyes flashed with defiance. They hadn't even started to process what the doctor had said, and he was already making a decision for them, for her.

"The baby is going to die," he said, taking Cristina's hand in his, "and you have already been through so much."

"Leo, get me out of here."

Leo helped Cristina out of the quilted, paper robe and into her clothes. He was silent now. Outside in the parking lot, Leo put the key in the car's ignition and told her that he was sorry and would support her in whatever decision she made. But his words came out flat. Like he was just going through the motions to placate her.

In the car, Cristina straightened up, gently fastened her seat belt, and looked him straight in the eye. "Men just don't get it. Whether it's keeping a baby or losing a baby, you just don't get it. And it's not fair. It's not just our bodies either. It's what will weigh on us for the rest of our lives. Who am I, who are we to play God? As long as this baby's heart is beating and the rest of his or her little limbs are growing, I'm not doing anything. Do you hear me? I will not play God!"

Leo knew that his wife was pro-choice, but he should have also known her well enough to know that she wasn't the least bit capable of terminating her own pregnancy. This call wasn't his to make, it was hers.

❧

In the early days of her pregnancy, no one knew how to talk about the baby's prognosis. Beatriz seemed to be the only person who treated Cristina like she was *really* pregnant. Leo and Isa asked about Cristina's health and level of comfort, but no one spoke about the baby. No one knew how to. Outside of the immediate family circle, no one knew just how bad the prognosis really was. They had been told that there was something wrong, but they didn't know to what extent. As a woman, she felt entitled to her own family, to raise babies, and to worry about them. Pregnancy seemed like an inherent promise that her body had made, just because she had been born a woman, but now her body was reneging.

Cristina quickly discovered that after a woman loses two babies, no one has any faith in her body. She's looked at as irrevocably broken, damaged goods, incapable of producing a quality product. More importantly, Cristina felt like society wasn't as generous with their sympathy. You received one pass, and after that, you were just courting self-induced disappointment. Pity gets replaced with a kind of victim-blaming that, in an ever-so-subtle way, shames women into giving it all up. Friends and relatives feign encouragement, pretend to be happy, but their body language and polite smiles always give them away. Insisting on a family, when you have had no luck the second time, is the equivalent of telling people that you're trying to get to the moon—on a bike. You can see judgment in their faces, can almost hear them say, *Your second loss was a sign. A biological baby is not for you. Get over it and move on.*

～❧

They drove home in silence. When they got home, Cristina went straight into their bedroom and into the shower. She cried as the warm water washed over her. She asked the question that everyone asks: "Why me?" Leo let her cry, then led her to bed and tucked her in. He held her hands in his and promised to have faith. Faith that it would all work out. "Babe, what is that you always tell me, 'Let go and let God'?" He whispered it in her ear, but couldn't let go himself.

～❧

Eventually, they both had to show up to work, pay bills, make beds, and get on with life. At some point, they both slipped into a kind of state of denial. They both behaved like nothing was wrong, like they hadn't been told what to expect; but as Cristina's belly grew, so did Leo's apprehension.

One night, Cristina came home from her parents' house and found that Leo had been drinking. He had started with a couple of beers and finished with half a bottle of tequila. He looked tired and heartbroken. When she tried to touch him, he bristled and walked away from her, the bottle of tequila in his hand. Then he stopped, pointed the bottle towards the ceiling and, barely able to stand, started in on her.

"Yes, first you, Cristina—then Cristina, and—wait, Cristina

again. Your needs. Mine don't count. It's like you've done it all by yourself. I just stand around and watch you make all the decisions. I'm supposed to walk around and pretend that I'm going to be a father, when in reality, I may never even meet my child."

Cristina followed him into the bedroom and watched him flop onto their unmade bed. He turned to face her and continued in his inebriated state, "I didn't even think we should have tried again." Cristina listened, in horror. Had he gone mad?

"Leo, what the hell?"

"Don't you understand, if you had *done it*, life would not be so hard right now? We wouldn't be here, living like this, not knowing. It would be done. It would all be *over*. We would have moved on."

Cristina took a second. She was about to apologize, when righteous indignation took over her, "No, no, sir! *You* would have moved on, I would be living with the consequences, with all of the *what ifs*. It would all be *on me!*"

As soon as she'd finished her outburst, Cristina felt guilty. This could not be good for the baby. If this was all the time her child had, she didn't want to waste it arguing. She started to get undressed and encouraged Leo to do the same. Leo began sobbing, and she held him in the crook of her arm. The last time he'd had had this much to drink was when his cousin Alberto had died. She tried to comfort him, but she was still smarting from his accusations. When was he going to understand? She hadn't had a choice! She didn't wake up one day and decide she wanted to make their lives so complicated.

Or had she?

Couldn't he see that she would be suffering just as much if she had terminated the pregnancy? It was *her* body! It was *their* baby.

When Leo started snoring, Cristina sat up, grabbed her keys, and left the house. She hopped into the car and drove north for two hours until her rage and grief had subsided. She stopped in a little town named Refugio for a bathroom break and decided to get a bite to eat. In Refugio, she found a Whataburger and ordered large fries and a milkshake. She maneuvered her growing belly into a booth. Sitting there, in a strange town, all by herself, she felt like God had abandoned her. Deserted them both. As soon as it started to get dark, the unfamiliarity of the people around her and the streets that she didn't recognize began to unsettle her. She wanted to go home. Whatever she had to face, she would rather do it with Leo.

﹋

That night, Cristina crawled into bed with Leo and dreamed about the baby for the first time. It was a baby girl, and the dream had been extremely comforting. The next morning, she tried to describe it to Leo, but she couldn't. All she knew was that after the dream, something had been lifted. Until then, she had been operating with twenty-five percent hope and seventy-five percent resignation, and the dream had flipped this on its head. It was now the other way around, and with every kick Cristina felt assured her that she had made the right decision. Her new priority was focused on meeting their baby. Holding the child in her arms and saying goodbye, properly. Whatever her fate, nature would decide it, and they would deal with it. Then and only then. But no sooner.

﹋

As her middle grew larger, however, she became more and more aware of what she had done. She hadn't told anyone at work that there was something seriously wrong with the baby. She felt like she was being a bit deceptive, but she didn't feel she had a choice. People would often respond in an incredulous tone when they learned about their many attempts to start a family. Sometimes she even wondered about her own motives.

There were other reasons. Cristina figured that if she told them, they would either want to talk about it all the time or not talk about it all—and she didn't know which was worse. They would probably do whatever they could to make her feel at ease. Perhaps even encourage her to start *letting go*. But how can you let go of something you don't even have? Cristina was waiting. And when the baby came, if the time came to let her go—because they could still be wrong—she would let go then. Then and only then.

Was she the selfish one for wanting a child, even if it was only temporary?

When her coworkers presented her with a shower that day, she could barely hold it together. Her friend Selma invited Leo over, and in an hour the festivities were wrapped up. That day, Cristina left her car at work and rode home with Leo.

ی

The next day they apologized to each other and talked about their expectations, and in the end, they settled on one thing: four minutes. That was all they asked for, four minutes to be with their child. They wanted to say goodbye. They wanted to tell their child that they had done everything they could. Just four minutes. One minute short of five, because five minutes seemed too much to ask for. They were exhausted and too tired to struggle. They would just see. Just wait and see.

ی

Not all days were spent thinking about the weightier issues. The day they found out the baby's gender, Cristina couldn't help but brag about her intuition. She had known all along and Leo did not believe her. They were having a baby girl.

"Yeah, you just got lucky," Leo had teased.

"No, a mother knows."

Initially, they had held off on knowing the baby's sex, but eventually curiosity got the best of them. They could no longer wait. The skin across her belly felt tighter and Cristina's breasts were heavy. She wondered if the baby would live long enough, or be strong enough, to nurse. Lying in the tub, Cristina watched her tears fall onto her swollen breasts. In these moments, she wondered what babies knew. Healthy babies, sick babies, babies destined to die—did they have any inkling of how loved they were? Did they know their fate? Especially since it was already written in their DNA?

꜀

In the end, as wearying as it all was, Cristina made peace with her child's undetermined future. True, there were some days when she felt the knowledge that her unborn baby would not live would kill her, but it didn't. She cried. She rested. She grew sad, a little mad, but in the end, she would move on.

What else was there to do? Quitting wasn't a choice. There were days when she felt as if she were floating over her own body, all five of her senses temporarily suspended. Coming down from these paralyzing moments was a slow and painful descent to her new reality. When she really looked at the baby's diagnosis, thought about what her child would have to endure, and not just them, she became anxious and worried, feeling like the most powerless parent. And the feeling would continue.

꜀

In the days and weeks that followed, Cristina discovered a group of supportive women online. It had all begun as a mad search for everything related to her baby's diagnosis, but she was also learning about various forums about mothers and children with anencephaly. Most importantly, she discovered that she wasn't alone. Minutes into reading, she had joined the forum, and started posting. She wanted to know if she was doing the right thing.

ᴗ᷅

Rena@grommy, thank you so much for answering my question. My name is Cristina. When my DH and I were told that our baby would have anencephaly I was a bawling mess. Finding this site and others like it has made me feel less alone. My heart and prayers go out to each and every one of you. Thank you! I also want to let Deena@ rasta (from South Dakota?) know that you should not feel bad about terminating your pregnancy. You are still so brave. Sometimes I feel like you are braver than the rest of us. Sometimes I feel guilty. Like I took the easy way out for selfish reasons.

Other people's perspectives helped Cristina. In these women's stories, she found both solidarity and solace in the words of kindred spirits:

No, I think that Fiona@starlight misunderstood me. Not selfish in a bad way. It's just that I truly believe that we are each on our own unique journey. Deena made the decision she needed to make. And instead of regret, I think that she should follow anna@cotysmom's advice: honor it, respect it and acknowledge it as her choice, her path.

ᴗ᷅

Cristina, welcome to our site. My partner and I buried our little one two years ago. Her mother (I refuse to refer to her as my mother-in-law), a cruel homophobe, said it was God's punishment for our lifestyle choices. Hard situations happen. When we made the decision to stay pregnant, we also had our doubts. We both wanted our baby so badly. Our loved ones who were supportive (and we are blessed to have more in this camp) feared for our emotional health. They encouraged us to terminate the pregnancy, for our sakes. But when our little girl was born, they couldn't fathom not having met her. Simone was born on my great aunt's birthday. She was very sick, but still so beautiful. We were able to know her for three days—the most blissful three days of our lives. I can assure you that as hard as it all will be, the day you get to hold your baby, you will be glad that you did it.

They all spoke the same language and negotiated similar fears:

As for Deena@rasta, God loves you. You did what was right for you. God does not see you as a sinner. Don't listen to Lady@lourdes. I know she means well, but she is not you and will never be you. And no, I don't believe that God judges like that. God is about love and understanding.

⌀

They lived in Cristina's world and Cristina lived in theirs.

DH and I just had a big fight. He won't admit it, but he is so afraid. When he sees the pictures and videos of babies like ours he doesn't see what we see. Sometimes, I feel so alone. Did anyone out there go through the same thing? Eventually, we made up, but it was still really hard.

⌀

She reached out, even when she wasn't feeling strong.

Sorry that I haven't written a word in three days. I've been in bed—A TOTAL MESS. Unwashed, unmotivated and depressed!

My mother dragged me to church; she doesn't even go to church, but she made me see a priest. How do you keep from losing it? Am I the only hypocrite, a believer one day, nonbeliever the next?

⌀

The day Cristina had written this last passage, she had experienced, hands down, the toughest week of her pregnancy. "Why am I even acting normal? Why am I still trying so hard? What am I doing?"

She crawled back into bed and didn't even bother to call work. When she didn't pick up her phone, one of her coworkers called Leo and he drove straight home. Cristina refused to get up. She didn't want to eat or shower. Beatriz moved in and didn't leave her daughter's side. She coaxed her into eating chicken broth and encouraged her to go on with her life. Cristina cried and imagined so many grim scenarios. During her lowest points, she wondered if she should stop eating and starve both of them to death. She could get into the car and drive into Falcon Lake. She could take something and never wake up.

On the third day, Cristina realized that she hadn't felt the baby kick throughout her seventy-two-hour pity party. And she was overcome with remorse. Was her baby dead? Had she rushed death? Beatriz made her a big hearty meal and Cristina devoured it. She showered and started to walk around. She pleaded. *Wake up baby. Kick me! Forgive me.*

chapter 4—Isa

Georgetown University Law School
Washington, DC, 2003

"I'm so glad that the baby is fine, Sis. I told you."

"It was just so scary, Isa," said Cristina, "I wish you weren't living so far away while I'm going through all this. I could feed off your strength."

"My strength? Are you kidding me?" Isa laughed.

"No, Isa," Cristina replied, "you are the strongest person I know, so sure of yourself."

Isa hung up the phone and felt like such a fraud. She had been lying, to herself and to everyone at home. For as long as Isa could remember, she had spent most of her time lying to others about her identity. She had never declared her love for a boy or a girl, yet she was already highly attuned to the strains of living a double life. When asked if a certain male movie star was attractive, she had answered yes, but mindfully noted that commenting on someone's looks was different from saying that she was physically attracted to them. It was in these little details that Isa stayed true to herself. And this meant a lot to her. That's why on the day that she declared her teen crush on Victor Carillo, she felt like she had betrayed herself. Up until this moment, she was still unsullied by labels. Pretending to be someone she wasn't was a bigger commitment than lackadaisical vagueness.

It was actually her sister Cristina's best friend, Ester, who forced to her to lie about her sexual preference. Ester spent many a Friday night at their house because Cristina was not allowed to sleep over at hers. Ester probably assumed that Cristina and Isa's parents were old-fashioned, which they were, but it was more than that. It was Ester's family lifestyle. Ester's father was a fairly high-ranking drug dealer in Rio Chico. It wasn't the *idea* of drug dealing that was scandalous. Far from it: they lived in a poor South Texas *colonia* where drug dealers were as ubiquitous as payday loan stores. Rather, they were more like the drunken or perverted uncle—everybody had one.

Since Ester's father was rumored to be fairly high up in the chain of command, Beatriz and Mateo didn't feel comfortable having their children spend too much time there. What if someone attempted to kidnap the man's children, and Cristina was with them? What if one of their six kids accidently picked up one of the man's many guns?

Ester actually preferred to be out of her house. On this particular night, Ester was spending the night and was watching a movie with Cristina when Isa joined them. Over popcorn, candy, and corn chips, they laughed and talked about their peers. In the middle of their reverie, Ester admitted that she was attracted to one of her brother's friends. Cristina sheepishly confessed that she had a crush on Beto, a known jerk who thought he was God's gift to all the freshman females. Then Ester turned to Isa, her eyes locked on hers. "What about you, Isa, is there a guy you are interested in?"

Isa felt trapped. How could she not reciprocate? So, she said the first thing that came to her mind.

"Your brother is cute."

"Oh, my God, Victor? You like Victor?" Cristina had squealed.

"Isn't he in English class with you?" Ester asked.

"But he has a girlfriend," Cristina had reminded them.

"So what?" Ester interjected. "What if he breaks up with her?"

Isa knew that Victor had a girlfriend—it's why she had blurted out his name. Even if she had been interested, guys like Victor didn't date girls like her. What she had not expected was the instant feeling of belonging that overcame her after "confessing" her crush. For one evening, she felt part of something. And it felt good.

⌐▄

Before she knew it, Isa was lying to herself. In English class, she found herself looking for Victor. Theoretically, could she even see herself with him? He was popular because of who he was; yet despite what his parents did, he was a decent guy. He was kind, polite, and never acted like he was better than anyone else. Victor was the son of a notorious drug dealer, and Aurora was an artsy girl who was being raised by a single mother. Better yet, he could be dating so many girls, but he was dating Aurora Trevino, a girl whom Isa actually happened to like. Aurora was one of those girls who wore what she wanted and not what school fashion dictated. She was in both the art club and the pep squad. Together, Victor and Aurora made a neat couple. She was actually happy for them, but more often than not, anxiety would creep back into her thoughts. What if he broke up with Aurora? And Ester told him about her "crush"? What if he asked her out? What if she said yes?

She went back and forth on the matter. Did she really have a crush on this likeable classmate, or was she just so committed to her lie that she was actually feeling things? It didn't help that Victor was such a gentleman. One day, he had stopped Isa right as they were leaving English.

"Hey, your backpack is open."

"Oh," Isa started to shake it off her shoulder, when Victor stopped her. "No, no, I got it. Here . . ."

Just like that, he zipped up the front pocket, and Isa was touched by his kindness and flattered by his attention. They were walking in the same direction, so he continued to chat with her. Isa tried to stay calm; she talked to him about their younger sisters' friendship.

"You know, your little sister is like one of the family?"

"Yeah, I think she spends more time over at your house than ours. By the way, you should come to my brother Lalo's party. It's in two weeks. Lalo is turning fifteen and my dad is throwing him a big-ass *pachanga*. We're calling it his dude *quinceñera*."

"Sure, yeah, I'll think about it."

Isa had never been to the Carillos' house, but she had heard all about it from Cristina. Victor had introduced her to his girlfriend, and when Isa discovered that she was even nicer than she had imagined, it was Aurora who caught her eye, not Victor. Aurora had fine, light-brown hair and a gentle smile. She seemed kind and self-assured. The only thing that worried Isa was what Ester had joked about, earlier in the week: her mission to get her and Victor together. The idea of Victor finding out was mortifying.

❧

Victor's palatial "narco style" mansion had everything a kid could possibly want. The five-car garage was littered with expensive remote-controlled toys and at least a dozen four-wheelers. There was a large walk-in bird aviary that held two lemurs, and several feet away stood an even larger chain-link enclosure with a plywood divider that housed the mini-pony and a very lethargic-looking llama.

Isa was trying to summon enough courage to go see the lemurs, but the terrible screeching noises they were making held her back. She was wondering if she should pet the mini-pony when Ester showed up with Cristina in tow.

"Guess what?" she asked, almost out of breath.

"What?" Isa answered.

"I think that Victor and Aurora just had a fight."

Cristina scrunched her face and looked at her friend. "Don't listen to her, Isa, I just saw them. They looked fine to me."

"Yeah, well, they have been fighting a lot lately, you never know."

Isa thought it was sweet that Ester liked the idea of the two of them together. It was an unlikely scenario, but stranger things had happened. Isa watched Ester drag Cristina over to the picnic table with all the snacks and desserts, and she wondered if anyone from her school would show up.

～♪

Eventually, Isa sat down at a table where a mother was trying to feed her baby without getting food on his adorable little suit. The toddler wore a gold chain bracelet on his chubby little wrist, and Isa wondered about its value. When she grew tired of staring at the blinged-out baby, she almost choked on a chip when she saw a man with a gun poking out of his holster. He was helping two elderly matrons with rosaries around their necks climb into a black Escalade. The older of the two reached out to the armed man to give him her blessing.

"*Que Dios te bendiga, hijo.*" May God bless you, son.

Isa made a mental note. This was one great anecdote for her mother. Beatriz loved nothing more than busting the sanctimonious types. She had very little respect for the kind of women who attended weekly Mass and went to confession regularly, but then turned around and reported gossip as fact.

These women were even worse. Beatriz would have criticized them heavily for such hypocrisy. Who did they think they were, Patron Mothers of Narco Spirituality? In Beatriz's book, you were either good, bad, or indifferent. She knew she was the latter, but to walk around with a rosary and bless known criminals? Well, that was just downright disingenuous. Isa and Cristina had been raised as cultural Catholics. They identified with Catholic traditions but didn't actively practice the religion. What Isa's mother could not abide, however, were *hipocritas*.

Here she was, worried about pulling off a fictitious crush on Victor Carillo (which might not even be necessary), when all around her nothing made sense. Nothing about the Carillos' lifestyle was normal, yet it was real and socially sanctioned.

⚜

The lucky birthday boy was Eulalio Carillo (a.k.a. Lalo), Ester's bratty brother who was in the eighth grade. Cristina had pointed him out to Isa earlier when he was seen walking around with a new eel-skin wallet and showing off the cash that his father's "associates" had generously doled out. Eulalio had been held back in school more than once and he had no problem reminding people that he was the only fifteen-year-old in junior high.

⚜

Isa was wondering where her sister was. She knew that Cristina was probably inside, but she didn't feel comfortable going in. She pulled an ice-cold can of Coke from one of the large coolers and sipped at it slowly—pretending she was waiting for someone. From where she stood, she could see more of the house, and it looked like the group of architects working on it couldn't agree on a single style. It's modern! It's ranch! It's confusing! There was an overabundance of stone on the façade, but it looked like they were inspired to do something different when the pool went in. The side of the house that looked out to the pool had a two-story addition with a balcony held up by Greek columns. Isa wasn't an expert, but she knew that decorative wagon wheels and anything reminiscent of the Parthenon did not mix.

Oh, but the horrors didn't stop there. She overheard one of the guests pointing out the fact that the monogram on the large wrought-iron gate at the entrance of the compound had been designed to resemble Mr. Carillo's custom-made Texas belt buckle. After that, she was comparing all the men's belt buckles with the gate—hoping to spot Mr. Carillo himself.

At one point, a pleasant woman came over to Isa and offered her a plate of *fajitas*, baked beans, and rice. The *conjunto* band started playing *rancheras,* and couples took to the improvised dance floor on the patio. Cristina came out of the house looking upset.

"Cristina? What happened?"

"I'll explain it in a minute, let's go."

"We need to call Dad?"

Cristina had taken Isa by her arm and urged her to "just walk."

Once they were both past the sea of shiny, double-cab pickups, on a makeshift parking lot located right outside the Carillo property, Isa stopped.

"What the hell? What's going on?"

"Just keep walking and I'll tell you."

"You're crying! What happened?"

Cristina had walked into the kitchen and overheard Ester's mom telling another woman that Isa was a *marimacha*—a lesbian. Someone at the party, who had a nephew who had worked with Isa—the summer she'd worked at Shop 'N Cart—had heard that Isa had been seen kissing a girl. Cristina had heard everything.

"Can you believe them, Isa? Why would they say that? Why? Then the other stupid lady goes, 'She doesn't look like one,' and then Ester's mom said something about some guy named Geraldo knowing everything," Cristina continued.

She imitated Ester's mom speaking in a hushed tone, "'Apparently, she was spotted by one of the guys who also works there during his break. He swears up and down that those two were making out.'"

"It's because they hate me." Cristina's voice was thick with emotion. "If they do, why invite us into their home if they are going to invent something so awful?"

Oddly, Isa felt relief. Someone had seen her after all. It had been raining, pouring actually, and they were on break. The other girl had quit the next day and ignored her at school. It was the only time she had dared to kiss another girl in high school. She had never in her wildest dreams thought anyone had seen them. Isa watched Cristina walk ahead of her. Cristina's steps were fast and purposeful.

She started walking more quickly to catch up with Cristina, then slowed down. She realized her sister wasn't giving the story any credibility; she was making it all about herself— and that worked for Isa. It was in that slowing down, in not reacting, that something inside of her shifted.

In that particular moment, she didn't feel like lying anymore. What if she came clean? Told Cristina everything. Just Cristina. No one else.

She thought about it, but when Cristina stopped talking, she chickened out. She was too afraid to say anything, so she figured she would say nothing. Cristina just continued to walk on ahead of her talking about the Carillos.

"They just think they are better than everybody, you know? Just because they are rich. I mean Ester is cool, it's like she isn't even part of that family. Well, so is Victor and the little sister—Amy, she's cool. Everyone else is awful. Just awful!"

Listening to Cristina rant, Isa realized that her secret wasn't even remotely on her sister's radar. How could it be? In South Texas people would rather believe in the existence of the *chupacabra* over the existence of homosexuals.

chapter 5–Cristina

Adelita Magnolia Alvarez was born on a Wednesday, thirty minutes before the heavens in South Texas delivered a torrential downpour. Leo would always remember the kind nurse who had burst into their room to announce the news—not about the baby, but the rain. Rio Chico residents talked about the rain for weeks afterwards, but Cristina didn't remember a thing. The only memories she could recall were the days that she first spent by her daughter's side. Outside, the water reservoirs in the neighborhood were filled to capacity. Children and adults had taken to the streets to soak up the water, but all Cristina had eyes for were her little one's perfect toes, nose, belly—every square inch below her damaged little forehead.

The rain had fallen for two and a half days. *Colonias*, as usual, flooded, so did the nearby creeks, causing many road closings. Beatriz had talked about kids in her neighborhood kicking and splashing in pools that ranged from ankle- to knee-deep. Children under the age of seven had never seen this kind of rainstorm. And they probably would not see one again for a long time.

Leo felt there was something comforting and special about bringing their child home under such auspicious conditions.

When Leo and Cristina held their little one, every second seemed worth the wait. Adelita's cheeks were rosy, and her thighs substantial enough for baby folds. Even the nurses commented on how fleshy her thighs were, and nicknamed her Chub Wubs. When the hospital hat was placed on her head and over her eyes, you couldn't even tell that anything was wrong. Her body was perfect, whole, and healthy. She almost seemed complete.

They walked her through each room of their home, including the living room, describing Leo's favorite recliner. "This is where daddy watches football." They told her the story of the infamous living-room set and how it had been delivered in a ridiculous shade of chartreuse before they received the right one. But the best part was ending the tour in their bedroom and telling Adelita the story of her new home. She was part of a new chapter in their lives, and they had come a long way, motivated, in large part, in anticipation of her arrival.

When Cristina and Leo were first married, they had initially rented a small, ramshackle apartment near the school where Leo was teaching. The rent was dirt cheap and the apartment was in the center of town. Cristina's dream had always been to buy one of the older homes in their town's historical district.

They soon found that none were for sale, so they started looking at the newer neighborhoods just outside of town, but not out in the *colonias*. It's not that Cristina was ashamed of where she had grown up, but her father had always insisted that his children do better than he had—and neighborhoods with no paved roads and subpar infrastructure were definitely not on their wish list. Leo suggested that they rent an inexpensive apartment so they could eventually save enough for a down payment and then be able to make comfortable monthly payments on their dream home.

They had rented for several years before the home they currently lived in became available. The former owners had filed for bankruptcy, and they found the government foreclosure before anyone else did. They planted grass, trees, and all kinds of flowers. Leo installed a sprinkler system and turned their backyard into their own private little oasis in a South Texas landscape that seemed to scorch all live vegetation.

They gave the baby a tour of the kitchen. They told her the story of the dispute they'd had over the appliances. When the cream-colored dishwasher died last fall, Leo suggested that Cristina wait a month to take advantage of Black Friday deals. But Cristina had not counted on him surprising her with a new white stove and white refrigerator. Had he consulted her, she would have told him that white was the new avocado green. Everyone was buying stainless steel appliances. Leo had called her ungrateful and shallow.

The off-white refrigerator humming in the corner of the kitchen was no longer an eyesore. They had a beauty baby girl to tend to.

ᴸᴬ

Adelita came into this world strong in body and soul, if not mind. Anencephalic babies like Adelita were missing not only a great portion of their brain, but also their skull and scalp, due to a neural tube defect. Cristina took great care in picking out a variety of knitted caps that covered this depression. Adelita, unlike less fortunate babies, had a good portion of her brain stem intact. But even though they had been told that Adelita could not see, hear, feel, or touch, Cristina and Leo were going to treat as if she were conscious of everything. If they were going to make their baby comfortable, they would make certain her last days, her only days on earth, were filled with love, grace, and dignity.

Adelita was able to take a bottle and coo—so regardless of what they were told, she was a real, living, breathing baby girl with her own personality. In her heart, Cristina felt like her child recognized the sound of her voice. They could also intuit that she had a sense of humor. She made the cutest little noise that sounded like a giggle. And when she chortled, she liked to kick her right foot. Cristina was convinced that this was Adelita cracking up at her daddy's senseless jokes.

Adelita was everyone's little darling. Initially, they all felt like she would break. She seemed so fragile. Mateo was hesitant to hold his granddaughter, but after he held her for the first time, he was hooked. His grandchild was so much stronger than anyone could have imagined.

Every day started with the same ritual. Cristina would change the sterile dressings on Adelita's head, pick out a lovely little outfit, feed her, and then place her in her car seat. Every morning, car seat perched up high on the kitchen island, Adelita and her mother listened to Cristina's favorite Spanish radio station and prepared Leo's breakfast. Despite Leo's objections, Cristina hesitated to let him change her head bandages or see her without her cap. She wanted things to be as normal as they could be. She wanted to spare Leo the baby's imperfections, even though it was not necessary.

Of course, not all days were idyllic. There were days when Adelita's abnormalities seemed to define her. Some days were spent at doctor's appointments. The second time Isa flew down for a visit, they celebrated and had a little party for Adelita. The baby was almost six weeks old. Adelita was already considered a miracle. But that's not how Leo and Cristina saw it, holding on to the possibility that Adelita would be with them forever. The last time that Isa had visited, she talked Cristina into scheduling a day at the spa.

"Are you kidding?" Cristina had said.

"Sis, you look like hell."

"Thanks a lot."

"No, seriously. Just a massage?"

"I can't."

"Look, I have already talked to Mom. You know that she can feed the baby and change her head bandages." Beatriz had watched her daughter and assisted in the highly skilled care that Adelita needed. Caring for Adelita meant taking meticulous notes for the doctor, feeding her with a special bottle that made it easier for the baby to swallow, using a triple antibiotic cream over the top of her head, and carefully covering her head with a Vaseline bandage.

"We will only be gone for a couple of hours. We'll skip the manicure and pedicure, come on, what do you say?"

"I can't leave her, what if . . ."

"Cristina, stop thinking worst case scenario. You look exhausted. Adelita needs her mommy to really be there for her. An hour massage? Come on?"

"You know what? Let's do it!"

⚓

The morning of the massage, Cristina was ready. She was feeling comfortable, secure that nothing bad would happen, that Adelita would be okay.

Isa had come over early and watched the baby while Cristina took a long, hot shower. It had been a very long time since Cristina had had the luxury of shampooing and conditioning her hair, shaving her legs, and just letting the hot water ease her stress. Thinking for the first time that maybe life could go back to normal. She didn't have to live in fear.

Spotting the pumice stone, Cristina thought of giving her heels a good scrubbing. She was leaning over the lip of the tub when she heard Isa scream. Cristina almost slipped in the tub trying to get out. She pictured her child on the floor. She managed to get out of the bathroom, sprint down the hall and into the baby's room soaking wet, not a stitch of clothing on her, barring the hand towel she had grabbed as she raced out of the bathroom.

Isa was standing in the middle of the room, holding Adelita and using her chin to point to the baby bottle on the floor.

"She started making a noise. A really odd hiccup noise. I thought she was choking. Is she okay?"

"Relax," Cristina whispered, relieved that nothing was wrong.

"That's normal?"

"It's one of the many little noises that she makes."

Still shaken, but reassured, Cristina walked back to the bathroom, threw on her robe, and came back to her child's side with a towel wrapped around her head. Gently she scooped her baby into her arms and sat in the rocking chair. She didn't have to say anything, Isa's look and demeanor was acknowledgment enough. She knew that they wouldn't be going anywhere. Cristina recognized that Isa had just experienced a taste of what her life had been like since Adelita's birth. Everything was unnerving.

"Silly girl," said Cristina, caressing Adelita's little arm, "you scared your poor *Tía Isa*."

In nothing but her mint green robe and the towel over her wet hair, Cristina cradled Adelita in her arms and sang to her. She felt so calm. So content. So blessed. Isa tiptoed out, and Cristina heard the car back out of the driveway, followed by the phone ringing. It was a teacher in-service day and Leo didn't think his peers would mind. Where had the morning gone?

⌣⚓

When Leo got home, it was time for Adelita to eat. He tried to give her a bottle, but she wouldn't take it. Cristina finally got dressed and found her husband and child lying on their giant king-size bed.

"You're going to be late," she gently reminded him.

"So what?" he said with a big grin. "I'd rather play hooky and hang out with my girls."

Cristina lay down, and they both looked up at the ceiling. Leo talked about the goings-on at school and about possibly going back to school for his doctoral degree. Cristina told him about their failed spa plans and the big fright that Adelita had given *Tía Isa*. Eventually, both parents turned on their sides and watched their little one sleep. They would watch the heaving of her little rib cage. Up and down. Up and down. Her pink, pursed lips. Her small hands and delicate baby skin.

Cristina was about to say something, when Adelita's little legs seemed to tighten. Her breathing did seem a little labored, and Cristina wondered if they should make preparations to take her to the hospital. Leo called their pediatrician and was told to wait an hour. Sometimes, Adelita needed an oxygen tank. Their silly "little goose" (Leo's nickname for her) would occasionally forget to breathe. But in less than half an hour, Adelita's color returned, and she even took her bottle. Leo called work and took the rest of the day off.

The three of them fell asleep. Cristina and Leo slept like they hadn't in months. Hours, six and a half to be exact, passed—a record. When they awoke, the sun was setting and their bedroom was filled with a stunning orange afternoon light. Cristina started to panic; Adelita had skipped two meals. How could it be so late? Leo reassured her that it was just time that their little one started to sleep for longer periods of time. It's what babies did. Adelita looked so peaceful, she seemed okay.

But way too still.

Cristina scooped the baby into her arms. She placed her finger over the baby's nose and looked at her husband. Afraid that his wife might collapse, Leo grabbed them both and gently led Cristina back to the edge of the bed. Leo checked for a pulse, but Adelita was gone.

They knew that she was gone, but they still frantically made the calls. They went through all of the motions. Cristina made Leo call an ambulance while she continued to hold her child, wanting her body's warmth to bring her baby back. Was this really happening?

By the time the paramedics arrived, Cristina was still. Numb, but unwilling to have anyone declare her child dead.

When Adelita was officially declared dead, they both asked everyone to leave. They needed to be alone.

They held her little hand and tried to keep her in this world. Had they been generous and selfless, they would have accepted and let her go. But they didn't. They clung to the present and willed her little soul to linger and comfort them. They nuzzled against her small body and inhaled their daughter's baby smell for the last time. Their nightstand would no longer be covered with her doll-sized diapers, lavender lotion, or milk rings left over from her nighttime feedings. Her bath towel and baby clothes would be stored away, not tossed into the laundry basket until their next use. They were grasping for a life that would no longer be. They were unable to part with her, so they lay still with a raw tightness in their throats.

chapter 6–Isa

Rio Chico, Texas, 2004

Isa had flown down as soon as she heard the news. Everyone knew it was inevitable, but that didn't mean that anyone was prepared for what happened. She knew that neither Cristina nor Leo would have the wherewithal to take care of what needed to be done. Cristina had refused to see to the details of a funeral before it was time, so Isa made enough calls from DC that by the time she boarded the plane, thirty-two hours later, most of the arrangements had been taken care of.

In Rio Chico, she hit the ground running. There wasn't much she could do for her sister and brother-in-law. Beatriz and Dora were responsible for greeting and feeding the guests who paid their respects at the house, but all they could do was to pass on their condolence to the grieving parents who sat on the couch, leaning into each other and looking lost.

Isa had to fly back at the end of the week, and by that time, Leo was starting to look a bit more like himself, but Cristina stayed in her room. Isa knew that there was very little that she could do. She kept assuring her sister that things would get better and she would be back as soon as she could.

❧

Two months later, Isa was back in town, and Cristina was still not doing well. During her absence, most of what Isa knew about her sister had come from reports from Beatriz and Leo. Isa understood. Her sister needed time, and she was hoping that this trip could be a nice turning point, to try to see past the sadness of losing Adelita and move forward, but when Isa saw her baby sister, she barely recognized her. No one had prepared her for what she would see—and she had many questions.

⸎

Had it been Leo and her parents' way of protecting her? How had they allowed Cristina to get to this point? When Isa saw her sister, her knees grew weak as she hugged her frail frame. Cristina started crying and so did Isa, but Isa didn't know who she was crying more for, Adelita or Cristina. Cristina was a bag of bones. She had dropped a little over twenty-five pounds, and her collarbone protruded from her tank top. Her jeans were loose on her, but the most frightening thing was the color of her skin and the state of her hair.

She was not just pale-faced, but a little yellow, and her hair was so thin and brittle that Isa felt that if she touched it would fall out. Isa's first reaction was to lash out at Leo and her parents. *Were they blind? Did they not see what she saw? Cristina looked like she needed to be in a hospital.* She could only blame herself. The sad truth was that it was Isa who had not been paying attention. Back in DC, she was busy trying to finish up school and lining up work, and she was hurried and frantic. And if she really thought about it, there were bits of the conversation that she had not given much credence to. Beatriz was always talking about trying to make her eat; Isa assumed that she was exaggerating. Leo had assured her that Cristina was never alone and she wasn't. Beatriz would spend most days with Cristina until Leo came home.

Isa had been so involved with her own life that she'd never stopped to think of what might happen to Cristina after her only child died. Her calls had been quick and superficial. Comforted by the knowledge that her mother was over at Cristina's house a lot, she never feared that Cristina was starving herself. She touched base with Leo every week and knew that he was in over his head at work, and most of the time that is what they spoke about. She knew it was his way of coping.

In the beginning, ensconced in his own level of self-denial, Leo spent longer hours at work. He started by keeping himself busy with all manner of paperwork, but then his middle school was hit with two big crises. Two of his seventh graders, twin boys, were killed in a tragic car accident. Leo was consumed with the collective grief of the school community and all of the matters that go along with handling such a tragedy. After that it was one fire after another. No sooner had the student body gotten over the shock of their peers' death when a different kind of crisis needed his attention: two eighth-grade girls came forward with claims about their basketball coach's inappropriate behavior. Leo's work life was an adrenaline ride and, sadly, a distraction from problems at home.

The longer Isa was home and questioning everyone, the more she understood Leo's lack of awareness about his wife's mental and physical health. During the day, after Mateo dropped Beatriz off with his daughter, Beatriz did laundry, cleaned up, and always made sure Cristina had lunch, and that dinner was on the table for both of them. Leo had told her that the dinner and all of the cleaning were not necessary—but who was he kidding? Beatriz and Mateo had been lifesavers.

Isa learned that the only time Cristina made it out of the bedroom was in the late afternoon when Leo got home. He had been assuming his wife was doing some of the housework, but through Isa he learned that Cristina stayed in bed most days, refusing to shower or drink more than a can of Ensure. When she did agree to bathe, she sat in the bathtub but never allowed Beatriz to wash her hair. Her scalp was too tender.

In the late afternoon with Leo, Cristina would muster up what little energy she had and pick at her dinner, while Leo ate and talked about his day. Then they would watch a series of mind-numbing television programs until it was time to go to bed. And that is how it had been.

❧

That evening Isa made two long-distance phone calls to Aisha and William. Aisha needed to hear this, and William—well, as her temporary roommate she had just confided a lot in him lately.

"It's not your fault, stop blaming yourself," Aisha had assured her.

"Yes, it was. Here I was only worried about finishing up my course work and exams."

"Look, honey, you have done a lot more than you think—as it is, you have to get used to the fact that none of your family members will be attending your graduation."

"Thank you, friend. I actually begged them not to come. Well, you know, Mom and Dad could never make it, but I couldn't have Leo and Cristina spending all that money. Leo insisted on covering my last two plane tickets, and that's already too much."

"Oh, and of course, I get to meet your new roommate, the loser who doesn't pay any rent."

"He's not a loser. We have become really good friends, and he's my default buddy for movies, eating out, and anything that requires a date."

"What kind of events require dates? You're not going hetero on me, are you?"

Aisha had laughed at her hetero references, but she felt little stabs of guilt when she thought of all of the times that William had flirted with her, and she loved the attention. Her life back in DC seemed worlds away now. Two days later, she would be calling her friend again with more news: Cristina's doctor had not only diagnosed her depression, but he thought that she'd actually had a nervous breakdown.

Many years' worth of disappointment and trauma had eroded and compromised everything that was holding Cristina together, until one day, she had just collapsed.

Isa had looked her brother-in-law in the eye and promised him that she would do everything that she could, while she was there, to get their old Cristina back. She was confident that she could do it.

⚓

Isa woke up and read the numbers on the alarm clock near the bed, scrambling out from under the sheets and walking into the living room. It was half-past eight, and Leo was long gone. There was a bowl of soggy bran cereal on the counter and a Hot Pocket that had been left in the microwave too long. Isa started the coffee maker, tidied up the counter, and then walked into her sister's room.

"Rise and shine, baby girl!" Isa said.

Out from under the sheets, Isa heard a muffled, "I'm tired, come back later."

"Cristina, I am only here for a week. Come on, you can do this, I know you can. You can't just give up."

Cristina threw the covers off, sat up, and leaned against the headboard. "Isa, I know that this is terrible. I feel so lame and pathetic. I feel guilty that Mom has to come over and make sure that I do stuff. But nothing helps. I just need time."

"Mom said that you stopped taking the medications the doctor prescribed."

"No, I didn't. I take them every day, but they make me so sleepy."

"Why would Mom say that you don't take them?"

Cristina looked offended and started to get up out of bed. "Isa, I am not a liar, okay? I'm depressed, but I am not a liar. Mom knows that those things make me sleepy, and if you want to know the truth, it's what I like about them, that they knock me out and then I don't have to remember. Maybe she thinks I need to be taking more, I don't know."

While Cristina went into the bathroom, Isa started to make her sister's bed. Cristina poked her head out of the master bathroom and looked disappointed. "Why did you make the bed? I'm going back to sleep."

"No, you're not. I have coffee brewing and we are going for a walk."

"Isa, please, don't. . . " pleaded Cristina.

"Sis, please, can we do this for one week, just one week, than I will leave you alone."

"Three days."

"Four days?"

"Two days."

"Okay, all right, three days!" Isa let out a whoop and motioned for her sister to get back into the bathroom.

◢◣

In the kitchen, Isa had bacon and eggs going, toast in the toaster, and two small glasses of grape juice. She poured two cups of coffee—it was her second—and watched Cristina emerge from the hall.

"Yay! You washed your hair!"

"Why wouldn't I wash my hair? I always wash my hair."

Isa didn't know if she should bring up how unkempt her sister looked, but she didn't want to argue. Then Cristina added, "I just don't use any shampoo or conditioner."

"Why not?"

"We're out of it."

"Well, let's go get some. In fact, after breakfast, let's make a list of everything you're out of."

"Sure," Cristina replied, very blasé.

"Wait, after our walk."

"I don't want to walk."

"Just one lap around the neighborhood, just one? Please?"

"Fine, just one."

Isa was nervous about her experiment, but she felt that just getting Cristina out of bed to eat had been a victory.

Isa insisted that her sister do things around the house: unload the dishwasher, start a load of laundry, and make a grocery list. To her surprise, Cristina didn't resist. Isa was even amazed when Cristina's unloading of the dishwasher led to cleaning the kitchen counter and then sweeping. She even found that their first morning walk had been a success.

On the second day, she had a little trouble making sure that Cristina was out of bed before nine, but the rest of the day went just as smoothly as the first. Cristina actually finished her breakfast and poured herself a second glass of juice. She was even looking a bit energized, but also motivated to get her home the way she liked it.

"Don't get me wrong, I am so grateful for *Ama* helping out with the cleaning and everything, but she wipes the dishes with the same washcloth that she scrubs the stove with—it grosses me out."

"Well, Sis, you have to admit, even my cleaning is no match for your OCD standards. That's why your husband no longer helps with the chores. You, my dear, are a control freak!"

On the third day, Isa awoke to the smell of coffee. She wondered if her parents had come by and started breakfast themselves. She leapt out of bed and called out.

"It's just me," cried Cristina.

"Awesome, this is great!" answered Isa.

"Isa, stop it."

"Stop what?"

"Acting like I'm not capable of doing anything."

"Cristina, I'm sorry. It's just that you were starting to really freak me out."

"Well, I'm good. I am."

"Are you sure?"

"Yeah, this is starting to feel more normal."

"Are you taking the medicine?"

"Yes, I am. . . "

"Okay, tomorrow we are going to see *Ama*. Dora is going to be there, she is making you *buñuelos*."

"No, I'm not ready, I can't."

"Yes, you can."

"I don't know, Sis. . . "

"Another thing, I'm spending the night over at Mom and Dad's tonight. That okay? I think that you and Leo need some alone time."

"Sure."

"So, I'll see you tomorrow, okay? Mom is counting on you, and so am I."

The next day Isa slept through her alarm in her old bedroom, while Beatriz worked outside in her yard, watering her plants. Startled by the loud noise that the old gate made, Beatriz dropped the hose and turned to see Dora, her neighbor and best friend, swinging open the gate that separated their yards. Dora, whose childhood polio had given her a permanent limp, drew closer and gestured toward the pool of water in front of Beatriz. "Are you trying to make the cement grow?"

The two made quite a pair. Beatriz was tall and robust, a substantial woman, while Dora was tiny, short, and thin as a rail.

"*Buenos días*, Dora."

"*Buenos días, qué paso aquí?*" asked Dora, pointing to a large puddle of water.

"Dora, it's just water."

Dora had hair like the fuzz of a newborn baby chick, thin enough that you could see whole sections of her pink scalp where her silver comb swept her hair into the stringy chignon that rested low at the nape of her neck.

"Beatriz, *qué te pasa*? I've been watching you from my window. You have watered the same plants twice. What's bothering you?"

"I'm just so worried about Cristina. She doesn't want to eat, she doesn't want visitors, and yesterday, Isa caught her packing away all of Adelita's things."

"Well, what's wrong with that?"

"It's too soon. The baby's clothes must remain untouched for at least six months."

"Who said that?"

"I heard an aunt say it once."

"You know what I heard an aunt say once?"

"What?"

That women should not enter swimming pools with men—because of their . . . you know…their ding dong . . . and what might come out . . . if they get excited . . . it could impregnate them."

"That's the most ridiculous thing I have ever heard!"

"My point exactly. That bit about the baby clothes, *pura superstición*! Our girls were raised here, and they have different ideas about those things."

"There has to be something that I can do to help her."

"You want to make her pain go away? Well, that's not going to happen. Just stand back and let her work it out. That's what her husband is for. They'll be okay."

"*Sí, comadre. Tienes razón.* You're right. They will work it out."

When she heard the phone ring, Beatriz jumped and handed Dora the hose. She feared that it might be Cristina, calling to cancel.

"Who was it?"

"It was someone speaking in English. I hung up."

"You heard Isa. She is doing great, she will come."

"Yeah, but Isa spent the night here, Cristina is probably not even out of bed yet."

"Well, *comadre*, tell Isa that I'm coming back later to say hello. I hope she comes, for your sake."

"Are you saying that I'm the one that needs the consoling?"

"Just a little," said Dora with a smile and a light tap on her friend's shoulder.

Technically, Cristina wasn't due for another hour. Beatriz had invited Cristina over to help her de-clutter her place. Her daughter had apparently perked up at the suggestion. For years, both daughters had begged their parents to clean out the house and the yard. Beatriz and Mateo had lived in the house for a little more than three decades, and almost every square inch had been turned into a museum of all things rusty, outdated, and electronically compromised. To Beatriz, every item on their porch was one or two degrees from being of some use, to somebody. Neatly and in a most orderly fashion, she and Mateo had lined up every appliance, electronic, and chipped household bric-a-brac item on their porch. In the far corner of the entranceway, Mateo had built a series of shelves that housed everything from old paint cans and portable transistor radios to his collection of spark plugs. Next to that, he kept three large plastic, industrial-size barrels where he collected aluminum cans and scraps of metal. An old refrigerator, two cooking stoves, and a dishwasher lined the longest wall of the house.

As they grew older, their home became more and more confining. They learned to carefully navigate their way through piles of plywood scraps and weathered-looking plastic kiddie pools (filled with sacks of potting soil and gravel) if they ever needed to find anything there. They couldn't remember a time when their porch had been empty. Clutter and domestic debris was just part of life in their household. It was only now, as adults, that the sisters realized that their parents' hoarding tendencies were not just unsightly, but a hazard. Four years ago, Beatriz's idea of a makeover had been to divide the clutter from the seating on the porch by having Mateo put down a piece of green Astroturf and use her collection of old tin pots with plants and a foot-high plastic garden fence panel as a dividing wall for all of the crap.

✦

Beatriz was standing over her jasmine plant, plucking off some dead leaves, when Isa walked out onto the porch holding a steaming mug of coffee and looking for a place to sit. When Isa spotted her mother, she pulled up another chair and asked her mother to sit a while.

"*Ama*, that's enough water, can I bring you some coffee?"

"No, *hija*, I had coffee already, and I really can't drink more than my one cup, or I'll get the shakes."

"So, are you really going to let us throw all this out?"

Isa had been smiling, but regretted it as soon as she saw how hurt her mother looked. This was her stuff, her treasures.

"Maybe we don't have to move everything, maybe just half of it?"

"*Mira hija*, if the thought of de-cluttering this mess gets your sister out of the house to take on a project, so be it."

Isa looked at the plants that lined the flimsy, small plastic fence. An idea came to her, and she leapt out of her chair, spilling some of her coffee. "*Ama*, why don't we repot everything in the same size terracotta pots, like after everything is cleaned up? I can go to Home Depot right after lunch."

"*Hija*, you kids have an obsession with everything looking the same. *No tienen mas que hacer.*"

Isa watched her mother get up to move the water hose and felt a pang of guilt. She looked at the mismatched collection of tin cans and only then realized that her mother had probably taken great pleasure in rinsing the cans, punching holes in them, and putting them to good use. They probably reminded her of her grandmother's courtyard back in México.

Isa sat up and changed the subject. "Do you think that I should go get her?"

"No, let's give her time. But I'll tell you, if she stays in bed again and doesn't come, I will be really worried."

"*Ama*, she will come. Besides she seemed well yesterday. I just think that you kind of did everything for her. You make their meals, clean their house—"

"Isa, she's not like you. You have always been independent. You're resilient. You know, when you were a baby, all I wanted to do was hold you on my lap, but you couldn't sit still. You either wanted me to walk around with you and show you things or put you down so you could be on your own. I had to pick you up when you were sleeping. I can still hear your father: 'Put that baby down, she's been asleep for almost an hour.' Your sister could sit on my lap and chew on a spoon forever. You, you were walking at nine months."

Isa smiled. Her mother rarely talked about their childhood, and she relished these recollections of the past, but the moment was soon over. Beatriz changed the subject, started sweeping, and moved on. Isa thought breakfast pastries might cheer her up.

"Should I go out and get us some *pan dulce*?"

"*Si, hija*, that sounds good."

Isa stood and realized that she couldn't go anywhere since her father wasn't home with the truck.

"Wait, no truck, I'll go to the *tiendita* and get us something."

Isa was just about to start walking towards the corner store when she saw her mom staring off into space, like something was amiss.

"*Ama*, what's wrong?"

"Isa, will you be moving back home after school?"

Isa felt like a deflated balloon. The morning had been going so well, and now this. How many times did she have to tell everyone that coming back home to Rio Chico was not in her plans? Her mother knew exactly how she felt, and Isa thought this was a pretty cheap shot. Beatriz was obviously trying to make her feel guilty because of what Cristina was going through.

"You could be a lawyer here. Buy a nice house."

Isa sat back down and started to strip the chipping paint off the metal rocking chair with her fingernail. Whatever she said would make her feel like an asshole, so instead of starting on any of the hundred reasons why she wouldn't, she said nothing. Eventually, she stood up and headed toward the corner store with a heavy heart. What if her sister wasn't coming? What if Cristina was going crazy? What if it was ultimately up to Isa to save her?

chapter 7–Cristina

Rio Chico, Texas, 2004
The Same Day. . .

Cristina dragged herself out of bed and into the bathroom. She had no energy to use soap, let alone shampoo, so she just stood there and allowed the hot water to wash over her until it started to get cold. Coming back to the bedroom after her shower, she opened the curtains and was surprised by how bright everything was. Stripped of Adelita's presence, the bedroom seemed foreign and forlorn.

When Adelita was with them, their bedroom had become more of a neonatal intensive care unit than a place of rest. The baby slept with them on their king-size bed every night. Both nightstands had been overtaken by special feeding bottles, gauzes, ointments, diapers, and a wide variety of specialized paraphernalia that her needs required. The bedroom furniture had served as a backdrop to the hectic but highly fulfilling life they'd led while the baby was alive. It had purpose, but now the bedroom was just a room with an assortment of meaningless objects. A place to rest at night.

Cristina had lived in pajamas and sweats since the funeral, and had no idea what she was going to wear today. She opened her drawers and pulled open closet doors. She still felt too lethargic for anything dressy, and the idea of what to wear was too overwhelming. Should she wear khaki shorts, yoga pants, jeans? Her life just didn't seem her own anymore, and she couldn't even decide who she was.

᠆ᴥ᠆

With the exception of breakfast, Isa had been been bringing in mostly takeout during the last two days, so the kitchen wasn't well stocked. Cristina peeked in the pantry and reassessed the fridge—to get reacquainted with her kitchen. She noticed that they were out of orange juice and creamer, and there wasn't a piece of fresh fruit anywhere. The fruit bowl contained one shriveled apricot and a heavily bruised green apple. She fried three eggs, heated up some tortillas, and made a strong cup of coffee. She ran a washcloth under the running water and swept it across the dark green, granite countertop. This inspired her to start throwing out everything expired and to clean the fridge. It was also the beginning of reorganizing all the things that her mother and Leo had moved out of place.

Maybe it was the antidepressants kicking in, or Isa's visit, or both, but despite the heaviness in her whole being, she actually felt capable of moving forward, like she needed to get things done. There was a modicum of hope. A week ago, she had seen absolutely no sense in doing anything. She would wake up with a sore back from sleeping too much, roll over, notice that it was only midday, and then crawl back into bed.

Maybe it was time to move on. Well-meaning people in her life kept telling her that her little one could see her and probably worried about her. Attributing that kind of caretaker consciousness to a dead baby seemed cruel to Cristina. Why should a baby have to see to the emotional needs of a parent? She was the mother. She should be the one taking care of and consoling her baby, not the other way around.

After her kitchen was clean, Cristina threw her bed sheets into the washer, cleared the counter in one of the bathrooms, and went around the house collecting mail. Small piles of market flyers, authentic-looking correspondence, and bills were all over the place. She knew her husband—this was all his handiwork. When she picked up the mail, she took it directly to the basket on the kitchen island. Some of Leo's mail ended up on the dining room table, some on the kitchen counter, but most of it ended up on the coffee table next to the remote control. As she culled the junk mail, Cristina finished her second cup of coffee, headed toward the door, grabbed her car keys, and forced herself to walk out the door. It was now or never.

✌

"*Ah, hija.* I'm glad you made it."

"*Amá*, why wouldn't I?"

"*No se*, I just worry about you."

"I know. I know."

"*Pasa*, come and sit with me."

"*Ama*, let's do something. I'm energized. I feel like I need to keep moving."

"Well, when Isa gets back, maybe we can go to that restaurant you like?"

"I had breakfast. *Gracias*. Didn't you want to go through some of the stuff on the porch?"

"*Ah, sí, pero . . .*" Beatriz hesitated.

"You promised."

"Yes, I just haven't talked to your dad about it."

"*Amá*? You have to get rid of some of this stuff. It's a fire hazard, and it makes the place look so junky." As soon as the words left her mouth, Cristina realized that she had hurt her mother's feelings and quickly apologized, "Sorry."

"It's our life, *hija*."

"*Sí*, Má, but, think of how nice everything would look if you freed up some space."

"Like getting rid of all of Adelita's things?"

Beatriz didn't mean to bring that up, but she was worried that Cristina would later regret erasing her own baby's presence before it was time. When Cristina was ten, and the girls got a new bedroom set, Isa couldn't bear to part with anything—not even some of her elementary school report cards. Cristina, on the other hand, had tossed everything into boxes and asked for new posters. Cristina was the type who changed everything on a whim and kept very little. Every object in her house had a purpose or a place. Nothing was superfluous.

"*Amá*, it's just junk. Useless items. *Para qué lo quieres?*"

"To you, it's garbage. To me, it's *mi casa. Mis cosas.*"

"Just things, *Amá*. Can't you picture yourself sitting on this porch with nothing but your beautiful plants and none of this?"

"I can. Actually, it's how I grew up. A clean courtyard. You should have seen this place when your father and I first arrived."

Cristina placed her hands on her hips, surveyed her surroundings and then, pulling one of the porch chairs out of the sun and into the shade, she sat down next to Beatriz. "*Má*, no worries. I'm not going to make you throw anything out." Beatriz smiled. They sat in silence. They watched the big yellow school bus pull up and swallow a bunch of kids at the corner. One mother waved at them as she made her way back into her yard.

"Cristina?"

"Yeah."

"Do you know that at your age, I was convinced that I would never have any kids?"

"Because you thought that you were an old maid?"

"That, and because I was told that I didn't have a uterus."

"What?" asked Cristina, giggling.

"That's what I had been told."

"What do you mean, you didn't have a uterus?"

"When I was sixteen years old, I had stomach cramps so bad that I actually fainted. I was taken into town to see the doctor. He suggested that they take me to the city for surgery."

"What was wrong?"

"Well, people were pretty ignorant and your grandpa let his sister, my *Tía* Cande, do all of the talking. She told everyone that the doctors had removed my uterus on account of lady problems."

"Uterus, on a sixteen year old? How did they explain your period later?"

"Ay, what did we know? When I got pregnant and I asked the doctor, he said that it could have been my appendix—but certainly not my uterus. I mean, what does *Tía* Cande know, she wasn't a doctor."

"*Amá*, you never said anything."

"*Para qué?* The past is in the past."

"So, did you ever tell Dad?"

"Yes, on our third date. Your dad got so serious, so quick. I got a little scared. What if he really wanted children? I told him and guess what? He didn't care. Your dad was forty years old when I met him. He figured, if he didn't have kids by then, maybe it wasn't meant to be."

"So, you two must have been so excited when you found out about Isa."

"You have no idea."

Beatriz reached over and took hold of her daughter's hand. She squeezed it firmly and said, "*Hija*, life has so many surprises. When I was your age, I was living in a rural *rancho*, and I barely went out. An old maid, by everyone's standards."

Cristina started to tear up and squeezed back, "I'm so glad that you're here for me, *Amá*. I can't imagine life without you."

⚓

"So, where is Isa?"

"She went off to the *tiendita* to get us some donuts."

"Shoot, I forgot, she doesn't have Dad's truck. I should have stopped for *pan dulce*."

"No worries, she was going to look for donuts."

Beatriz watched Cristina pick away at a stray piece of string on a wobbly iron table.

"You know, *hija*, before this home was stuffed like a *guajolote* on Thanksgiving, it was an empty canvas. Oh, you would have loved it. This *colonia*, this little corner of the world where you grew up, was once nothing but a bunch of dust and unpaved roads that had been sub-divided into small one-eighth-acre lots and sold to poor Mexican immigrants like us."

"How did *Apá* even know about it?"

"He had this second cousin, who had been here since the fifties. By the time the sixties rolled along, all over the Rio Grande Valley, developers were offering farm workers and immigrants the opportunity to buy lots. This part of the US may not be paradise, but it gave us all the chance to own a piece of land, for pennies on the dollar. With his meager life savings, your father made a modest down payment on the property, and in return for no title—until the full balance was settled—he could make a low monthly payment."

"*Amá*, I can't imagine you and Dad in a house without all of this in it."

"Well, believe it or not, that's how we lived for a long time. When I first saw our place, it was small, half the size it is now, but tidy and new. It still needed a coat of paint, but despite that, it stood apart from the others. While other yards showed signs of children's toys, plants, and trees, ours was a clean slate. No one had yet opened and closed the screen doors one too many times, or left the doorframes mangled, or torn through our window screens. The asphalt shingles on the roof were new, and our yard, unlike the neighbors three yards down—who had lined their driveway with rusty steel drums—still looked nice. Full of landscaping potential. I was so naïve back then, I actually thought that your father would make it look like the houses he once took care of up North."

"That's funny, Dad mowed rich people's lawns for so many years, why didn't he bother with his own?"

"Oh, we tried. This soil just won't grow a lawn."

"*Sí*, Má, but what was the inside of our house like?"

"Looking back, it all seemed so easy. Simpler times and new beginnings. Our bedroom, for example, had nothing but a little closet and a mattress and box spring on the floor." Beatriz's eyes lit up and she started to rock in her chair. "Oh, let me tell you about the first time that I actually walked into this house. Your father was talking a mile a minute and rattling off a list of things that would eventually get done: coating the exterior walls with stucco, adding the porch, and if he found extra work, maybe even enclosing the entire lot with some fancy chain link fencing. I was barely paying him any mind; my eyes had locked onto my new kitchen. Your father had meticulously installed confetti linoleum, and had someone come in and built custom, floor-to-ceiling cabinets in the kitchen. That day, all that I could think of was waking up every morning and making and eating our meals in such a lovely space. Our bedroom was practically empty. Your father had shoved a cardboard box with all his clothes, work boots, and toolbox into the small closet."

"So, let's start making it all simple again."

"*Mija*, at the time, things didn't feel simple. Just as your future won't feel like it does today. I wanted a family, and didn't think that I would ever get one. And look at me now, two beautiful, grown daughters. What your little house looks like now will not be what it will look like years from now, and don't be surprised if there are young people begging you to throw out things out too."

Cristina leaned her head on her mother's shoulder.

chapter 8–Isa

Georgetown University Law School
Washington, DC, 2004

When Isa left, she had warned Beatriz not to step in if Cristina retreated back to her old ways, but her advice had been unnecessary. Two days after Isa left, Beatriz broke her ankle on the steps to Dora's house, and Cristina had no other choice but to step up and be around for her mother.

Thinking about how everything had unraveled, Isa wondered if Dora had been right. One day, after Cristina had gone home to greet Leo, Beatriz, Dora and Isa had stayed on the porch talking. Watching Cristina get in her car and drive off, Dora said, "She needs some trouble in her life, that's what she needs."

"Troubles? She has troubles," Isa had said, shocked.

"No, hear me out. This is what happened to a *comadre* once. There she was, complaining and protesting about her life. Her husband was unemployed, she hated her job, and her daughter was unwed and pregnant."

"I would be complaining too. . . "

"Wait, *espera*, I'm not done. Her husband eventually found a better job, but until he did, all she did was feel sorry for herself. She was mortified about her knocked-up daughter and how little money was coming in, until her daughter was in a car accident and died."

"Oh my God!" cried Beatriz. "Dora, that's terrible . . . that's an awful story."

"I never said anything, but I just kept thinking, her former problems paled in comparison, *que no?*"

"Yeah, I'm sure she would give anything to have her daughter—and grandchild—back," added Beatriz. "Problem is that my daughter has already lost it all."

"Has she?" asked Dora.

"Well, she has lost a lot," replied Beatriz.

"But not everything," Dora added.

⚓

Isa felt like she had accomplished a great deal. She had even considered having Cristina fly back with her for a change of scenery, but not only was Aisha going to be visiting soon, but her sister was thinking of going back to work a couple of days a week.

Two months came and went. She was looking forward to Aisha's visit—she always did—but this trip especially. She had some news for Aisha that could only be delivered in person—something that was going to leave Aisha with her mouth wide open. For once, she had done something completely crazy. Until then, she had to buckle down, finish classes, and continue studying.

Right now she was having a hell of a time trying to catch up. Isa was never behind on her reading, but now that she was back, she was cramming and suffering from information overload. Her head felt heavy with facts from dense cases, and legal jargon swam around her head, making no sense. She needed a break. Lately, she had taken to fantasizing about taking all of her study materials and every study note, right down to her stack of curled-up post-it notes, and setting them all on fire like a pile of dry leaves.

Isa decided to call it a day and go to bed. She was picking Aisha up at the airport the next day.

When Isa parked her car in the wrong airport lane, the angry security officer blew his whistle and motioned for her to move on. She was about to move out of her space when she was startled by a big loud noise. She slammed on the brakes, horrified, and craned her neck to the rear, fearing that she had hit someone. It was Aisha slamming her small bag on the rear of her car.

"Shit, Aisha! You scared me!"

"I was waiting in the other lane, about to try your cell, when I saw you."

"Well, get in, quick. That cop is giving us 'the look.'"

Aisha tossed in a small suitcase and a quilted, floral duffel bag, and hurled herself into the back seat. "You are so paranoid. Always were."

"He was yelling at me, telling me that I had parked in the wrong place."

"You did, my dear, you were in the shuttle lane."

Laughing, Aisha leaned over the front passenger seat and gave Isa a big hug.

"So good to see you, honey! Sarah says hello. Girl, you are looking good. The extra weight does suit you."

"I have an ass now," Isa said proudly as she squinted and tried to cut back into the airport exit lane.

"I wouldn't go that far, but you actually have some curves. You no longer look hungry."

"Hungry? Aisha, come on! That's just wrong."

"Woman, I'm not going to lie, I have always been jealous of your whole fashionably gaunt look."

"Well, I have filled out. It's probably all of the junk I've been eating, but I'm kind of loving it."

"Remember sophomore year? You were so stressed out that you didn't get a period for six months? I know when you drop below your regular skinny weight. I worry. We don't want your hair falling out again."

"Stop it! That only happened once!"

"Once is one too many times, my friend."

Isa reached over to the backseat and patted her friend's leg. "So good to see you! I can't tell you how long it's been since I just took a whole day off—well, there was Texas, but that so doesn't count."

⚓

"You study too much."

"No such thing here, honey."

"So, tell me, how is your computer love lady doing?"

"Stop calling her a computer lady," Isa said grinning.

"Honey, you're pretty and smart. You're a catch. What are you doing lurking online?"

"Lurking? You make me sound like a pedophile."

"I just think that you should be getting out more, meeting real women."

Isa grabbed a stack of papers and swatted Aisha playfully. "Aisha, get with the program already. Join the twenty-first century. This is how smart and discerning people are meeting each other now."

For the past three months, Isa had been chatting with a woman—"Nancy"—whom she had met through an online dating service. She was curious to see if a series of questions and keywords could match her up with someone with shared interests, but who was radically different in a way that still allowed Isa to be herself. Isa's chats with Nancy went something like this:

"I want to meet someone who is okay with a partner who will be working late."

"I'm okay with that, as long as you're working and not cheating on me."

"I don't want someone who will try to change me. I have no interest in being the poster girl for Latina Lesbians. I decided a long time ago that I was comfortable being invisible. It suits me."

Nancy didn't care. She had dated women who announced their sexuality every day on their commute to work, via outrageous in-your-face bumper stickers. She had also slept with women who had been married—women who would deny any and all lesbian dalliances if confronted.

Nancy was okay with Isa being open about her "issues." She would rather know the truth than be misled. Isa loved the idea of doing everything backwards. Online, she could disclose all her baggage, while flirting and simultaneously "connecting." And when they did meet, if they decided to meet—which was highly likely—they would only be pleasantly surprised by each other's positive attributes.

That night, Isa and Aisha caught up, while Aisha confessed to being jealous of her online "friend."

"Well, you can either believe it, or not. Every time I trust her with my innermost thoughts, I see it as an intimate act, one that only deepens our connection."

"*Cringe alert!* You sound like a Hallmark card."

"Shut up!" Isa blurted out, laughing, and drove them home.

⋈

Aisha, now married, living in Vermont, and working at Middlebury College, was sitting on the floor helping Isa fold clothes in the middle of her apartment. Shoving Isa's law school books aside, Aisha rolled her eyes and acted like the whole lot was a pile of toxic waste. "I still can't believe that you want to be a lawyer?"

"Correction, I'm *going* to be a lawyer. It's my last semester, in case you haven't noticed."

"Well, it took you long enough to decide on something."

"Seriously," Isa mockingly glared, "this coming from a woman who has had five secretarial jobs in three years?"

"My wife is a tenure-track professor. As long as she's employed, I can be happily undecided."

"Yeah, must be nice, but when are you going to do anything related to your degree?"

"When are you going to come out of the closet?"

"Touché."

"Maybe she'll help you?"

"Like I said, she could care less. She likes me for me."

"So, if coming out isn't the big news, what is it? If it turns out your secret is that you had a one-night stand and cheated on your computer screen, I might just have to hit you. Hard."

"Stop it! Be serious."

"What? You either did or you didn't?"

"No, I didn't meet anyone. Yes, I did have a one-night stand."

"Oh shit, did you hook up with that professor you were crushing on?"

"No. Why would I sleep with my professor?"

"People do."

"Okay, be serious. This is big news. I've done something that you, my dear, have never done."

"Oh, this I have to hear." Tossing a pajama bottom at her friend's face, Aisha demanded, "Tell me now!"

"William."

"William what? What about him?"

"Well, the night before he left, we were hanging out, thinking who knows when we will ever see each other again, when we got really, really drunk."

"No, no, please no. You didn't."

"Wait, it wasn't like that."

"You slept with that moocher?"

"I barely remember it."

"And you waited until now to tell me, Isa, while I'm folding your clothes? This is what you should have told me when you picked me up at the airport. No, the very night it happened."

"You mean the next day?"

"I need a drink."

Standing up, stretching her legs and walking toward the kitchen, Isa started to laugh, "Look, it happened. If we could get over it, so can you."

"Get me a beer and bring your ass back in here, you got some 'splaining to do, Lucy," Aisha called out to her.

"Here," said Isa handing Aisha a cold beer. "Seriously, it's no big deal. We were both really drunk and horny."

"Wait, back up, how drunk were you?"

"We were hammered, and we were having this really interesting conversation about why we were attracted to our own kind, and he started in on how he has always been attracted to me."

"Yeah, but he had a boyfriend?"

"Well, yeah, he was . . ."

"Shut up, I don't want to hear it!"

"Just listen, okay, so, he leaned in to kiss me, and I kissed him back . . ."

"No, this shit doesn't just happen."

"Well, we're friends, and . . ."

"We're friends, you don't see me jumping you!"

"Look, all I'm saying is that it felt good for both of us. I think. I mean, we did do it. I guess, since we both trusted each other, it was something to try. Aren't you the one that said something along the lines of sexuality is fluid?"

"I said no such thing. Isa, seriously, I'm shocked. Look at you, not even out of the closet, but an expert all of the sudden on everything on the whole sexual orientation continuum."

"Well, it's actually what we were talking about and probably the whole reason that it happened. William has such a healthy view of his sexuality. Our bodies, our orientation, to him this is beautiful, not dangerous stuff."

"Okay, where is the repressed friend that I know and have come to love?"

"You know, William really helped me see things in a . . . kind of different light. My parents didn't even have 'the talk' with me. There was no awkward way of telling us about the birds and the bees. It was just our implicit understanding that our bodies were our own worst enemies. Sex meant itchy bumps on your genitals or unwanted pregnancy. Then add lesbian sex into that nonexistent equation? You have one messed up . . ."

"You!" blurted Aisha.

"Yes, you have me."

"I thought it happened because you were drunk?"

"That too," Isa said with a grin. "You can't turn off sexual desires."

"How did you feel in the morning? Are you going to do it again? Are you bisexual now?"

"Oh God no, absolutely not, Aisha. If anything, it just confirmed things for me. And yes, we talked—a lot—the next morning. We got all that awkwardness out of our systems. No one is falling in love with each other or anything; we are grown adults. Sex is sex. Actually, I think he just got me out of his system. He was never in mine—that way, you know?"

"Well, yeah, it was Mr. Bisexual's way of getting into your pants and then skipping town."

"Whatever, now I can say I slept with a man. And it's not

for me. William is the closest that I have ever come to living my heterosexual fantasy—a life with zero complications."

"Isa, what have I told you about romanticizing heterosexual life?"

"Well, it beats living in the shadows."

"It doesn't have to be that way."

"Aisha, we have gone over this. I can't come out. Home might not be the place where I want to live, but 'home' as in the place that I can visit anytime—well, it's sacred to me."

"See, now you're romanticizing 'home.'"

"No, I am talking about familiarity, my mom and dad, the old neighborhood. Everything. The food of my childhood, Spanish television in the background . . ."

"Okay, I get it. You're still sentimentalizing the town you've always disliked. And family? All those cousins who thought you were a snob because of your bookish ways, did they all suddenly embrace you?"

"We all get along differently. See each other on holidays. We have fun—as long as my stay is brief and sweet."

"For a few hours, and then you leave and don't see them for another year."

"Whatever, maybe I needed to leave in order to know what family is. What I was always taking for granted."

"I still want to know how you ended up in bed with a man. It makes no sense."

"Look, it happened, and in a way, it was good."

"Okay, talk."

"I realized that I love women. Always have, always will. I think that somewhere, deep, deep inside of me, I thought that I might just chicken out, move back to Rio Chico, trap a man, and live the truly closeted life."

"Well, at least something good came out of this. Does this mean you're going to tell your sister?"

"Maybe, someday."

"Wow, well, thank you, William," Aisha said as she lifted up her beer and made a toast.

"Does Nancy know?"

"That's why I am so smitten with her. She knows everything. Absolutely everything about me."

"Only, you haven't met her?"

"She's gonna fly out."

"When?"

"Soon."

"So, where is William anyway?"

"Prague."

"Prague?"

"Yeah, following a really hot guy, who is also very rich. He barely even writes, he's forgotten all about me already. See? No need to worry about anything."

"So, he dumped you?"

"No, we were never together. I just think William latches on to whoever is close to him."

"Well, I'm glad. I feel like while he was in town, he was an emotional leech. What does he think about Ms. Nancy?"

"He thinks she's The One."

"How the hell does he know?"

"I think he's right, sweetie. I think I'm in love."

"With someone you've never met?"

"You just don't get it."

"What if your dream gal is really a middle-age man living in his parents' basement? Just using you to get his crotchety parts tingling?"

"Eeew! You are so gross! And I thought I was the cynic."

"By the way, Isa . . ."

"What?"

"Did you two use protection?"

"Duh."

"Just saying."

"As drunk as we were, I knew that much. He's as vehemently opposed to having children as I am."

"Well, Sarah and I really want one."

"A baby?"

"No, a puppy."

"You live in Vermont. Don't they just hand out babies to doting and devoted lesbian couples?"

"You're an idiot."

"But you still love me?"

"Hey, by the way, how is your sister doing?" asked Aisha.

"Cristina is . . . holding her own, I guess," Isa said.

"Do you think that Cristina will ever try again?"

"Honestly, I don't know."

"How can you not know? I mean if I had a sister, we would talk about everything."

"It's complicated."

"I'm sorry. Whatever issue you guys have, it's her fault. There must be something about her that you don't trust."

"Aisha, what are you talking about?"

"She's your only sister? How can she not know you're gay? How can she not be accepting of her only sister?"

"Well, that's it. I don't know. She might be accepting. I'm just afraid to go there."

"You two are just weird! You're close to her, but at the same time you guys are like strangers."

"It's my fault, probably," Isa said. "I just don't like to know stuff. So she doesn't ask about my stuff."

"Stuff?" asked Aisha.

"Yeah, like Cristina would always ask me about men. Was I

in any relationships? Pestering me about waiting too long. One day I told her off and she stopped telling me . . . about her baby troubles. And we kind of kept it light after that."

"Oh, my God, Isa, maybe Cristina knows?"

"No, I don't think so."

"You know, Isa, you spend so much time thinking of worst-case scenarios. Latinos love their gay children too. Maybe all this time it would have been okay. Your parents are not the first Latino family to have a gay child."

"I don't think that they would stop loving me, it's just that it would be different—different in an alienating kind of way. There is so much about our lives that is scary and unfamiliar. I can't. I won't."

"Okay, okay, forget I asked. We have only been having this conversation since college. How is your dad?"

"Dad is supposed to be retired, but he's working at my uncle's auto-salvage yard. It keeps him busy and out of my mother's way."

"Why isn't he home relaxing?"

"The man is seventy years old. He does what he wants to do."

"Isa?"

"What?"

"What if your parents die and you never tell them?"

"I would be sad that they died, but not that I didn't tell them. Aisha, please, please, just drop it."

"How can I drop it? You're my best friend. I turn around for one minute, and you sleep with a man."

"It was nothing. Besides, what if it had been, you know, like I discovered that I was bisexual? What, you wouldn't be my friend anymore?"

"No, sweetie, it's too late. You're like a sister to me, Isa, but I do think that the closer you get to finishing law school, the more the 'real world' looms over you, the more scared you get."

"Aisha, if you're worried that you'll lose me to the hetero-sexual world, it's not gonna happen."

"Sometimes I don't know. Women have been doing it for years. Why not you?"

～❧

After four days of talking into the wee hours of the night and cramming study sessions while Aisha shopped or saw a movie, Isa drove her friend to the airport. The reality of not sticking to her study schedule weighed heavily on Isa, but instead of getting right back to work, she tried to impose order on her cramped quarters. She tidied up the bookshelves, gathered dirty linens, and threw out a variety of takeout containers from the fridge. As Isa walked around her tiny apartment, picking up trash and straightening out cushions, she silently fumed over her guilt. Aisha had reminded her of the toxic "internalized homopho-bia." And Isa resented her for this. She could tell Aisha that she was okay with not being out, but deep down, she wasn't a hundred percent comfortable with it. When it came down to it, she knew that she wouldn't be free, free to just be, until she told Cristina and their parents.

～❧

Isa often wondered if her own parents would accept her like Aisha's had. But then she would get real. Telling her par-ents—let alone sending them pictures of her lesbian nuptials in Vermont—was not something she could *really* contemplate.

Aisha was always accusing Isa of driving women away. "You're like the guy, the total alpha butch wolf in femme's clothing. Isa, you don't like to communicate." Of course, Isa resented that. She was attracted to other femmes and always stuck to partners who wouldn't push her to come out. When she dated women, she always kept them at arm's distance in public. Isa loved the fact that she could safely move through the mainstream world without anyone's preconceived ideas of what she should be. And the women that she was attracted to were, oddly, closeted just like her. It was almost a prerequisite.

Maybe she should keep William in her life. He had given her a neon-yellow index card with his new contact information, and Isa wondered where she had put it. She couldn't find it anywhere. Well, he knew her address, maybe he would write to her first. He also had her e-mail. After straightening up her place, Isa made a mental note to visit the Health Center. She had been feeling tired and achy. The last thing that she needed was to get sick. Her throat was also scratchy, so she was going to get a strep test. She could not afford to get sick; she was in the home stretch now.

❧

Isa loved when her work space was cleared of all clutter. Her books were on the right, notebooks and file folders on the left. In the center of her kitchen "desk," she had placed a small, square-shaped glass vase where she stored her favorite pens. She pulled her planner from her favorite canvas bag and laid it open on the table. Whenever she needed to quiet her mind and start over, all she had to do was to look at her pretty planner. It was meticulously color-coded. She pulled a bright red marker from the short vase and marked out the days that had passed while Aisha was over.

She took a deep breath, and just as she was about to refer to her study schedule notebook, an odd feeling came over her. It was just a funky feeling, almost like déjà vu, but not quite. Rather, instead of feeling like she had already seen or experienced something, the sensation was of being in a familiar place where she felt comfortable and at ease. Maybe it was time, time to call Cristina and tell her everything. That's why everything had happened the way it did. Sleeping with William was like coming clean, to her. Get it all out in the open. Just face it. A weird rush of adrenaline overtook her, and she picked up her cell phone. She held it in the palm of her hand, dialed, and for what seemed like an eternity waited for Cristina to pick up.

"Hello?"

"Cristina?"

"Isa? What's up? What are you doing?"

"Aisha just left, so it's back to studying, not much else. What about you?"

"I'm sitting on the floor, prying hair and gunk off the vacuum brush. It's disgusting, makes me want to go out and buy a new vacuum instead of cleaning it."

"Sis, how are you feeling?"

"Some days are easier than others, you know."

Isa sensed that she had asked about Adelita too prematurely, she usually waited for Cristina to say something. She was quick to change the conversation.

"Oh, wait, there is something new. I have curves."

"What?"

"Yeah, I weighed myself while Aisha was here, and I've gained like fifteen pounds."

"What?"

"Yeah, it's pretty awesome. I should go out and find me a new pair of jeans."

"You're nuts! Everyone is trying to get your boney figure, and you're all excited about gaining weight."

"What can I say? I think it's my age. I better start watching what I eat now."

"Yeah, well, I'm sure you're not enjoying regular periods. I always thought you failed to eat just to suppress your period."

Isa paused. Cristina kept talking, but for Isa time seemed to stand still. Her period. It hadn't come. She tried to stay calm.

She reminded herself to keep calm and to breathe. Then, she just felt sick, sick with worry and dread. Was this really happening to her?

"Isa? Isa? Are you still there?"

"Oh, yes, yes, sorry . . ."

"Everything okay?" asked Cristina.

"Yeah, yeah, it seems like someone is at the door, can I call you back later?"

Isa hung up the phone. *I am not pregnant. I am not pregnant.* She repeated it like a mantra. She found comfort in this. She had to remain cool until she could be sure.

﹋

"Five months!" Isa blurted out.

"Five months," repeated the lab technician at the doctor's office.

"Oh, my God! How could I not know?"

"Have you not had your period all of this time?"

"No, I've been underweight most of my life, and I've missed a lot of periods."

"Not anymore," said the technician as she cleaned the cold gel off Isa's fairly flat belly.

"That's why I had a body all of the sudden?" whispered Isa to herself.

"Look honey, count yourself lucky. Most women are dreading the weight gain . . . not many have the luxury that you do. I'm still carrying thirty-five pounds from my baby boy, and he is going away to college next year."

Isa left the doctor's office. Standing outside the building, still in shock, she started walking towards campus and her favorite café.

She knew the familiar dips in the sidewalk; she could see the wars that the university's lawn maintenance team had waged with the thick tree roots. And it looked like the sidewalks always won. She used to love to see the clever ways landscapers had rerouted sidewalks where the old ones had shifted or cracked. Now, they would just remind her of this day.

Walking toward the café, she felt like her stomach was bulging out, though it was pretty flat this morning. It was amazing to think that a simple pronouncement could make you feel different. In an instant, she wasn't the same person that she had been the day before. Yesterday, she was voluptuous. Now, she was pregnant. Self-conscious. Protruding. Being aware of her body's new status, its new role, made her feel different.

The nurse had given her a slip of paper with the brand of some prenatal vitamins and an appointment in two weeks. She slipped the paper into the back pocket of her jeans and swung open the door to the café.

❦

She initially questioned her choice of beverage, coffee or tea? Her sister Cristina had never had so much as an ounce of caffeine during any of her pregnancies, but Isa figured that today's cup wouldn't do too much damage. She ordered the strongest coffee she could and waited for her favorite seat to become available. She wanted to get the processing of her new reality over with. She needed to figure out what she was going to do.

Everything had changed. It wasn't just her perception of herself, but her old surroundings. Even her favorite coffee house now looked different. The owners had made the place look like someone's quaint country cottage; if you pretended to ignore the sugar and dairy stations, the strangers bent over laptops, you would actually think you were holed up in some cozy country cottage—all by yourself. The two large bay windows were the most coveted areas of the café. The window-box seating was soft and welcoming, filled with a bunch of throw pillows in varying shades of yellow and green. The walls were painted in a light turquoise shade. All the pieces of furniture were in different styles, colors, and stages of distress. Isa always favored a square, low-lying table, wedged between two bookshelves. Her desk faced the wall, but the light from the skylight fell right down on her spot.

When Isa sat down, she realized her hands were shaking. She was a mess, and the coffee tasted horrible. The coffee had tasted just fine yesterday and the day before. Was she bringing on her own pregnancy symptoms? She pushed the coffee away and felt the waistband of her pants pinching her. The bottom of the top of her jeans was pressing into her gut, and she wondered if she should undo a button. She kept her eyes on the cushioned window seat until the two young women had thrown their backpacks over their shoulders and left. Then Isa, suddenly physically uncomfortable, wanted to sit by the window, soaking in the golden rays of autumn, and watching the traffic go by. What if she went to the movies and watched three back-to-back shows? Could she trick her body and her mind into thinking that there was no pregnancy, no major dilemma for at least another two days? Could she close her eyes and make it all go away?

⸺ ⸺

She was too far along to even consider the other option. And how would William react? Did she even have to tell him?

But then she thought of Cristina. This baby was inextricably linked to Cristina and Isa's mother's age-old dictum that *everything happens for a reason*. Ever since Isa could remember, those words had been uttered by her mother and served as both a moral and pragmatic compass. They could be pulling out of the driveway on a last-minute decision to go out for burgers as a family, when their mother Beatriz would declare, "I left the iron on. It's a sign. We are not meant to eat out tonight." Everyone would get out of the car and push the warm greasy burgers and crispy fries out of their minds because they knew that there was no talking Beatriz out of her favorite edict—as silly and superstitious as it was.

Even her skinniness was part of the grand design. Anyone else would have noticed such dramatic body changes—unless she was built like a tall, skinny man. She was pro-choice and had absolutely no moral compunctions about terminating a pregnancy. If she hadn't been so far along . . . And yet, here was her mother's saying again, *everything happens for a reason.*

Still, it was too late, and she wasn't mother material. Everyone knew that. It's what she had heard her whole life. As a child, she liked to play the role of teacher, doctor, or lawyer. The idea of taking care of a little one always gave her a sick feeling in her gut. It was the same sensation she got when she was told that she would have to wear a bra and put up with a monthly period. Even in high school, she had run from the idea of pregnancy when she had participated in a simulator program, one designed to deter teenage girls from getting pregnant, and she had found the whole thing laughable. Isa already knew that no amount of societal pressure was going to get her anywhere near child entrapment. And yet, here she was.

Oh, the irony.

chapter 9–Cristina

Rio Chico, Texas, 2004

Saturday was a good day. It was pure and filled with an unadulterated sense of joy and anticipation. Unlike Sundays, which merely signaled that there were a mere twenty-four hours until Monday morning, Saturdays were clean slates, full of potential. Anything could happen, and if it didn't, there was always Sunday. For Cristina, who was now working again, and for Leo, there was nothing better than Saturday mornings.

They were not jolted out of bed by the jarring interruption of the alarm. They did not have to go through the motions of their morning routine with dread and anxiety. They didn't have to be anywhere on time, and there were no coworkers to see or deadlines to meet. For both Cristina and Leo, Saturday mornings meant getting out of bed because they wanted to and not because they had to. Before Adelita was conceived, Leo had one of his best ideas ever. To take their minds off things, and try to focus on something other than starting a family, he'd suggested they build a brick-and-stone patio in their backyard. It was a big project, and they had spent many weekends digging, hauling gravel and stones, and then setting them. The only thing they didn't do themselves was tackle the landscaping around the new patio; that they left to one of Leo's friends, who would come in periodically.

The bushes and plants flourished while Cristina was pregnant with Adelita. When she was born, they had forgotten about the patio, but now their backyard retreat was a little oasis where they looked forward to working on Saturday mornings. The garden required maintenance, so on Saturdays they had the ritual of drinking their coffee as soon as it was daylight, and then working until it started to get too hot.

This particular morning, Cristina was up before Leo, and in the mood for an elaborate breakfast. She had already chopped up green chilies, onions, tomatoes, and cilantro (her secret ingredient). Making salsa from scratch and delicious *huevos rancheros* was one of her few culinary talents. The look on Leo's face made the effort worthwhile.

By the time Leo came shuffling down the hall from their bedroom, Cristina had already laid out three fried eggs on a bed of lightly fried corn tortillas and topped them with a tomato-based chili sauce.

⚓

"Those *huevos rancheros* were great, honey, thanks."

"Thanks! I thought that they were pretty tasty myself. Hey? Are we going to Paco and Wendy's barbeque tonight?" asked Cristina.

"Babe, I don't know. Didn't you want me to put in the trellis in the garden?"

"We can always do that next weekend."

"I'd rather get it finished."

"Why can't we do both? Paco and Wendy have three kids under the age of eight, and Paco is still hosting the barbecue and singlehandedly retiling both their bathroom floors."

"Yes," said Leo, "but they're used to it. I'll take our life over theirs any day."

Cristina became very quiet, and slowly started to clear the

table. She could see that Leo had instantly regretted his choice of words. He knew what had just happened. His poor choice of words had disrupted the delicate balance. As difficult as life caring for a special-needs child had been, it was a routine, a lifestyle that they missed.

"Cristina, I'm sorry."

"Leo, it's okay. I'm getting pretty sick and tired of feeling useless and fragile."

"You're not useless."

"I know, but I feel inept. What am I doing with my life? Nothing. I'm not where I ever wanted to be."

"Cristina, you know that I'll support you if you go back to school."

"I don't want to go back to school. I want to be a mother. I just want to hold a baby again."

꙳

Cristina went back inside. After Adelita died, she had gone to church for help, guidance. No one in her family had ever been very religious. The only thing the Catholic Church symbolized for them growing up was that Mass was always followed by a party—*quinceañeras*, weddings, baptisms, even graduation ceremonies. It's where families went to get their blessing to celebrate. She had gotten into the habit of going to church every Sunday now. She was never able to pay attention to the sermons, no matter how hard she tried. She would stand and try to sing along or follow along in prayer, but in a matter of seconds, her mind was always elsewhere. Still, she felt that the special characteristics of the place—the marble floor, large vaulted ceilings, colorful windows, and the smell of natural flowers—invited a state of grace. One where she could find peace and the ability to forgive.

She had promised Adelita that when grief threatened to overtake and paralyze her, she would let it go and begin again.

Today, in their bright kitchen, Cristina inhaled and exhaled. *Let it go. Begin again. Let it go. Begin again.*

She tried to keep her mother's words in mind. *No one was put on earth to suffer the whole time; something good had to be around the corner.* It just had to be. As soon as she was resolved to have a good day, Leo poked his head into the kitchen and asked if she was okay. Cristina stood straighter and put a special pep in her voice. "I'm going to make my famous potato salad."

"Really?" replied a very surprised Leo.

"Yes, really. I'm good."

"You're up for it?" he asked.

"Yes. I think I'll even go to the hardware store with you."

Leo walked over to his wife, grabbed her by her waist, and pulled her toward him. He planted a kiss on her soft lips, and Cristina responded by kissing him long and hard.

It was a while before they made it out of the house and to the store.

❧

That evening, after the barbecue, Leo and Cristina came home around 11:30. They had eaten way too much, but had a terrific time.

"I'm so beat," cried an exhausted Leo from the garage.

"What?" answered Cristina.

"I said, *'I'm worn out!'*"

She walked toward Leo and into the garage. "You know, we should have them over next time. They haven't seen our cool patio."

"Yeah, but I can see their kids trashing it."

"You are so mean," Cristina chuckled, "Is that the phone?"

"Who the hell is calling at this time of night?"

❧

Cristina rushed back into the living room and moved the seat cushions around, trying to find the phone. When she finally found it, she saw that it was Isa and plopped herself on the couch.

"Isa, is everything okay? It's so late."

"Cristina, it's 11:30 on a Saturday night. What are you, in fourth grade?"

"Unlike some single people, our lives are pretty boring."

"Are you sitting down?"

"Oh, no, what, what—you met Mr. Right?"

"Not really."

"Then what?"

"I have some news."

"Good or bad?"

"I don't know, it's complicated."

Cristina was trying to discern the tone of Isa's voice. Getting information from her sister was like drawing blood from a stone. For years, Cristina had taken Isa's silence and withholding ways personally, until she finally realized that's just who Isa was. She kept to herself, shared the bare minimum. It made Cristina feel awfully lonely, but she had finally made peace with this Isa. Over the years, their relationship had run hot and cold. One minute they would be sharing an old memory, and then Isa would retreat like a little hermit crab, leaving Cristina feeling like she had said something wrong.

"Isa? Are you there? Okay, now you're scaring me."

Isa took a deep and audible breath. "I'm pregnant."

"I'm sorry, what?"

"I am going to have a baby."

Cristina didn't even know how to respond. Her nerdy, overachieving sister, who had moved clear across the country, hundreds of miles away from any blood-related kin, the same one who swore that she was never, ever going to have a baby, was pregnant! Leo had once asked Cristina if she had ever considered that her sister didn't like men, and well, here was their answer. Yes, she did. Apparently, she liked them a lot.

"*Jesus!*"

"You sound like *Ama*, Cristina."

"Mom knows? Isa, is this a joke? Because if it is, it's not funny. Who is the father? Why didn't you tell us about him?"

"It was a one-night stand. I don't even know where he lives," Isa lied.

"Shit!"

"No, he's not even in the country, I think."

"Isa, seriously, you think?"

"No, I know he mentioned being from out of town, like way out of town."

"You never talk to me about your boyfriends and now you just lay this on me? What are you going to do?"

"Cristina, it was an accident, and I'm too far along."

"How far?"

"Five months."

"Five months, and you're just now telling me?"

"Honestly, I didn't know. I get missed periods all the time, and all of the weight I've gained has gone to my boobs and thighs."

"My older sister, with hips?"

Cristina was trying to keep the conversation light. She wanted to sound supportive, but she also felt betrayed. She wanted to get off the phone and cry in Leo's arms. Before she had to get used to being an aunt, and welcoming a niece or nephew, she would cry, throw herself one long pity party. She deserved it. Cristina got so choked up, she could barely speak.

"Isa, wow, this is great news."

"Cristina, I can't do this."

"Isa, honey, you don't have a choice. We will all help you.

Move back to Rio. You, me, Mom, we can all do it together."

Cristina realized that Isa was talking, saying something about her whole life changing, but already she was miles away. "Isa, I have to go. Let's talk tomorrow, okay?"

"What's wrong?"

"I'm tired and well . . . shocked?"

"Cristina, I didn't mean to hurt you in any way. In fact, it's because of what you are going through that I had to let you know first."

Cristina hung up and then her body started heaving and convulsing. Leo ran to her and held her as she sobbed and blubbered something about a baby.

"It's not fair. It's just not fair."

"What's not fair? What's going on? Who were you talking to?" asked Leo.

chapter 10–Isa

Georgetown University Law School
Washington, DC, 2004

Isa's reality was both inconvenient and a little bit cruel. But if she couldn't tell her own sister, who could she tell? She had not planned on being pregnant, and now she was going to have a child. And her sister wasn't. Cristina needed time, and that was okay.

～

The next day, Isa hit the books—which meant that for four hours, she kept reading the same paragraph over and over again. When she gave up, she decided to drive to her favorite neighborhood in DC. If everything went well, and the firm where she last interned hired her, she knew exactly where she was going to live. This was the neighborhood she had fantasized about calling home someday. Isa had attended the H Street Festival, the yearly party held in the neighborhood, and there was something about the place that felt welcoming. Walking down the streets, she admired the elaborate ornamental pressed-brick structures, the row houses built in small groups, each façade more imaginative than the next.

One of the handfuls of reasons that she had never considered

Rio Chico home was because she never felt that the homes there were anchored to anything. Unlike stone homes, brick structures, or even large Victorians, most of the houses back home seemed so precariously built they seemed untethered, as if, like a balloon, they could just up and float away. Sure, the *colonias* had their own history, but aesthetically most of the houses looked shoddy and provisional. Nothing dated back for decades, let alone a century. There were no cobblestone streets; hell, most neighborhoods didn't have asphalt roads yet. Her own street was still unpaved and didn't have city trash removal. Might as well be living in Mexico.

It wasn't just the homes, either. Mature trees were a rarity—non-existent in the *colonias*. It was always so hot that people couldn't even grow bad crab grass to hold anything down. The wind and the oppressive heat seemed to kill everything.

⌐◄

Two years after leaving Rio Chico for college, Isa had been asked by one of her old middle-school teachers to come back and speak to her students. Isa had expected the students to seem eager and excited, but very few of the students in Mrs. Segovia's classroom seemed the least bit interested in going out of state for college. They didn't seem the least bit curious about her school, Notre Dame, either.

The teacher had asked Isa if she was coming back to live in Rio Chico after college. Isa remembered getting stuck on the answer. She knew that the correct answer was to say yes. Something along the lines of mission, duty to give back to her community, blah, blah, blah. But she couldn't. She did remember the kinds of questions they had asked.

"Did leaving your family behind make you feel sad? Were you lonely?" one student asked her.

Isa had skirted the issue. At the time, she had felt a little ashamed. What was wrong with her? These kids, like her, had been born and raised in Rio Chico, and they were invested in it. They were rooted to its physical landscape and its culture; anyone would be crazy to leave. Because if there was anything that did keep you rooted, it was all the happy cultural traditions—socializing at all the important milestones in a person's life. Mexicans celebrated a baby before birth (the baby shower), at its baptism, then communion, *quinceañera*, graduation, and then marriage . . . only to start the party all over again when the couple had their first child.

Isa's life had centered around these cultural traditions, which were missing outside of Rio Chico, Texas, and she didn't know how people could bear it. Most importantly, for her and Cristina, their social lives had happened mostly south of the border, in Mexico. Unlike some of their peers, most of their relatives still lived about an hour's drive away. Their parents' childhood homes in Mexico held and would always hold a special place in their hearts.

When Isa was young and read in books about the big houses that some of the characters resided in—with formal dining rooms, sitting rooms, multiple bedrooms, and bathrooms—she yearned for such luxury and privacy, but also remembered what made her childhood unique. Hers wasn't the childhood with the tire swing on the green lawn; it was spending weekends and sometimes entire summers on her grandparents' ranch in Mexico. It was the best of Mexico, without the problems.

Maybe that's why Isa didn't feel a hundred percent rooted in Rio Chico? Mexico was special, and her allegiance was divided. But ultimately, neither area was home. In Mexico, she was the *Americana,* and in Rio Chico, the *first generation newcomer.* That day when her former teacher had asked, Isa had answered it with her own question. "Why do you think I left?" She had felt ashamed of herself.

But then it hit her, as she walked around one of the oldest and most architecturally diverse communities in the Washington, DC area, that for her, maybe *home* meant privacy. As she observed strangers cross the street or step into shops, *home* was where no one could reject her because of who she was. And outside Rio Chico, she could always live anonymously, only accountable to herself. *Home* was feeling comfortable in her own skin, and the only time that happened was when she was surrounded by strangers who couldn't judge her.

◄

She didn't know a single soul in this neighborhood, yet she felt like she could instantly walk into any one of the houses and call it home. It was the fact that no one knew her. They were all outsiders. No one could claim to be a native and keep others out. All her life, Isa had felt like an outsider. She was an outsider in Rio Chico, on account of her parents' not being born and raised there. Back in Mexico, she was considered an interloper for having left. Her fellow classmates didn't find her interesting, since she wasn't into any of the mainstream activities that represented their interests. Isa had been more concerned with being authentic than popular, and that hadn't endeared her to anyone.

In DC there was an energy and intensity around the gathering of people from all over the world that you just couldn't find in small towns. Isa was grateful to Rio Chico, thankful it had been her home for so many years. It had served its purpose, but like a small and tidy little bird's nest, it was also a launching pad for a very critical point of departure.

◄

Two stores down, Isa spotted a mother wrangling a toddler back into a double stroller. The other compartment seemed to hold a newborn. That would be her soon. And she hadn't even given thought of everything that came with motherhood: strollers and Sippy cups, wipes and diapers and the loss of her identity. She would have this baby—she had no choice—but everything would change if she kept the baby. Everything. And it scared her—the longer she walked and imagined herself with a child, the more thoughts of motherhood consumed her, and she found it distressing.

She had grown up with her mom's own narrative about women who either had abortions or gave up their children. There was the big speech that her mother had given both her and Cristina when they found out that the school counselor's daughter had gone through with an abortion.

"Why?" Beatriz had shouted, to no one in particular. "Why? That poor unborn child, how much room can a baby take anyway? That young woman knew what she was doing when she opened her legs, and she should just deal with the consequences."

Isa had tried to argue the point. "But, *Ama*, if she keeps the baby, she might drop out of school, and then she is one more young, uneducated single mother who probably wouldn't even know how to raise a child anyway."

"Let me tell you girls something," Beatriz had said, staring at them, both hands on her waist and practically boring a hole into their adolescent skulls. "If you ever get into that kind of situation, and chances are you never will, but if you do, don't you dare go taking the life of an innocent child. I'll raise that baby myself if I have to."

"Babies cost money," Isa had countered.

"*Hija*, have you never heard of the saying, '*Todo bebe llega con un pan bajo el brazo*'?"

Back then, Isa could never have imagined that she would be in a situation that would require her to recall these lectures, but here she was. And the saying that every baby came into this earth with a loaf of bread under his arm made even less sense now. How had that saying helped women in Third World countries with undernourished children? Her mother's logic probably only applied to the old days in Mexico, when no one gave a second thought to having one more child. Not only did they not have a choice, but there were plenty of siblings to help with childcare, and the basic staples were always available. People in her family were always saying, *where there is room for four, there is room for one more.* The problem? Isa was not about to raise a baby in rural Mexico. She didn't have a village. It would just be her. And no one else. No husband. No mother. No in-laws. No safety net.

In order to juggle her career and a baby, there would be so many decisions and arrangements to be made. Who would care for the child? What about evening hours? Who would take on night care duty? No, the idea of a baby coming was not as easy as fashioning a crib out of your bottom dresser drawer. She was looking at a future as a struggling single mother with zero chances of doing well in her career.

~

Isa stood in front of the hall mirror and examined her body. The recent changes suddenly made sense. What seemed like late-blooming body parts were nature's way of cushioning for a baby. The curves and the softness that had overtaken her once slim and boyish frame all made sense now, but she still could not believe it. Just when her world had come to seem predictable, it wasn't.

There was a child growing inside of her. Was she supposed to feel some kind of automatic bond? Because she hadn't yet. She barely had a bump, the weight seemed to have spread everywhere but her stomach. She was cognizant of the changes, but she wondered if she was expected to get a sudden surge of maternal feelings. Was she some kind of a freak? She just couldn't handle it. She didn't want to become a mother. The intensity of care that children require was just not something she could offer. No matter how many times she thought of her predicament, flipped it over and inside out, she knew in her heart that she could not make a commitment to motherhood.

But her sister did.

And the idea was crazy.

How would you even start that conversation? "Trade you my unborn child for your favorite sweater?" It's not what women did. Or was it? Her mother would never allow it. She could almost hear Beatriz, "*Estas loca*? Women do not give their children away, they just do not!"

What if she used the *everything happens for a reason* card?

She was emboldened. Cristina and Leo could raise the baby as their own. She could be the doting aunt. Isa even surprised herself by saying the words out loud: Cristina and Leo could raise the baby as their own. How can one idea seem so sensible and ridiculous at the same time? She wondered if she should run it by Nancy and Aisha. Part of her felt that both would do their best to talk her out of it. She had dialed her sister's number, but then hung up. She called Aisha, and Aisha recommended that she speak to a counselor.

Two hours later, her friend had phoned back. She had found a counselor on campus for Isa to speak with. "Be there at ten a.m. sharp, okay? You need to talk to someone, a professional. These are the kind of decisions that women make and always regret. You will regret it. Everybody does. Its just what women do. The sun eventually comes out. People eventually die. Women who give up their children regret it. It's not just a trope on Lifetime Television, it's the truth!"

The next day, Isa found herself sitting across from a dour-looking, middle-aged woman wearing green suede Mary Janes with heels fashioned out of cork material. The counselor wore an oversized cardigan and a small, early-eighties-style floral print blouse. To tie the whole ensemble together, she wore her long hair in a dismal braid, the kind that started out thick but eventually tapered down to something that resembled a rodent's tail.

Isa didn't mean to be so harsh in her assessment; it's just that the counselor seemed, from the beginning, to be highly inconvenienced by her presence. Put out. And to make matters worse, the counselor didn't even seem to be entirely present. She was doing some breathing exercises, and Isa felt like she had interrupted her mid-morning meditation routine. When Isa offered to come back at a different time, the woman sat up and tried to appear more engaged.

"Was your mom the nurturing type?"

"Yes. She was very nurturing. She never worked outside the home, and there wasn't a day that my sister and I didn't come home to a warm and nutritious meal, a warm and loving home . . . she just wasn't the lovey-dovey type."

"What do you mean?"

"Well, we don't say "I love you," or hug a lot, but families rarely do, right? That doesn't make us dysfunctional."

"They never said, 'I love you'?"

Isa resented the counselor's tone and responded defensively, "My parents are older and traditional, and they don't need to smother me to show their love."

"No, sweetheart, you misunderstood. It was just a question. Your parents are normal, you are normal, and I am just trying to understand some things," she said gently.

They talked for another half-hour and the session was almost productive, but there was one question that caught Isa off guard, one she hadn't expected.

"Isa, don't you think that you're asking too much of your sister and brother-in-law by offering them your baby?"

"Seems win-win to me."

"What if you changed your mind?"

"Why does everybody assume I will change my mind? Honestly, I think that a woman who would change her mind wouldn't even have thought about it, not for a second. In fact, the more that you and everybody try to talk me out of it, the easier it feels to just do it."

"I think that there is a legitimate fear that you would want the baby back, and they would be, like any parent who is adopting, heartbroken about taking you up on the offer."

"But I wouldn't take the baby back."

"That's what you say now."

"No, it's my final answer."

⚓

Isa left the counselor's office that day, and she felt shitty for so many reasons. The counselor had told her to take some time and listen to her instincts. But her instincts were telling her, *loud and clear*, that she was not ready to become a mother. That she wasn't mother material. Maybe it was the repressed Catholic in her, but the question kept coming up. What if this was God's way of making Cristina a mother?

⚓

Even when Isa looked at a future with a child, her options were few, and the few unpromising. To begin with, her child would be in some kind of daycare all day. Instead of being raised by two loving parents, her child would live his or her life in transport:

123

single mother's apartment to daycare. That poor child would be one more name on a list. Then, Isa had a terrible thought. She pictured her child, a little brown baby in a sea of potentially blond, blue-eyed babies. What if they ignored her child? Every day, a different worker would give her a bottle, change her diaper and look up at the clock, waiting for their shift to be over.

This, Isa thought, must be her maternal instincts kicking in; or were they just the concerns of an ordinary, sympathetic person?

Isa was desperate to talk to Cristina again. Cristina and Leo had probably thought it over . . . and well, how can they not accept?

chapter 11–Cristina

Rio Chico, Texas, 2004

Cristina stood by the door of the old nursery and looked around to see what was left. They had donated the baby's furniture and most of her clothing—practically given away everything that they hadn't saved as a keepsake. Cristina wanted no reminders, and now Isa was pregnant. Isa could have used it all.

When the phone rang, Cristina surveyed the room and wondered if maybe they were better off moving. Starting over in a new house. One where there would be no expectations, no memories.

"Hello?"

"Cristina?"

"Yes?"

"Listen to me. It's important."

Isa couldn't drag it out any longer.

"I would like you and Leo to adopt the baby, raise it as your own."

"Isa, you don't mean that. You think that you don't want a baby, but once you have that baby, you will."

"Cristina, Mom and Dad wouldn't even have to know."

"What?"

"Trust me, I have thought about this. I have a plan."

"Isa, just come home."

"Cristina, you know how Mom always brings up that whole, *everything happens for a reason* saying?"

"Yeah?"

"Well, as much as I have always dismissed it, think about it. What are the chances of me getting pregnant and you not being able to?"

"But Isa, it's a baby, not a sweater. And if you want to go that route, maybe it was meant to be. Maybe it was God's way of showing you what you thought you didn't want."

"But . . . having this baby means that I have to give up my job, my career, and probably move back home."

"Isa, you're acting like you're the first professional, single woman to raise a child."

"There is no way I could raise a baby without family help. And let's suppose that I did get a job in the Valley, where I have never wanted to live, can you see me spending my days in a small town? The same one I've spent my whole life running away from?"

"Isa, I love this town and you would too if you gave it a chance. You're such a snob. Guess what, if you move here, I'll start a petition for a Starbucks."

"Funny. Let's face it, I would be one of those bitter mothers who would always resent her child."

"You wouldn't. Trust me on this one."

"Look, I know this is a lot to digest, just think about it, okay? Talk to Leo. I have already started looking into all of the legal aspects."

Silence.

"Cristina, you know that I have never wanted children. It's just not who I am," Isa said, her voice trying not to crack.

"Oh, don't cry, Sis. Now you're making me cry. I'm just . . . well, how would we do this? *Ama* would never let you do it.

Actually, let's call Mom, because if there is anyone who will talk you out of doing this, it's her."

"Don't you dare!"

"She will eventually know."

"Nope."

"What do you mean, no?"

"You know as well as I do that Mom would never let me give up a child that is biologically part of the family. She would never forgive me."

"But even if we raised the baby, it's not like I can fake a pregnancy."

"Look, this baby is coming in four months. I saw Mom a month ago. I was already pregnant and didn't even know it myself. I hold off on seeing her until the baby is born. Meanwhile, you and Leo take a short sabbatical and spend four months with me."

"Now you're being ridiculous. This is not happening. People in real life don't do stuff like this."

"Cristina, listen. I have thought about this. I have sat with this for a week, thought about multiple scenarios and made more lists than I care to elaborate on. The only way that I want this to work is for everyone, the baby included, to think that he or she is yours and yours alone."

"That's impossible."

"No, I don't want the kid to have psychological baggage, wondering why I gave them up. And I'm like right there in their life, the greedy, pathetic aunt who wanted to live her own kind of life so bad. No way, I don't care for that. I want no part of that."

⤚

Cristina hung up the phone and stood in place, until Leo, hearing the annoying off-hook tone, hung it up for her.

"Who was that?"
"Isa."
"Everything okay?"
"No, it's not."

~*

"Cristina, people, sisters especially, don't call up and promise you a baby."

In her heart, Cristina knew that her husband was right—women did not easily give up their children. Isa had only known that she was pregnant for a week, she was freaking out and thinking of easy solutions. But part of her appreciated her sister's gesture. She also hated herself for indulging in the fantasy of taking her up on it.

~*

That night, Cristina called Isa back and thanked her, but told her that it was all too soon. Cristina urged her sister to take some time and think seriously about the baby.

~*

The next day, the alarm went off, and Cristina realized that Leo was already out of bed and in the shower. After registering the sound of the water running, the next thing that popped to mind was a pregnant Isa. That's all that she could think about.

She avoided the topic at breakfast, acting like Isa's news didn't matter, but the truth was it was all she could think of, and it made her feel so alive, so full of hope. Then it hit her: Isa would have to move back, and she could help her raise the baby. She could be the doting aunt who would be there for her niece if Isa's motherly instincts didn't kick in. Isa could buy a house in their neighborhood, continue as the workaholic that she is, and she could raise the baby. It was win-win—kind of.

Leo headed off to school and Cristina to Fernandez Insurance. At work, Cristina entered the most recent batch of new claim reports into the system and made it her mission to tackle every piece of paper on her large metal desk. She worked straight through her morning and lunch breaks. Usually Cristina was slow and fastidious, the ultimate perfectionist. This time she was bypassing all attention to burdensome detail, delegating work to her co-workers and ultimately clearing everything off her desk. She couldn't remember the last time that her IN or OUT bins were empty. For the first time in months, she could see the entire surface of her workspace.

Fueling her newfound sense of energy was an adrenaline rush from just thinking of the possibility of adopting her sister's baby. Because at exactly this time, one week ago, there was nothing interesting happening in her life. Right now, all that mattered was that someone's situation was going to change, either Isa's or theirs.

What Cristina was experiencing was what Leo had coined a 'crisis bonus.' It was a change in situation or some kind of reward that came after a crisis or was born in the midst of one. They had come up with the term three years into their marriage when they were fed up with their frugal lifestyle and felt like they were living in near squalor in order to save up for a down payment on a house. "We must stay focused," was what Leo would always say, "and stay within the budget."

Initially, Cristina and Leo had rented a rather dreary, almost windowless space—the place used to be someone's two-car garage—for almost three years. The small apartment had a total of three small windows. One was a frosted windowpane in the bathroom; the other two were small, rectangular slits above the kitchen sink. The converted garage was long, dark, and narrow. The owners had converted it into an in-law suite in the late sixties, and the only bright thing in the whole place was the avocado green shag carpeting in the tiny living room. As newlyweds, Cristina and Leo had decided to rent this space for almost nothing, so they could save every penny. Cristina had tried all manner of cheap designer tricks to try to brighten up the place. The small space had dreadful seventies wood paneling that made any kind of decorating attempt futile. The linoleum was chipping, and the plumbing was unreliable.

Their running joke was that they couldn't even live in their car if they wanted to. Before Cristina had her own vehicle, they had shared a fifteen-year-old Camry that had a terrible stench. Leo had accidently spilled a half-gallon jug of milk in the back seat, and no amount of cleaning could get the stench of spoiled milk out.

Each day, Leo and Cristina would get into their car, roll down the windows (regardless of the weather), and pull out of their rental, feeling like all of their hard work and savings would never amount to anything. Back then, the good thing was that it was all temporary—living in a rental, driving a jalopy, and being childless were all part of their newlywed dues. The best was yet to come.

The crisis came one Friday afternoon when the couple realized that the meager amount they usually allotted for the weekend entertainment had already been blown on an unexpected insurance deduction. Cristina had had it.

"That's it! Let's spend a weekend at Padre Island! Let's check into a nice hotel and eat great seafood for one whole day!"

"Are you crazy? Do you know how much that would set us back, babe? Be strong!"

"Leo, I am so sick of this place!"

"Cristina, we have had a zero balance on our credit cards for three months. Three months."

"It's just, on days like this, I get the whole instant gratification thing. Living for the moment."

"Or we can live forever and three years from now, we can be chasing babies around this same place wondering why we never saved up for our own place."

"Okay, say no more. Let's rent a movie."

Their plans changed when, not half an hour later, one of Leo's co-workers, a new science teacher, and his wife invited them over to their apartment for dinner. Excited about the change of plans (and free food), they both freshened up and drove across town, towards the outer perimeters of Rio Chico. When Cristina and Leo had married, Cristina's parents had suggested that they live with them. Beatriz thought the idea of renting made no sense, when they could live in her old bedroom and save money. Leo had insisted that they start off their marriage separately; Cristina had begged him to rent a new apartment. That, too, was out of the question—the converted garage apartment was the best compromise between the two—but going to Leo's coworker's place for dinner reignited the old rent debate. The luxury apartment was so seductive.

Once they had parked their smelly car under the carport in the visitor's parking lot, they proceeded to Apartment 42B and couldn't help casting their covetous eyes over the place and its amenities. The Torress's apartment was small, but it was like a showroom. Cristina just wanted to sit on the couch and take in their friends' picture-perfect domestic paradise. The living space was flooded with natural sunlight.

It was shortly after this visit that everything started to go wrong. They were battling one crisis after another. The same week that the Camry's engine caught on fire and the car had to be towed away, they also received notice to move out of their low-rent abode. Their landlords were selling the house, and the new owners were not interested in tenants.

Their luck finally changed, when Leo's boss offered to take him out to lunch. Leo was being offered to take the position of vice-principal on the condition that he enroll in a master's program.

This position was more than double his pay. By the time that lunch was over, Leo had talked himself into buying a new car and asked Mr. Velasco to drop him off at one of the local dealerships. There he test-drove a new car and talked the car salesman into driving it straight over to Cristina's workplace.

"Well, what do you think?"

"You didn't buy a car!"

"No, that's why I'm still here," chimed in the salesman. "Hi, I am Raul, from Keely Automotive."

"You don't say?"

The salesman hurriedly shook Cristina's hand, then jumped into the back seat. "He hasn't bought this yet," she asked. "Nope, but it's definitely an option, and you two have excellent credit."

"Just get in here," Leo had said, as he got out of the driver's seat and handed Cristina the keys.

꙳

Leo was ecstatic; with his salary almost doubling, they could now move forward. In less than two weeks, the pair had purchased a new car, rented an apartment in the same complex as the Torres's, and started talking to contractors about building their dream home.

Anytime some unexpected crisis led to a spontaneous and serendipitous bonus for the better, Cristina remembered this windfall and referred to anything remotely similar to it as a crisis bonus. She could really use one now.

꙳

That day, before heading home, Cristina called Leo at school.

"Babe? It's Cristina."

"Everything okay?"

"Yeah. Um, can we go back to talking about adoption?"

⚓

Cristina was ecstatic; Leo had never liked to bring up the subject of adoption, and here he was willing to give it a go. Maybe it was a macho thing, something about raising a child that wasn't his. Maybe Isa becoming a mother was the nudge Leo needed. Now, both sisters would be mothers. The next day, Cristina spent every spare moment Googling adoption options. And two days later, by the time Sunday rolled around, she had seen enough to turn her off adoption forever. It just seemed that everyone and everything was constantly colluding to make parents who chose to adopt as unsuccessful as possible. The whole ordeal left her with such a bad taste in her mouth that she cleared her entire Internet history browser and told Leo that she would never, ever research the topic again.

⚓

She hadn't heard from Isa in a while and assumed it was because Isa was already madly in love with the idea of a newborn. She probably had come to her senses.

Cristina waited for Leo while starting dinner. She cut tomatoes and bell peppers, sautéed onions, and in less than an hour the food was sitting on their white tiled kitchen table. The *fajitas*, their favorite meal, just sat there. Neither of them could eat. Leo leaned over the table and tried to touch Cristina's hand. Cristina pulled it back as if she were pulling burning flesh out of the fire.

"I'm sorry," she apologized as she stood, grabbed her plate, and threw the perfectly good food into the trash. "I just don't know how to go about my life right now. I just can't pretend that my sister just offered us a child and we said no."

"Cristina, come on. I'm not a woman, I don't have to be, I just know that even I couldn't give my child away. What if we get all excited and she says no at the last minute. I wouldn't be able to handle that. Would you be able to handle that?"

"I'm not mad at you," Cristina yelled, "I'm mad at *everything*. Why should we even be put in this position? It's like God is up there pushing buttons and seeing how much we can take. It's like saying, 'Here's a million dollars. If you take them, life will be complicated; if you don't take them, life will still be complicated and suck.'"

"I understand."

"I don't! I'm so mad. So angry. I want to—"

"Be angry, it's okay."

Cristina froze.

"You okay?"

"You know what? I'm craving burgers from Lalo's place."

"Seriously? You just threw out fourteen dollars worth of premium beef *fajitas*."

Wanting to avoid a meltdown, Leo pushed his chair away from the table and said, "Okay, I'm game."

"Thanks, babe."

As soon as Leo was out the door, Cristina started pulling out all of her dishes out of the kitchen cabinets. In seconds, the counter was covered in saucers, plates, cups . . . anything and everything that could break. She walked over to the laundry room, emptied the laundry basket and started to fill it with the yellow and silver-rimmed "Classy Casual" dinnerware set that had once been a treasured wedding present.

She couldn't lift the basket now, so she dragged it across the kitchen and out the back door into the garage. She ran back in, grabbed her car keys and pulled her car out of the garage. Inside the garage, with the doors closed, Cristina turned up the volume on the dusty boom box that Leo kept there. She started with the mugs. They shattered against the interior red brick wall. She didn't care if a rogue shard ricochet off the wall and cut her. With every piece she hurled, she released bits of anger. Anger that had been taking up precious real estate in her body and mind. The only thing that she regretted was not hearing the noise she was making. The music was too loud, and she didn't want her nosey neighbor Caro to hear her. She was so into it that she never noticed Leo coming in.

"What are you doing?"

"I'm doing what I should have done when the baby died."

"Break all of our dishes?"

"I'm going to replace these shitty dishes."

"Now?"

"Yeah. Here grab a plate," said Cristina, handing him a saucer. Leo got into position and told her to step back.

"You know, if my mom saw this, she would think we were crazy."

"Are you hungry?"

"Famished."

After dinner that night, they made love. And it was more than just comforting sex, it was a kind of letting go. Starting again. Shortly after, Leo went straight to bed while Cristina watched television. She had been watching some reality crime show marathon for two hours when Leo walked in and startled her.

"Leo! You scared me. I thought you were asleep."

Holding the hand over the phone, Leo sat down next to Cristina on the bed and said, "It's Isa. She's giving the baby up for adoption."

Cristina, still struggling to understand what was happening, sat up, looked at Leo and asked, "What? Let me talk to her."

Leo smiled and, looking at his wife, spoke into the phone.

"Isa, if it's okay with you, we would like to adopt the baby."

Did her husband really say that? She would never forget that moment. Before he handed her the phone, he hugged his wife firmly. When he held her tightly against his chest, Cristina felt that his squeeze was keeping her anchored to this world, because if he let her go, she would just drift away.

～

After they had both hung up with Isa, Cristina, still in awe, looked over at her husband and said, "Where did that come from?"

"We are over-thinking it. That's it. I thought that she would not go so far as to really give the baby up for adoption, so it might as well be us—and as for it being complicated, of course. Bring it on!"

Cristina's eyes filled with tears. She made the silent gesture for *wait right there*, and ran off into the kitchen for a couple of beers. She handed one to her husband and then clinked hers against his. She hated beer.

"You're a beer drinker now?" cried Leo.

"Yeah," said Cristina after taking a swig of her beer and making a face.

"You still don't like beer, do you?" asked Leo, laughing.

"Nope, it's still disgusting."

That night, Cristina and Leo found a way to move forward with their lives. It would be a challenge, but they were both up for it.

chapter 12–Beatriz

"*Puras mortificaciones!*" cried Dora, as she limped into the yard, chain link fence slamming against its hinges.

"*Que te pasa mujer?*" asked Beatriz, rolling up an old piece of green grass carpet.

"What the hell is that?" asked Dora.

"Just another piece of garbage that Mateo hauled in."

"Where are you planning to put it?"

"He thinks that we can cut it up and use it as a bathroom rug, want a piece?"

"No, thanks. Nancy just bought me a nice matching rug set—the pretty one from Kmart too, not the flimsy stuff from Casa Hung Emporium."

"So, what's wrong with you?"

"It's Belen, *esa niña*. I thought that marrying off that *muchachita* would put an end to her craziness. She's talking of leaving Pancho."

"What? Why? He's so good to her."

"That's the problem, *comadre*. Pancho is a good person. He works a lot, always pays their rent on time, and wants to hold off on her having a baby until they have a real house. The kid has a really good head on his shoulders."

"So, what's the problem?"

"Well, you know Belen. She is complaining about him. She whines about him being too cheap, that he doesn't take her out. She is used to buying new clothes and going out. I think she thought that she could continue her single life after she got married. And Pancho keeps her on a budget, won't even let her have a credit card."

"*Bruta*, why did she stop working?"

"Beats me. *Pobre mija*, maybe she thought that Pancho would give her everything."

"No, *que pobre mija* nothing, *comadre*, she needs to learn. This is the real world. You spoiled her."

"She's my daughter."

"*Comadre*? Come on? She lived with you for nine years after graduating from high school, that's different. She held a decent job; she never helped you and Canutero out. All she did was buy shoes and outfits."

"She paid for her car and her insurance."

"You still overindulged her. Before Cristina moved out, she paid the electricity, the water, and the cable bill. She also pitched in for groceries, she was responsible."

"Well, *comadre*, you got really lucky. Your girls are perfect. No drama."

"Dora, you have four kids. Three of them are perfect. In loving relationships with their spouses. Smart, thoughtful grandchildren. Even Arturito, after Manuela died, he found another wonderful woman. Belen isn't even that bad. She is just a little spoiled."

"*Para que nos quejamos, comadre*. Life has been good to us. You're right. We did right by them, and they did right by us. I just wish I didn't feel their problems as much as I do."

"What are you going to do about it, right? I still have faith that God will give Cristina and Leo a baby and one day Isa, as well; she is going to surprise us all. When she is ready to settle down, she is going to show up with a husband and a baby on the way."

"They are good girls, your girls. My girls. My boys. I mean, look at Isa. None of my kids went to college, and she not only went to college, but also worked and saved up to pay for law school. You have nothing to worry about with your oldest. She is so self-sufficient, so happy."

"*No creas*, I worry. I mean, I'm so proud of Isa, but she is so far away, and when she does find that man and settle down, I can almost guarantee that she will not do it here. You know Mateo and I can't travel. We can't be in the car for more than an hour before everything is hurting. Imagine hours of that? And fly? No way, never. I will see my grandbabies once a year, if I'm lucky."

"Trust me, Beatriz, you might be better off. I love my grandkids, but having them so close reminds you of everything they need and want. Paco's oldest just turned fifteen, and she is doing great; she is just like Isa, studious. But his little one, El Mickey, we are afraid he will turn bad."

"Stop thinking like that."

"Anyway, Belen will be fine, right? A new baby would be nice. If that's what she wants."

"Ay, Dora, slow down. Stop counting babies; the girl doesn't even know if she wants to stay in the marriage. Belen needs to get her act together first."

Making the sign of the cross and knocking on a nearby wooden bench, Dora exclaimed, "No, *divorcio no*! If she can't make it with Pancho, no one else will put up with her. No, *comadre*, just consider yourself blessed that both of your girls are happy and not weighed down by such crazy problems. Not a care in the world."

That evening, as Mateo shuffled out of the shower and started to get into bed, Beatriz sat on the edge of the bed, taking off her necklace and telling him all about Dora's daughter Belen.

"*Esa niña*. She has never known what she wanted. Ever. Dora doesn't know that I know, but that girl has had two abortions. And not with the same guy. She isn't going to make it with the nice boy because of God's punishment."

"Don't talk about those things."

"That girl of hers is a bad seed; I don't blame her for not wanting me to know. Belen is probably already cheating on her husband."

"Okay, *mujer*, this is how all of this *chisme* gets started."

"Dora talks too."

"Both of you talk too much. Both of you have daughters. Imagine if they said that about one of our girls, and it wasn't true."

"Ay, Mateo, I know everything there is to know about Isa and Cristina.

"Well, at least she's married now, not running around leaving children for Dora to raise," Mateo said.

"Mateo! Are you saying what she did was the right thing?"

"No, *mujer*, I never said that! Good night!"

⚓

Beatriz slipped into bed next to her husband, but far enough away to let him know that she wasn't too happy. Any mention of cheating transported them to the past. He knew what she was thinking. She thought of that awful night, more than twenty-five years ago. The girls were little, and they had taken the girls to a *feria* across the border in Mexico. It was the town's yearly fair and one that they always attended. Traditional Mexican crafts were sold at every corner. Delicious fruit cups filled with *jicama*, pineapple, grapes, and mango were sprinkled with chile powder and savored by all. There were warm *elotes* slathered with creamy mayonnaise, chile powder, and salt, and topped with fresh-squeezed limes. The men could buy beer in a cup or the all-time *feria* favorite, Clamato juice. The Ferris wheel was at the center of the grounds, and not too far away were the bumper cars. To the north was the main plaza's gazebo, where a local band played while they waited for the featured *conjunto*.

The local *ferias* put everyone in a festive mood. The kids walked around with balloons, and the mothers purchased homemade aprons, pirated T-shirts, and baseball caps for their kids or, if they were into it, their favorite celebrity photo shellacked on a piece of wood. What Beatriz remembered the most about this night was the fact that she had received the bad news at the beginning of the fair. They had just left Mateo's sister's house in town and packed both their girls and all four of their nieces and nephews into their vehicle. Entering the arches, brightly lit, Beatriz counted the six kids and hoped that her sister-in-law wouldn't take too long doing her hair. The crowd was large, and her sister-in-law's kids had the tendency to scatter and never report back.

As soon as she was sure she had all of her brood, a clown on stilts appeared before the kids and started to dance. A shorter clown, who must have been his assistant, carried a portable boom box and played music that Beatriz could not identify. It was in English and something that the kids were really into. Mateo had headed off to the beer stand and found some friends, so Beatriz looked around, hoping to see someone that she knew.

Chatting with old friends was one of the best parts of the yearly fairs in Mexico, that and showing off her new lavender dress and strappy sandals. It was a little dressy, but all the women wore their best. She will never forget how she was busy smoothing out the bottom half of her dress when a younger woman wearing an inordinate amount of makeup and tight red jeans came right up to her and asked, "Are you with him," pointing across the way towards Mateo.

"*Si, porque?*"

"He gave me a night to remember, and even left me with a present."

The woman had clearly been drinking, and her companion, a man with plucked eyebrows and bright-red lipstick, laughed and pulled her away. "*No seas pendeja!*" he said. Beatriz knew exactly who they were, everyone did. They were both local prostitutes and one had just pointed to her husband. Beatriz knew that her Mateo had visited the local brothels before their marriage, but he promised her he would never do it afterwards. What was this woman talking about? Before or after? She left the kids with the two clowns and ran toward the crowd that had swallowed up the pair, until she caught up with the woman in the red pants.

"When?" asked Beatriz.

"When what?" answered the woman.

"When was he with you?"

"I don't know, I don't write down the dates."

"Was it more than five years ago?"

"*Ay, no, mija*, it was sometime in the last year."

"*Mimi, callate pendeja, vamonos,* you're drunk and you're going to get both of us in trouble!"

Beatriz watched the young man escort his friend away, and she started to shake. Mateo had been with another woman, and not just any woman. He had been with an unclean, probably diseased woman. And what had she meant by present? Had he impregnated her? Forgetting about her children and her nieces' and nephews' whereabouts, she headed straight to the beer stand and confronted him.

"*Estas loca!* What are you talking about?" Mateo had said, trying to speak below a whisper.

"Did you get someone pregnant?"

"How would she even know that it was mine? She's a whore!"

"You did sleep with her."

"I just did it twice. Everyone else does it."

Sickened, Beatriz walked away from her husband and said that she was ready to go home. The kids had cried in the car. They couldn't understand while they were leaving so early. And they drove back across the border in silence. Beatriz didn't speak to her husband for a whole week.

After a week of silence, Mateo asked her one simple question.

"Are you going to leave me?"

Beatriz didn't answer and she watched Mateo walk away. That night he slept on the couch and his eyes were red. He was still lying there after the girls had gotten on the school bus.

"Well, aren't you going to go to work?"

"Beatriz, without you, nothing matters."

These were the most romantic words this hardened man was ever going to speak. It wasn't a lot, but it was enough. Beatriz decided to forgive him, but she remained angry with the woman at the plaza. Anytime she remembered the incident, she boiled over with anger and seethed, attacking any woman who seemed the least bit promiscuous. Dora was the only person who knew about her secret, and it was because Dora's husband flaunted his visits to Mexican brothels in his wife's face. Dora didn't care too much and actually preferred that she be left alone rather than bothered with her husband's amorous overtures.

"Better a stranger than me. Hell, if I had it my way, I would have one of those women in a back room every time he fondled my breasts, just so he would never have to jump on top of me again."

"Dora, you're crazy," Beatriz would answer. "Mateo isn't

like Canutero, he did it when I wasn't able to be with him, after that surgery."

"And you bought that excuse?" Dora answered.

"I believe him. It's those whores that I don't trust. They're just out to break up good families. All they do is have abortions."

"I don't blame those poor women."

"What do you mean, poor women?" asked Beatriz.

"*Comadre*, I know that you have some sense. Who on earth would take up whoring as a career?"

"*Putas.*"

"Well, before they became who they are, those girls were someone's daughter, mother, and sister. They still are. Somewhere, something went very wrong and they didn't have a choice."

"Are you saying that they are not to blame? It takes two, you know?"

"Ay, Beatriz, sometimes it's like you don't have a brain."

"Dora, these women are bad. Why are you defending them?"

"You shouldn't blame everything on the other woman. Your horny husband had nothing to do with it? Ay, ay, *pobrecito.*"

Beatriz had grown up demonizing such women. They were all whores to her, and they didn't deserve her pity. They all wore purple lipstick and bright red, painted-on jeans. They all looked like the woman at the fair. It was always black and white for Beatriz. And nothing in between.

chapter 13 – Cristina

The wheels were in motion. Cristina and Leo were going to be parents. In less than four months. They made a pact. No negative thoughts. But there were. All the time. Staying positive didn't change the facts.

"Honey, I'm just so afraid. I don't know if I should get my hopes up or treat this like it's not going to happen, and then be pleasantly surprised if it does."

"Well, I'm all in. You should be too. We lose nothing and gain everything, and our new motto is, 'We'll cross that bridge when we come to it.'"

"Leo, you know what's keeping me up at night?"

"The faking it part? Keeping it from your parents?"

"That's bad enough, but it's being able to forgive her if she doesn't go through with it."

"Well, I wouldn't have agreed to all of this if she wasn't so serious about giving the baby up for adoption. I know your sister. When she says she will do something, she means it. I feel that if we let her go the route of giving the baby to complete strangers, she will do just that."

"Why does this have to be so hard?"

"You would forgive her and move on. You're that kind of person, honey."

"All I know is that right now, she has really convinced me, and you know what gives me hope?"

"What?"

"That we are going to be right there with her. "

⚓

Leo asked for a six-month leave of absence. Cristina quit the insurance agency. If Isa changed her mind at the last minute, they would deal with it then. Together, the trio got it all together. The plan was in motion. They would tell everyone that they were in DC to get away and see a fertility specialist. They would live with Isa and help take care of her, but once there, they would "discover" that Cristina was already pregnant. They would wait there until the baby was born.

They would keep to the plan and their secret, unless Beatriz and Mateo showed up at their doorstep. This was highly unlikely, but if they did, they would all just come clean and let the parents deal with it.

Once all three of them had turned the plan on all its sides and considered every angle, to the point that they felt like they had successfully mastered an emotional Rubik's cube, they all agreed that they didn't care if people back home in Rio Chico asked questions.

"Surely, someone will wonder, why all of a sudden, we up and left," Cristina had said.

"To hell with them!" Leo had shouted.

"What will we say? If they don't think I look like a woman who just had a baby?"

"You know what, honey? That week, when Isa first brought it up? I was walking around school feeling like we had already announced the plan and felt that everyone was onto us."

"Really? Why?"

"Well, wait, get this. Then I met with Letty Lara, the new science teacher?"

"The recent divorcée?"

"Yeah, that one! Well, she asked to take four weeks off because she was going to have bunion surgery, on both feet."

"So?"

"Well, my secretary, who has to process all the paperwork, and all her friends in benefits know that she will be having surgery, just not on her feet."

"What's she having?"

"According to the secretary, thigh liposuction and breast augmentation."

"And she doesn't think anyone will notice?"

"That's not my point, babe. My point is that this stuff is pretty commonplace. In the years I have been working in the school district, I have been privy to all kinds of explanations for absence, medical leave, et cetera. People are ashamed of everything from hemorrhoid surgery to taking care of a stomach hernia. The point is that people don't ask more than superficial questions."

"But won't people wonder why this woman's bunions moved up to her pecs?" joked Cristina, pointing to her breasts.

"Okay, that's a visual that I don't want in my head. My point is that people don't really care, they will talk about you regardless of what you are or are not getting or doing."

◆

Initially, Cristina worried so much about the amount of lying that she was going to be doing that she broke out with a cold sore the size of Montana.

"See what you get for worrying?" Leo told her.

"It's just, why does everything have to be so involved?" asked Cristina while she dabbed some medicinal gel on her lip.

"All that I know is that we will be out of town, and for me, the timing is perfect. I'm suffering from major burnout. I need to see new faces; everyone is saying a sabbatical was a good idea."

"I just—well, I talked to Isa about breaking down and telling Mom and Dad about it. They could keep a secret, I mean, Mom knows everything about me. That is what has me sick."

"What we do need to worry about is all of the legal paperwork and expenses."

"Yeah, Isa said that she was looking into all that. I feel sick. Just sick," said Cristina, walking toward their bedroom.

⁓

They had enough money to pay for the trip and to help Isa with apartment expenses, but not legal and adoption fees. Leo had already started looking for area schools where he could work as a substitute teacher; meanwhile, they would live off their savings. When Cristina thought of all of that hard-earned money disappearing, she would mentally picture their baby. Six months ago, Cristina and Leo had considered blowing half of that money on an exotic getaway. Luckily they'd held back, and this, she thought, was divine intervention.

⁓

It was the craziest thing they had ever done, and the most thrilling. Cristina finally understood what her mother meant by trying to see life as a new adventure. On the drive to Washington, DC, it all felt like a dream. She could not believe what they were doing. They both felt like teens playing hooky from life and lying to their parents. Leo, who was already prematurely graying, felt he had gotten a new lease on life. He was looking forward to temporary work as a substitute teacher. He was looking forward to putting a high-stress administrative job on hold and going back to the classroom. Cristina, who had never lived outside Rio Chico, was looking forward to living in a new place. For a moment, all their woes just slipped off their shoulders, and they felt free from everything. As soon as they crossed the state line, they were just looking ahead. It seemed like the further they drove away from town, the less important all of their concerns were.

◄

Beatriz and Mateo understood the couple's need for a change of scenery. Cristina had told her mother that they would be living with Isa. Maybe a fresh start would result in a pregnancy. She had reassured her parents that Leo would still have his job when he returned. They had enough in savings to pay the mortgage, and they would be back in the spring.

Beatriz and Mateo hated that no one would be home for Christmas. The trio had thought their parents would understand that it was one more added expense, and they did. Beatriz had wrung her hands on her apron, but she had understood. "Yes, it's the only reasonable thing you kids seem to be doing, staying put for the holidays. Flights are expensive and it just makes no sense. Four months, we can wait four months." Cristina and Leo felt terrible about the bold-faced lie. Their plan could also work because traveling was out of the question for Beatriz and Mateo. The drive would be too hard, and both had vowed to never, ever get on a plane. This was one time their mother's phobias had actually worked in everyone's favor.

◄

It was raining hard. The streets looked deserted, and visions of a nice fall landscape, the one Isa had told them to anticipate, were nowhere in sight. Isa's apartment, though big by DC standards, seemed cramped. Leo and Cristina had mailed half a dozen boxes ahead of time and the boxes were everywhere.

Cristina looked at the new Isa, fleshy and more voluptuous. She wiped her eyes, looked around and joked, "Wow! What a mess."

"Sorry Sis, it's definitely nothing like your house."

"Nonsense," said Cristina as she stepped toward her sister and gently patted her belly.

"Not much to look at yet."

"No, not yet, but soon. Look, you take care of the baby and study. Unpacking all this stuff will actually give me something to do, besides cooking and cleaning."

～

That night Cristina and Leo slept on a futon in the living room. It was so uncomfortable that they decided to put the mattress directly on the floor. The soft drumming of the raindrops eventually made Cristina sleepy.

Isa's furniture, the boxes, and the carload of things they brought cluttered the place, and Cristina just couldn't picture how she was going to make it a space fit for three people. They had all decided that Isa should take the bedroom so she could fit her bed and computer desk in there.

～

It took weeks before Cristina had settled into a routine, one where the new sights and sounds of her new street felt comforting and familiar. Leo would be long gone by the time the women were out of bed.

Cristina wasn't at ease if the dishes weren't done or the beds not made. So after Isa left, she would fold the futon, tidy up the place, shower, and then go for a long hours' walk around the neighborhood. She finally understood what people liked about city living. Back in Rio Chico, the only two densely populated commercial areas were a medium-sized strip mall and the supersized Walmart. In between lay a smattering of fast-food establishments, and it was only during the peak of the lunch hour that all the fast food and small restaurant spaces were filled with the lunch crowd.

Cristina rode the metro for the first time and came face-to-face with disparity, handing out her meager change to the countless homeless people, the same ones who sat less than fifty feet from trendy restaurants.

Cristina wanted no part of that world. There was enough poverty back home, and she hadn't come to DC to see *tristezas*, sad things, as her mother always put it. True, poverty in Rio Chico looked different, less gritty and sad, dressed in its charming rural garb, perhaps because it was more familiar. The financially deprived landscape looked different and thus seemed "safer," but the results were the same: high dropout rates, incarceration, drug problems, and poverty that could easily give DC some healthy competition. The only difference between a McDonald's in Rio Chico and a McDonald's in DC was that, in DC, McDonald's had posted security guards and in Rio Chico, the average person's salary was half of what that same DC security guard made.

When the leaves finally did change, the fall was breathtaking. Everywhere she looked, Cristina took mental snapshots, memories she wanted to keep in her mind, hoping to revisit them when South Texas was at its driest. It was on one of these days that Cristina noticed a job announcement on the window of the neighborhood gym, a medium-sized place with a small playroom. Cristina applied on a whim and was pleasantly surprised when she received a call two days later for an interview.

In less than a week, Cristina was reporting for childcare duty. She loved holding the smaller babies and tickling the adorable toddlers who often fell asleep in her lap. Frazzled looking parents would drop off their children eagerly. Cristina swore that she would never become like that. She was quick to judge all the parents who, she imagined, had just picked their children up from daycare and then rushed them off to another one so they could fit in their workouts.

～◢

Pretty soon, the trio felt like they had been living together for a long time. The more time that they spent together, the more emotionally invested they became in the plan, the more real it all seemed. Gone were the days when Cristina and Leo feared that Isa might change her mind. Neither Cristina nor Leo knew if Isa spoke to the baby privately, but while buttoning up a shirt or getting a glass of water, Isa would say things like, "Oh, baby, if your parents are going to spoil you as much as they spoil me, you may never want to leave the nest."

At the gym daycare, Cristina's coworker, Leidy, was fascinated by her life and in total disbelief about what Cristina told her. As a Dominicana, Leidy, like Cristina, also comfortably switched languages, one minute Spanish, the next English.

"So, *mami*, let me get this straight? Your mama, back home, *no tiene ni la menor idea* that you and your sister are about to swap babies?"

"Well, we're not swapping."

"You know what I mean. Like, swapping situations. I'm not good with words, but I know you're following me. You think your *mami* don't know? I'll tell ya, my mom would know. She would just know something was up. *Ella sabe. Eso te lo aseguro.*"

"How?"

"Woman, you've had a baby before, why are you acting so ignorant? The way you walk, hold yourself, or even complain about peeing on yourself if you sneeze."

"Leidy, I don't think anyone will even notice."

"So why hide it?"

"One of Isa's stipulations was that the baby not know until she was of age that she was adopted, because we live in a small town, and someone would eventually say something."

"Well, that makes sense."

"And because, secretly, I think that my sister knows that my mother would talk her out of it."

"True that. *Eso es.* That's what it is, I couldn't put my finger on it; that's what my mama would probably say. I can hear her now, reprimanding my sister and me: 'Well, you two can't even share a pair of pants or lend each other earrings, much less a *lil carajito.*"

Cristina had become silent and started picking up the scattered toys, and noticing it, Leidy had chimed in, "Ay, *mami*! Don't be getting sad. I'm just playing with you. Everything is going to work out. Besides, this baby is coming, and from everything you say, your sister is not mother material. Shoot, I had an aunt like that. She went on to have three kids. Hated and resented them all. And it wasn't baby blues either, she just never cared for them."

"That's sad."

"It is what it is. She didn't have any fancy options like your sister, neither."

⚓

For the most part, it was all smooth sailing. Their first victory had been the phone call home to announce her "pregnancy." And the call had been made a week and a half after arriving in DC. Cristina called her mother and told her "the great news." She was five months pregnant and had never even known about it. Before the call, Cristina had worried about Beatriz asking a hundred questions. Cristina was terrified of hyperventilating on the phone, and feared that, like a guilty child, she would just blurt out the truth. But Leo and Isa had assured her that all

153

would go well, reminding her that there was no reason why her parents would doubt the story. What kind of parents would ask or even think that their daughter was making up a pregnancy? In fact, when Cristina did make the call, while holding Leo's hand, it had been rather anti-climactic.

"*Hijaaaaaaaa!*" Beatriz had cried.

"*Ama*, can you believe it?"

"*Claro que si! Ya vez*, God was looking after you. Waiting to bless you with such good news after so much *trajedia*."

Just like that. Beatriz even insisted that part of her had seen the changes in Cristina's body.

"Your hips seemed wider! You'd been eating more."

Oh, the wonderful things that the mind can make up when it sees what it wants to see. After Cristina had talked to her father, she had passed the phone on to Leo and then Isa. And it was hearing Isa talk about being an aunt again that made Cristina feel the first twinges of guilt. There was her sister, half-full with child, pretending like she wasn't. When Beatriz asked the inevitable—"So, are you coming home now?"—Leo very calmly told her, in as soothing and nonchalant tones as he could muster, "The doctor doesn't want her traveling, given her previous problems. We're going to have the baby here and go home as soon as the pediatrician allows it." Both Cristina and Isa gave him a thumbs up.

ᵕ✦

Isa was studying hard and experiencing a textbook pregnancy. Every night the three had dinner together. Cristina took over all of the cooking and cleaning in Isa's apartment. They were impressed with Isa's commitment. Fortunately, Beatriz wasn't much for pictures, because she never asked for any. There would be plenty to see after the baby arrived, and it's not like she hadn't seen her daughter pregnant before anyway.

◄

Cristina and Leo had thought that waiting for their baby would take forever, but before they knew it, Isa's due date was fast approaching. Days, weeks, and eventually months had passed, and there were never any signs that Isa would let them down. When she spoke to the baby, she referred to herself as "*Tía* Isa." Isa was the consummate professional. The perfect surrogate. A more clinically detached person could not have been found.

When Isa moved about, pregnant and cumbersome, Cristina was in awe at how much weight a slim woman like her sister could gain. There were instances, when trying to maneuver around the breakfast counter, where Isa's natural instinct was to put her hand over her stomach, protecting her unborn child, leaving Cristina both equally touched and worried, concerned that her sister's full maternal instincts would come barreling out of her system, just like that child eventually would. And at night, lying down, head on her pillow, staring at the ceiling and counting down the days, she would confide in Leo her feelings, her doubts, her suspicions. And Leo would do his best to assure her.

"I'm going to quote Mrs. Delfina at work," Leo started to say.

"Yes," interrupted Cristina, "worry is like a rocking chair. It gives you something to do, but it gets you nowhere."

chapter 14–Isa

Washington, DC, 2005

Three weeks before the baby was due, Leo and Cristina scheduled a long weekend away. They had already visited the National Mall, the US Capitol Building, the White House, and enough other monuments and museums to last a lifetime. They had also taken the train to New York, checking the Big Apple off their bucket list.

The sport they had never done, and were intrigued with, was skiing. It was the one sport that Leo had always wanted to try and one that Isa was actually familiar with. In the past three years, Isa had been skiing every winter and really loved it. When her friends Marjorie and Tom invited her to their place in the Poconos, she declined but asked if Cristina and Leo could take her place.

"You guys will love Tom and Marge," Isa said excitedly, while she had Leo pull a large cardboard box from the top of her closet.

"But maybe they want to be alone," protested Cristina. "We don't even know them."

"Oh, trust me," Isa laughed, "these two are absolutely no good alone. They don't know what to do with themselves. I think that is why they take me every year— so they don't have to talk to each other."

"That's so sad," said Cristina.

"No, they are made for each other. They're just better off in a group, that's all."

"Cristina, it's free lodging, just go with it," said Leo.

"Okay, Cristina, you will find everything you need in that box over there—for the trip. Leo, for you, we will hit the local thrift shops, if you don't mind outdated ski clothes and used snow boots."

"No, not at all."

"How far is this ski lodge in the Poconos?" asked Cristina.

"Five hours, I think," said Isa.

"Are you sure you'll be okay? The due date is so close now," said Cristina.

"I still have three weeks. Besides, if I go into labor, I'll call you, and you can be here in time. What are the chances that I'll have the baby five hours after I feel a contraction?"

"Better yet," added Leo, "what are the chances that the baby will come three weeks early? Stop worrying, woman, don't ruin this."

"Besides," added Isa, "I need some alone time. I love you guys, but it will be nice to have this place all to myself again."

⚓

Since they would be gone for three whole days, Cristina had cooked several meals for Isa and made her promise to call several times. "Jesus, woman, you're only going to be a stone's throw away in Pennsylvania," Isa had assured her. Isa was going to miss them, but she would have her apartment all to herself for the first time in a very long time. Her bedroom was the only space that was off limits to Cristina's obsessive cleaning, and Isa felt that the one thing that she wanted, out of the whole three days, was to create a clear and calm study area in her bedroom. She was so big that the most comfortable place to study had been her bed, making her desk the drop pile. The pile had gotten out of control.

⁓

By the time Cristina and Leo were due to leave for Pennsylvania, *The Plan*, as they all had come to refer to it, was that Cristina and Leo would be at the birth and, when the baby arrived, the baby would be handed to Cristina and Leo. It had been Isa's idea and she was confident that it was best for everyone, that she not get to see the baby immediately after it was born. She didn't want to risk bonding with the baby. Reluctantly, Cristina had urged her sister to reconsider. It was the right thing to do, but she was secretly relieved when Isa insisted on *The Plan*.

When they found out that the baby would be a girl, Isa had suggested that Cristina and Leo have a baby shower when they got back to Texas. She also gave Cristina permission to shop to her heart's content, leaving the entire baby trousseau to her. In the hall closet, Cristina had squirreled away some basic items for the baby's layette. She and Leo had also purchased a car seat. Everything else could wait until they got back to Texas.

The baby's first contact would be with the woman and man who would raise her as their very own. Isa wanted to avoid laying eyes on the child and, in a separate room, have someone lay the newborn baby against her sister's naked breasts. For her part, Isa had played this out in her mind. She would be calm and cool. And she would be so exhausted that she planned to catch up on sleep, getting her old body back (maybe even keeping the curves), and looking forward to starting her career. Isa would not be the first to see her baby. Her true parents would. And shortly after the birth, mother, father, and baby would be on the way home. And everything would be perfect.

⁓

The day before Cristina and Leo were due back in DC, Isa woke up to see light snow outside. She hoped that enough would fall to create a winter wonderland, the perfect setting for Cristina and Leo to come home to. No longer able to sleep in, on account of her ever-expanding stomach, Isa took refuge in her bed and surrounded herself with highlighters and pens, notes and reading material. It wasn't until she decided to take a break and catch a *Law and Order* marathon on television that she read the severe winter storm alert on the bottom of the TV monitor. Tired, and feeling like she had studied enough, Isa decided to call it a day.

It snowed. The trees outside her window looked so beautiful. There was a period that Isa named the "gray space," a void that Mother Nature seemed to deliberately force on the human eye in order to make the changing of the seasons a true and transformational feast. This morning, as Isa looked out, she saw that enough snow had accumulated to cap all the trees that lined her street, the wires, and the cars. It was nature's way of magically pulling the wool over the grittiness of dull cityscapes in winter.

⚓

Isa had ordered a cheese pizza for lunch, and was told she was their last customer on account of the storm. She sat back on a mound of pillows, throws, and blankets, thoroughly enjoying her piping hot slices of pizza while the banner at the bottom of her television read *Severe Weather Watch*.

After she was full of pizza and milk, she fell asleep with the television on, and slept straight through the night and into midmorning. When she awoke, Isa was famished again, and her bladder felt ready to burst. She looked out the window, and her eyes were blinded by the whiteness of it all. There was more than two feet of snow on the ground, not a soul in sight, and the only things visible were the lights coming from a snowplow in the distance. The world seemed to have come to a grinding halt, and Isa couldn't be happier. When normal routines like this were interrupted, she always felt like God was hitting the pause button and everyone had the right to stop whatever they were doing. For Isa, it was worrying about the bar exam.

Even though she had slept so long, her body still craved more sleep. Moments like these reminded her why she wasn't cut out to be a mother. She knew that women in her condition had young children to look after, but the idea mentally exhausted her. The best she could do was to get up, wash her face, reheat the leftover pizza, and down a glass of milk, a quarter of a banana, and half a yogurt, then crawl back under the covers. She knew the street crews were going to start the hardest part of their job, clearing streets and taking care of everything, so by the time Cristina and Leo came back, they would even have a space to park in. This is what she was thinking about when she noticed the blinking lights on the answering machine; Cristina and Leo had called three times while she was sleeping. They were having a great time, but they were worried about the storm. They were probably going to have to stick around until the roads were clear.

Isa lay like a fat cat on her bed. She grabbed a handful of highlighters and thought about getting back to her reading, but then changed her mind. She grabbed the TV remote and fell back on her pillows. As soon as she turned the set on, the familiar notes of the *Law and Order* theme song caught her attention. Her heart leapt; the marathon was still on. Isa was engrossed in the final part of the show—where all the lingering issues of the episode are resolved and order is restored—when she felt a cool sensation on her inner thigh. She slowly realized that the coolness was actually wetness. Was she so enormous that the pressure on her bladder was too much? Or worse yet, was her water breaking?

Isa wasn't in any pain, so she refused to panic and call an ambulance. They had all taken a childbirth class, and their instructor had recommended that they spend as much time as possible in the comfort of home before they had to go to the hospital. The hospital was not too far away, and she was confident that she could do all the things she needed to do before her contractions started. Her hospital bag was ready to go and waiting in the front closet. After showering and putting on clothes that weren't designed for sleeping, Isa tidied up her bedroom, scooping up all the books, notes, and writing utensils into a basket. She made the bed, emptied the white wicker wastebasket into the large one in the kitchen, watered the two small plants in the kitchen, and then called Leo and Cristina. None of her calls were getting through. Thirty minutes later, Isa started to panic. She wanted them by her side. And she wanted them *now*.

When Isa finally did get a hold of Tom and Marge, she was told Cristina and Leo had already left. She assumed that they were on their way, so she wrote a note and called a cab. In her right hand, she had her overnight bag and her purse, and in her left, two thick, beach towels for the cab seat. She was still leaking. Luckily, she lived on a busy street, so the snow had been cleared, but when the cabbie pulled up and saw her noticeable bulge and the way that she was delicately trying to get into his cab, he advised her to call an ambulance.

"Oh, lady, if this is what I think it is, I'm not your man."

"I'm not having the baby right now."

"Lady, I don't deliver babies."

For a minute Isa thought he was really going to make her call an ambulance. Then he laughed, grabbed her bags, and helped her into the back seat.

"I'm just joking," the driver said.

Isa assured him that she was fine, and was only going to see her doctor, who was in the same hospital building as the maternity ward. She wasn't in any pain; she was just anxious. She didn't bother to call her doctor; she just didn't want to be alone. If he needed to be called, someone would notify them from there. Not one single contraction, and it could be hours before any action even started.

Later she remembered discreetly placing the towel under her bottom and then sitting back and enjoying the view. The cab was nice and warm and, fortunately, very quiet. All around them, the city felt still. It was as if everyone had decided to stay home and skip everything: work, school, and play. The cabbie was chatting about the number of inches the city was expecting when they realized there was a holdup on the highway, just as they got on the ramp.

"Must be an accident," she said.

"No, it's scaredy-cat drivers who slow us all down. It's a good thing you're not in labor. We're going to be here a while."

The cab continued to crawl along behind the traffic, and Isa sat back and sighed. *Everything would be fine.* She had a good feeling. She wasn't going to be one of those women who dramatically went into labor on the road. There was already enough drama in her life.

~🐦

Fortunately, Isa's doctor's office was located within the hospital, because when she arrived she was almost nine centimeters dilated. Isa was given a room and told that the baby was coming. She was shocked. How do you get to this point without contractions? Apparently, she was one of those fortunate women. Once the real contractions hit, it was all about getting through the process alive. Isa had never felt so alone in her life. All of the sudden, she wanted her mom, she wanted her sister. But there was no going back; calling her mother was not an option. The shock would probably kill her mother. The nurses on call were extremely sympathetic. They probably thought she was some poor, single mom who didn't have a soul with her. As it turned out, she was. Four hours later, the baby was born.

&

The baby was placed on her chest, and she immediately burst into tears. After being cleaned up and attended to, Isa was handed a tightly swaddled little being dressed in the standard hospital blanket and cap. She gently lifted the tiny pink lip of the cap and stole a glance at the little tuft of dark, downy hair. The nurse left them alone. No words were spoken. Isa just held her. Mia, the perfect name. It would not dawn on her, until much later, that Mia's Latin origins is "mine" or "wished-for child".

&

A day passed. No word from her sister. And then the bonding kicked up a notch. She didn't even see it coming. There she was, staring at her child, when a young nurse leaned in and exposed Mia's little leg. She said something about needing a blood sample. Before Isa could even react, the nurse had already rubbed alcohol on Mia's little thigh and pierced the baby's delicate skin with a needle. Isa watched in utter horror as the baby wailed.

Standing behind this blood-sucking nurse was a second nurse. The consultant was saying something about now being the ideal time for the baby to "latch on." She would find it soothing, comforting after the shot. Isa must have nodded, given some kind of visible form of consent, because next thing she knew the lactation consultant was positioning the baby onto Isa's bulging breasts and trying to get the baby to latch onto her nipple. Isa didn't even know when she had even opened her gown, but before she knew it, Mia had greedily started nursing and stopped crying. As the baby tugged, Isa stared in wonder. Her body worked. Despite it not even being her intention, it worked. Holy crap!

"Oh, this little one is a pro. And you have great nipples, yes, the pair of you, you're going to be just fine."

It was a bit painful at first, but it felt so right. So natural. Isa had carried this child, created this child, nourished her, kept her safe, and now that she was outside her womb, Isa still had the ability to feed her. It was very rare for the first time to go so smoothly. The lactation consultant said, "Count your lucky stars."

When the nurses left, it was just Isa and baby Mia. A fresh batch of tears crawled down her cheeks, and she had to keep them from coming down onto Mia's head. How on earth was she going to give her away?

❦

While Cristina and Leo were stuck at a motel half-way between PA and DC, Isa was tucked away in Room 142 with nothing but a staff of caring nurses and her little one. When the nurses suggested that the baby sleep with the other babies, Isa objected, and the baby slept nestled in the crook of her arm. When she wasn't asleep, she was nursing or having her diaper changed. When Cristina called and asked Isa how she was doing, her voice cracked, and Isa knew why. Cristina's worst fears had come to life, and Isa didn't reassure her. Isa didn't have any words, beyond the dreadful small talk that escaped her lips every time she opened her mouth. Gut instinct told her that Cristina knew. *The Plan* had gone horribly wrong.

❦

At the hospital, Isa spent every waking hour staring at Mia. She looked so much like her. The baby had inherited her caramel skin and dark hair. She'd been born weighing six pounds and seven ounces, and was twenty-three inches long. She would also be tall.

Leo had hoped that the baby would be as light-skinned as Isa told them William was.

"I'm not being racist," he'd joked.

"Then what is it?" Cristina had said, playfully hitting him on the shoulder.

"I'm just saying that it would be better if she matched us."

"She's not an outfit," Isa had blurted out.

"I don't care what *mija* looks like. I just can't wait to meet her," Cristina had said, as she folded baby clothes.

≈

Mija. My daughter. Words that Isa had never pictured herself ever pronouncing were now carelessly slipping off her tongue every time she kissed and caressed the soft little bundle in her arms. She felt equal parts fierce love and remorse when she remembered *The Plan*. When the baby slept, she would lie there and consider so many different scenarios.

Could she just take her back from her sister, like a shirt? Could they both run away, be accountable to no one? Show up years later when all would be forgotten?

Leo and Cristina were stuck in Pennsylvania for two whole days. This was one of those snowstorms that everyone had downplayed and almost dismissed. Roads were a mess and Leo was too afraid to drive under conditions he knew nothing about.

One minute Isa was convinced that she could take Mia back, that she had every right to her child. The next, she remembered her obligation. Her promise. Cristina's face would occasionally come to mind, and Isa realized how much her decision would hurt her. Hurt them both. She had practically forced Leo and Cristina to take the baby. She had made them uproot their lives. She had promised. Many times.

This would also be the fourth baby her sister would lose. Isa couldn't do that to her, could she? Her resolve swayed back and forth like a pendulum.

～☙

When baby Mia slept, Isa slept. She found comfort in listening to the reports of closed roads on the television mounted just above the foot of her bed. She watched old reruns and news reports, and she prayed that the winter storm would continue to rage and bring everything to a standstill. On the television, the sight of reporters fighting the wind in front of tall banks of snow comforted her. Citywide devastation, so long as no one was hurt, and reports of State Highway officials urging residents to keep off dangerous side roads meant she had time. The baby spent the first days of her life this way, ensconced in the crook of Isa's arm, waking and sleeping to the tune of her heartbeat while footage of stranded cars and closed businesses looped endlessly, and bundled reporters acted as if it were the end of the world. When, in reality, it was just beginning. For her and Mia.

～☙

Years later, Isa could easily recall that small hospital room. The muted patterns of light salmon, blue, and coral colors, swirled wallpaper and the matching window seat cushions. The stingy windows and the partial view of the wing that led to an even more grim building. It was only after the baby was born and within her reach that Isa noticed the one potted tree outside, a small bit of nature. In only a matter of hours, Isa had become accustomed to the daily structure: the hourly routines, change of nurses, dispensation of medicine, diaper changes, meal trays, and the Percocet-induced naps which provided both her body and her mind with the kind of comfort that only familiarity and repetition can bring. There was nowhere to go, nowhere to be. High on the fumes of her baby's smell and touch, Isa slept, nursed, ate and repeated the process. Pure bliss.

⁓

One evening, while the baby was nursing, Isa examined a noticeable birthmark on Mia's left hand. Engrossed, mesmerized by the pleasure that she took in mapping the nuances and contours of her newborn's body, Isa felt like someone was watching. But it wasn't a nurse or a doctor. When she looked up, staring from the threshold of the room's entrance were Cristina and Leo. How long had they been standing there?

Isa felt a mixture of shock and disappointment, a look of disillusionment and sadness. She felt she had been caught in the wrong, had broken a promise. They must have sensed this, just as Isa sat up, unintentionally pulling her breast out of baby Mia's mouth and upsetting the baby, causing baby Mia to squirm and pull back. Like a pro, Isa placed the baby back into position, while bouncing her about and calming her down. Neither Cristina nor Leo was prepared.

Leo stiffened, unsure what to say or do. Cristina walked straight up to both Isa and Mia and kissed them on their foreheads. Isa could see that every cell within her sister had shifted, regrouped, and had gone at all costs and with great hardship into comforting mode. It was classic Cristina—compassion and kindness—she was a good person, always had been. Hesitantly, Leo followed Cristina's cue and came forward, hugging them both.

"She's so beautiful," Cristina said, breaking into tears.

"She's a mini you," Leo said.

"Yup, no *güero* genes here."

"Can I hold her?" Cristina asked. Isa hadn't realized how tightly she was gripping the baby.

"Oh, yeah, yes."

"She's so light. I forget how little they weigh," Cristina said as she sat down on a nearby chair with the baby. Cristina started to say something, but immediately broke out sobbing, "Isa, she is your child. You have every right to change your mind. We have no right to walk away with her."

Isa watched her sister's body shake with grief as Leo took the baby away, fearing that his wife would collapse. Isa, unable to speak, watched Leo look down at the baby and slowly return her to her Cristina's arms. Thirty seconds seemed like an eternity, before Cristina regained her composure. And while Cristina held herself together, Isa prayed. *God, give me a sign. Tell me what to do. Help me.*

Isa had to be honest. She now wanted, more than anything, to make a life with Mia. And she thought that she had found it, until she looked deep into her sister's eyes and saw the pain reflected inside them. And looking into Cristina's eyes and now knowing what it was like to love like only a mother could, Isa wavered.

Cristina deserved a better life, a better sister.

Looking down at the baby, Isa tried to visualize their future. She had forgotten about the realities of becoming a single mother. Baby Mia growing up without a father. Life would be so hard on both of them. All the practical matters floated back to the surface. Isa was caught up in this sense of overwhelming responsibilities when Cristina leaned in again, tried to touch the baby's hands, and finally managed a smile. Maybe she was tired of hoping and had finally given up. Tears streamed down Isa's cheeks, but through blurred vision, she saw Mia's little hand. When Cristina ran her hand down the baby's wrist and into the palm of her hand, the newborn instinctively wrapped her small, puffy hand around Cristina's pinky.

"Oh my God, look! Look!" Cristina cried.

"What is she doing?" Leo asked.

Smiling, trying mightily hard to look like she was at peace, but with her heart in her mouth, Isa said, "Choosing. She's choosing."

chapter 15—Beatriz

Rio Chico, Texas, 2005

In the beginning, Beatriz would pick up the phone to call her daughter, and then realize she wasn't in Texas. Why hadn't they come back when they found out that she was pregnant? Why did all of Cristina's pregnancies have to be so difficult? And then there was the big fight that she had with Mateo over visiting them in DC. Beatriz had wanted to be near her daughter, especially for the birth. Mateo was too old to drive and neither of them was about to fly. They had argued for over a week, before they just left the whole thing alone.

"What if we take the bus?" Beatriz had suggested.

"What if one of us gets sick?" Mateo had responded.

"We'll make sure that you have all of your blood pressure meds."

"It's not me that I'm worried about."

Mateo did have a point. The thought of either one getting sick on a cross-country bus trip, where the kids had to come and get them—well, they would be more of a nuisance than any help. But after many months, the kids were coming home, and both Beatriz and Mateo were just beside themselves. There had been days when both feared that Cristina and Leo would fall in love with DC and decide to stay there. The idea that both of their girls would be living far away made them feel alone and unsure of anything. If it hadn't been for her best friend, Dora, her longtime companion in all things related to mothering and being a wife, she simply wouldn't have made it.

～

Back when Beatriz moved to the *Los Polvos Colonia*, Dora was the first real friend she had made. Over the years, they had raised six children between them, and Dora was already the proud grandmother of five grandkids. Granted, all of Dora's grandkids had come early and regularly. Dora's oldest daughter had married right after high school and given birth to twins. Dora's oldest boy moved to Tennessee, married a white woman, and had two kids too. The youngest grandchild, everyone's favorite, had just visited and christened them both with new nicknames. Gregory, only four, had referred to Beatriz as Big Bird and to his Grandma Dora as Tiny Baby Bird. No one had to ask what the child meant, because anyone could see the resemblance of the pair to the larger-than-life Sesame Street character and a baby bird.

Beatriz was a tall and rather large, big-boned woman, while Dora was a tiny, little wisp of a thing. What Dora lacked in physical fortitude and appearance, she more than made up for in persona and innate high spirits. Dora was a joker with deadly comedic timing. She loved to talk smack, and her friends and relatives could always count on her to be the life of the party.

The women had become best friends, not only because of close proximity, but also because neither knew how to drive a car.

～

On this particular morning, impatiently awaiting the arrival of her daughter, son-in-law, and new granddaughter, Beatriz stood on the only patch of lawn not cluttered with big pieces of metal or rusting appliances, watering a scrawny tree she hoped would actually grow. Two days ago, it had been so cold she hadn't left the house, and this morning, it was already seventy-five degrees. She walked out onto her porch and stretched out like a lazy cat, surveying her neighborhood. How it had changed. Once so spacious, it felt like all of the lots had shrunk, and the houses were on top of each other.

Smaller homes and mini-trailers had sprung up like mushrooms. Grown married children either built their own temporary starter home right next to their folks, or the once small houses were made larger to accommodate growing families and grandchildren. The far side of the *colonia*, which had been the last to develop, had sat empty for years. The kids had turned these four acres of dusty desert into a three-wheeler track.

All four acres belonged to Juanel Juarez, a notorious drug dealer who had many plans for the land. On one side, he had built a McMansion that sat on top of a small, manmade hill, and on both sides, smaller versions had been built for his son and his daughter.

Everything felt so cramped, and now her husband had made matters worse in their own shrinking lot. Now that there would be a new addition, Mateo had gotten it into his head that they needed more space.

"Mateo, the kids are not moving in."

"But we're getting grandkids. What if they decide to stay the night?"

"Why would Cristina stay the night? She lives five miles away!"

"Well, Isa will eventually marry and have kids. I doubt that she will come back home, so she will be visiting with her family."

Beatriz had liked the idea.

Two weeks after Cristina and Leo had driven out to DC, Mateo had started the big building project. It was more like he was picking up where he had left off months before; he had laid the foundation, but work at the salvage yard had stopped any more progress. Everything he had moved to build the foundation eventually wound up on the foundation, and now he was hauling all that junk away. Beatriz looked around and felt totally overwhelmed by the piles of building materials—some new, most not so new. Mateo was the type to bring scrap lumber from yard sales and buy nails from the clearance bin at the hardware store. There were sawhorses, cinderblocks, bags of cement, and pieces of asphalt tile shingles all over the place. Worse yet, there were patches of ground where mixed cement had fallen, patches guaranteed to kill the grass and anything that tried to grow around it.

꠸

Surveying the littered landscape, Beatriz wished the yard could revert back to that blank slate that they had once driven up to. When they had first moved into *Los Polvos*, before the girls were born, life seemed so simple in their sparsely furnished, three-room home. In these heady early years, Beatriz could dust, sweep, and mop and have her home tidied up in less than an hour. She even had the time and motivation to sweep the hard-packed dirt in their front yard, where the grass always refused to grow. Back then she didn't appreciate the simplicity of minimalism. She had wanted rose bushes, a gravel driveway, a fancy chain-link fence to keep out the neighbor's dogs, and she'd wanted to feel like they had been there and made a home.

But as grateful as she was for her home, she didn't appreciate the open and largely empty space. As much as she had loved her new home and its outer surroundings, the empty spaces all called to be filled and decorated.

Maybe the arrival of the baby and Isa's new job meant the arrival of a new phase in everyone's life. A fresh start.

Optimistic and reenergized, Beatriz grabbed a mildewed carton box that had once held a window fan and began tossing in items she didn't think Mateo would ever miss. In went a can of rusty nails and a barbecue-grilling brush from two decades ago, and out came a sigh of relief and lightness that she was making room for the new. Her children were coming home, and she was going to make it all better for them.

chapter 16–Cristina

Driving south from Washington, DC,
back to Texas, 2005

"We're going home!" cried Leo.

"Home," answered Cristina.

"Stop worrying."

"I just wish that it was 1950-something—no car seats, just holding your newborn."

"Never mind the babies that died."

"Okay, Mr. Morbid, I was just fantasizing about holding Mia in my arms. She's all by herself back there. She hasn't been out of the womb for a week and now she's just all by herself."

"Then join her, you doofus!"

"Are you sure you don't need company, to stay awake?"

"Well, I'll tell you what, it's been about seventy-five miles since I saw so much as a patch of snow, so let's pull over. You can hold her for a while."

No sooner had Leo pulled over when Cristina unbuckled and crawled into the back seat to take the baby out of the car seat. Mia was fast asleep and looking quite angelic in her yellow-and-green-striped sleeper.

Holding her daughter tightly against her, Cristina inhaled the already familiar baby smell and kissed her daughter's head.

She knew that stops like these were only making the road trip longer, but she couldn't help it. The baby needed her. She needed the baby.

In the end, Isa had kept her promise, but Cristina knew that something had changed. Part of her felt like they were making a fast getaway out of town, just so Isa couldn't catch up to them. The more distance they put between them and their child's past, the better it was. For everybody.

～🕭

Whether Cristina and Leo were consulting a map, switching between radio stations, or drinking bad gas station coffee, lingering right beneath the surface was the awful feeling that they were doing something wrong. Sometimes it felt that Isa's palpable grief dogged their newfound joy.

～🕭

In Tennessee, Leo pulled into a La Quinta Inn. He showered and slumped into one of the double beds, while Cristina slept in the other bed with their baby. Like the baby, she had been sleeping most of the day and she was more than prepared for the nighttime feeding shifts. Like an excited new mother, she stared at her newborn and eagerly anticipated the baby's every movement. The confines of a hotel felt like a neutral zone; she didn't feel shame or guilt.

～🕭

The following late afternoon, in Refugio, Texas, almost two hundred miles from home, weary and tired of being on the road, Cristina, who had her feet up on the dashboard, put them down abruptly and looked at her husband.

"Why does everything have to be so hard, so damn hard?"

"I know that your sister is weighing on you, and she weighs

175

on me too, but as an outsider, I think that I can see things a bit more clearly than you can. I think that you don't have to live in fear that she will always regret this or—"

"Come back for the baby?"

"I'm going to be honest with you, Cristina. After all we've been through, if I see you heartbroken again, so help me God, I will never speak to your sister again."

Mia slept most of the way home, and Cristina and Leo talked about the color of her crib, her room, the irony of now having a baby and none of the equipment needed to raise one. They had given everything away. It was only when they were immersed in the small details, like stopping at Walmart for a plastic baby tub, diapers, wipes, and formula, that they stopped thinking of everything that could go wrong.

chapter 17–Isa

Washington, DC, 2005

As soon as Isa discovered that the Percocet that her doctor had given her for pain soothed and relieved her anxiety, she started doubling up on it. She knew the drugs could be addictive, but she was in real physical pain, and if the side effects were also helping to ease the terrible separation anxiety she was experiencing, so be it. Her private parts felt like they had been hit by a bowling ball, and her breasts were engorged. The best she could do was to sleep, wake, change her clothing, struggle to go to the bathroom, and then repeat the whole process again.

This was the loopy state she was in when Cristina and Leo called from Texas. Isa had been both waiting for the call and dreading it, but when it did come, she summoned all her strength and pretended that she wasn't two steps away from collapsing under the weight of her own remorse. When Cristina asked Isa how she was doing, Isa answered, "I'm doing great. Tell me, tell me all about the trip. How is Mia? How is she doing?" And she couldn't believe herself. Who was this woman speaking?

⟶⟵

Isa was going to give herself just one week after leaving the hospital to hang around, rest, and groan and moan. After that, it was back to studying and continuing her job search. Her friend Margo had brought over her own study materials and had taken up the entire kitchen table with them.

"Okay, hon, I'll be in the dining room. Get some sleep," said Margo.

"I feel guilty. I should be studying. It's not like I have to rest because I have a newborn to look after."

⚓

The day before she was supposed to take her exams, Isa had slept in and was unable to drag herself out of bed. In the last three days, she had cleaned up her apartment, gone shopping, and even picked out a suit should she be called in for a job interview. There wasn't much for her to do but study and be sad. She had taken the last Percocet the day before and wished she had used them more sparingly. She had walked around the entire apartment and gotten rid of any trace of her sister, her brother-in-law, and her pregnancy. She wanted a new start; she wanted to leave the past behind her. She had made a decision, a promise, and she had to keep it.

⚓

Four hours later, when Margo knocked on the door, no one came. Still having her extra key, she let herself in, only to find her good friend still in bed. Isa was sitting up, staring out the window. Her hair was greasy and unwashed, and she hadn't even changed out of her pajamas.

"How are you feeling?" asked Margo.

"Sleepy," answered Isa.

"You're depressed. This is normal. You had a baby, now the baby is gone—whether you intended to be a mother or not. It's only natural. Your body is grieving, and it's okay."

Margo sat on the bed next to Isa and patted the area over the covers where Isa's feet were.

"Are you having second thoughts?"

"Margo, I'm beyond second thoughts, that door is closed."

"Is it?" asked Margo.

One Year later. . .

PART TWO

chapter 18–Cristina

Washington, DC, 2006

Dear Isa,

We were really disappointed that you couldn't make the baby's first birthday party. Mom and Dad worry about you. They think you work too much. But working a lot is better than not working, right? Mia loved the birthday gift you sent. Well, she chewed on it and said a couple of syllables, so I took that as a good sign. She was almost five months old when you saw her last; can you believe how much she has changed since then? Especially the picture where she is wearing the purple dress? It's all going too fast.

Isa, I hate that we are no longer as close as we used to be. I don't even know where to start. Or what to say. I have written and rewritten this letter in my head so many times, and it never gets easier. I want you to know that I am sorry about causing you so much pain.

I knew that I should have never accepted Mia that day at the hospital. I could see it in your eyes. I knew that we both shared the same tightness in our throats. I wanted to do the right thing. I was waiting for your cue. I was waiting for you to speak up and claim Mia. But you didn't. I was relieved that you didn't change your mind . . . but I still had mixed feelings. The urge to walk out of that room as a mother, Mia's mother, was so strong . . . I can't explain it. And I kept walking. I never looked back.

When we drove back to Texas and knew that you still had time, I waited for you to call. I swear to you, I waited. I was torn between bonding with my child and letting her go. Your visit was so short last time. Not that I blame you. I can't imagine how hard that must have been. But believe me, hermanita, when we left DC, every time the phone rang, my heart stopped. Would you change your mind? Would you show up unannounced? Would you come and take her? I changed diapers, pulled fresh onesies over Mia and folded her small little clothes with so much care and joy. And every day, I worried about having to pack up her things. It reminded me of the days when I had to be strong for Adelita. The threat of losing our daughter was always there.

My fear is that the difference between you and me is Mia. She is the reason that I live. Sister, please forgive me, but I just want you to know that if there ever was a time that I would have accepted you taking her, it's gone. And I need you to know that.

I am doing Mia a disservice by living with this fear. Adelita had a life-threatening illness, and I had no choice. Mia is whole and healthy. We love her so much. She has filled a hole in our lives that nothing, nothing could ever fill. No words, not this letter . . . nothing could ever express what this child means to me. To us. And that's why I know what she means to you.

I just wanted to let you know that in the beginning, I was prepared to do the right thing. Give her up. But you didn't call. I knew that you were hurting. And I didn't do anything.

When you came to visit us, I wondered if perhaps I had gotten it all wrong. I was hoping that you and I could have a fresh start. But then I saw you. You could barely talk in Mia's presence. You looked so helpless. I felt so guilty. I still do.

Isa, I understand your pain. I feel your pain. I will never forgive myself for putting my needs first that day. Eventually, I realized that in gaining my precious Mia, I lost you, hermana. I chose her. I chose her over you the day that I walked out of your hospital room with her. I'm sorry. I want you to know that I love you and will always love you. I don't know if either of us will ever be at peace, but I wanted to let you know that I miss you. I miss you so much.

I know the chances of you forgiving me are equal to those of my returning the baby. But this is no longer about us. It's about Mia. She's ours now. Please understand that. Please, please forgive us and help us move on.

Love,
Cristina

chapter 19–Isa

The first time that she read it, she wanted to tear it up. There were a thousand ways to get rid of that letter, but not one single way of forgetting what was inside of it. The plain white envelope seemed innocuous enough, but the guts, its contents, felt vile and offensive. Final. Certain phrases and words stood out. To haunt and taunt her.

> ~~Dear~~ Isa,
> . . . *waiting for you to speak up . . . claim Mia . . . you didn't . . . waited for you to call . . . doing Mia a disservice . . . to do the right thing. Give her up . . . you didn't . . . you changed your mind . . . didn't do anything . . . gotten it all wrong . . . guilty . . . will never forgive . . . this is no longer about us. It's about Mia. She's ours now . . . move on.*
> *Love,*
> *Cristina*

Isa had actually purchased a ticket and boarded a plane with the hope of arriving in South Texas and reclaiming her child. In Houston, right before she needed to board her connecting flight, she'd had a change of heart. There, two seats away from her, a father was trying to calm his infant. His wife, two rows ahead, was putting something away at the last minute. The father was trying to explain the baby's hysteria: "He's used to his mother." As the baby came out of his intense sobbing and gasping, his shuddering breath and inability to settle down had completely traumatized Isa. If this baby's world was coming apart because his own mother was out of sight, what would that do to Mia?

She headed back home on another plane, feeling exhausted and bereft.

~🔹

The letter sat on her bureau, an indictment of her as a parent and as a sister.

But every once in a while, Isa was overtaken by a righteous kind of indignation. She felt affronted by the letter's contents and by her sister. If there was anyone who knew what it felt like to lose a child, it was Cristina. So why write such a letter? What kind of person would ask a suffering mother to move on?

~🔹

Sometimes Isa started to write to Cristina, but she would stop herself. The words in the letter would come back to her. *She's ours now. Please understand that.* Simultaneously sensible and hostile. Every attempt at trying to craft a genuine response to Cristina was either mean or vindictive, or it sounded false and contrived. The effort always left Isa feeling like she was running out of air, struggling to breathe.

chapter 20–Cristina

Rio Chico, Texas, 2006

After three days of thirty-degree winter weather, South Texas went back to its seasonal norm of eighty-five degrees. Cristina had kept the baby home on account of *el norte*. It was just too windy. During this time, Mateo and Beatriz had visited, but on a day like this, the grandparents had insisted that Cristina bring the baby for a visit. Sitting on Beatriz's porch, they both watched Mia crawl around on a quilted blanket that Beatriz had put down for her.

"*Que cosas*," sighed Beatriz. "It's like I am looking at Isa at this age. It's unbelievable how much they look alike."

"Yes. I guess it's a look that runs in the family genes?"

"Your sister is probably going to marry a *gringo* and have a baby that looks like you. Wouldn't that be funny?"

If Cristina lost a pound every time someone reminded her how much Mia looked like her sister, she would have disappeared into the ether. Cristina loved her child, every inch of her, exctly as she was, but she did wonder whether things would have been different if Mia didn't look so much like Isa. Would that have altered the tension between the sisters?

chapter 21–Isa

When Isa wasn't working, putting in more hours than anyone else at the firm, she was shopping for furniture. It had all started when she'd bought her first piece of grownup furniture. Her first purchase was an original Edmund Jorgenson open bookcase, circa 1965. Isa loved its smooth walnut finish and magnificent grain. The whole piece was raised on dainty legs that tapered down to delicate-looking brass feet. One of her New Year's resolutions had been to stop shopping for Mia, a habit that had gotten out of control, and to replace all her garage-sale findings and Ikea furniture with nice things. Three weeks after buying the piece, the dealer called and asked if she was interested in seeing a 1960s Danish retro dining table in perfect condition. These two pieces started Isa's love affair with sleek furniture and minimalist design. They also led to the third, and most problematic piece, a vintage bar cart.

"Woo-hoo, look at you!" gushed Aisha the first time that she had seen it. Holding up a stainless steel pestle, she said, "What the hell is this?"

"That, my dear, is a muddler."

"A what?"

"One of my many bartending accoutrements. It's what you

189

use to mash, or muddle, whatever, fruit or spices at the bottom of your glass."

"Why does it have to be muddled?"

"To release its flavor."

"So, now you're into everything cocktail?"

"Hey, I figured if I was going to buy a $2,000 bar cart, it should be well-stocked."

"Cheers!"

What Aisha didn't know was that Isa's bar, while clearly displaying a couple of expensive vodkas and a rainbow's worth of brightly colored liqueurs, wasn't her "working stash." The level of liquid in the bottles displayed on the beautiful Lucite cart remained consistent. What didn't were the ones stored in the bottom cupboard sideboard in the dining room.

Isa's drinking had started slowly. There were the business lunches, the after-work happy hours, and eventually, there was the drink at home that led to two, and then three. Isa would come home late, after eating something at the office or on the street, peel off her work clothes, and slip right into her pajamas. If she hadn't brought anything from work (a rare occurrence), she would put her feet up on the couch and fix herself a cocktail.

⌐⌐

In the beginning, Isa didn't have to drink every day. She quickly gained the title of the most work-obsessed lawyer in the office. She would stay at work until midnight every night, and be the first one in the office, way before any of the paralegals. She didn't turn down work, ever. She loved her apartment, but she didn't like missing Mia. The void that Mia had left was sometimes crippling, so when she couldn't throw herself into her work, she numbed her pain with spirits. Her child was sometimes the first thing she thought of in the morning and the last thing she thought of at night. It was exhausting.

Drinking is what she did when she couldn't stop thinking about the baby, like the one Saturday when she discovered the hospital bracelet that she'd been wearing when the baby was born. Or the times when she became particularly sentimental and couldn't let something go, like when a colleague had wished her a great weekend when she was dreading having to fly out East for a deposition and not to Texas, where her daughter would be celebrating her third birthday.

"Have a great weekend!" Vicky, one of the new paralegals had shouted in the parking lot. Great? What was Isa going to say? Smile, and with as straight a face as she could muster, just answer, "No, not great. I gave my baby up. My weekends suck, all of them, this one in particular. It's Mia's birthday."

꽈

Flying back from Texas was always difficult for Isa. On one particular trip, she found herself settling into her seat and trying her best to keep from sobbing out of sheer misery. It was during these times that Isa had to remind herself that things had gotten better, that slowly she was at the very least building and shaping a relationship with her daughter, something most other birth mothers couldn't do.

When Isa had visited the baby for the first time after the hospital, Mia had just entered the separation-anxiety stage and would start to cry as soon as Isa walked into the room. Leo and Cristina had tried to get the baby to go to her, but Mia had seemed to resent every effort made to pass her to this total stranger, so she would cling tightly to one of her parents and turn away. There was nothing more depressing than watching your own child turn her head and start howling when you reached out for her. To Cristina and Leo's credit, they made many attempts. Isa could see the frustration in their faces. She could tell that they both felt terrible. But what had she expected? That Mia would fall into her arms, cling to her tightly, and never let go, knowing Isa was her biological mother?

Visiting Mia had never been easy, but the more of a little person she became, the harder it was for Isa to daydream about taking her away from Cristina and Leo. Mia's little voice and personality, her wants and desires belonged to her, and the love that she felt for her mother and father were like a physical fortress, a boundary that Isa dared not cross.

"My mommy makes eggies this way. *Papi* built me a swing set."

Cristina and Leo would always be Mia's parents, not her. Isa had wondered many times what would become of her life if she did disappear with her daughter. Start a life in Mexico? Not in the north, where her parents were from, but in the far south, or better yet, lose herself and Mia in the anonymity of Mexico City. She had enough money to start a small business. They were all crazy dreams, though; Isa knew that the only banishment she was doomed to live in was exile from motherhood. Deep down, she could find comfort in the idea of traipsing around the world with her daughter, running from their past, but she would always come to her senses.

The last time Isa had visited, Cristina and Leo had given Mia a party at a pizza place with an indoor playground. Mia was excited, and she was at that fun stage where she appreciated having Isa as the doting aunt who spoiled her. Isa had returned to Washington with a picture of herself with Mia. By chance, both were wearing red, and with their striking resemblance, the picture was almost a dead giveaway. She wondered if it had been hard for Cristina to see the similarities. The picture was an eerie reminder of what had transpired. How had Cristina managed to part with it? The picture now sat on Isa's mantel. Visitors to Isa's place always commented about the similarities between her and her niece, and Isa just nodded, her eyes vacant.

chapter 22–Cristina

Rio Chico, Texas, 2010

It was one of the coldest Februaries on record in Rio Chico, Texas, and Cristina had bundled Mia up so tightly that the little girl waddled when she walked. Tomorrow was Mia's fifth birthday, and she had a 103-degree fever. Mother and daughter both pushed the heavy clinic glass door open, and Mia ran toward the children's corner of the doctor's office.

Cristina kept an eye on her while she spoke to the receptionist. Meanwhile, Mia started to take off her jacket and gloves. She had even kicked off her shoes and was sitting down next to the brightly colored Lego table.

"Mia, please put your shoes back on."

"No, Mommy, my feet are hot and my neck is sweaty."

"That's because you're sick, baby. Come on, let's put your shoes back on."

Cristina set her purse down on the closest chair and scooped her daughter up from the floor and onto the rigid chair. She knelt down beside Mia and picked up the bright yellow-and-pink boots with fleece trim. Once done, Cristina sat next to her daughter.

"Want to sit up on Mommy's lap?"

"Mommy, I'm not a baby anymore. Tomorrow I'll be five."

"Oh, well excuse me, Miss," teased Cristina.

Once free of all of the extra clothing, Mia sat patiently until she became bored and started to swing her legs back and forth, making a pinging sound with the buckle on her boots against the chair. Cristina looked up from the magazine that she was reading. "Mia, please be still."

"Mommy, what if I get a shot? Shots hurt."

Cristina gave her a stern look, and Mia sighed heavily, stood up, and walked toward the window. Once there, she turned toward the lady next to her.

"Poor baby, you're sick on your birthday," commented the woman sitting next to Cristina.

"I'm not sick, and my birthday is tomorrow. We're having two *piñatas* and a pizza party," answered Mia with a croupy cough.

"She has a fever," added Cristina.

"You wouldn't know it. She looks so happy."

"She's really excited about her birthday."

Cristina whipped out a coloring book and a box of crayons from her oversized purse and walked over to the window.

"Mia, let's color while we wait, okay?"

Cristina sat on the carpet with Mia, and together they started to fill in the pages. On the other side of the waiting room two women sharing a bag of Doritos were talking so loud that the rest of the patients couldn't help but overhear.

"Some people," said the old man sitting next to Cristina and Mia.

"It's worse when they're on a cell phone," snickered Cristina as she handed Mia a different color.

"What makes people think that we want to hear their conversation, anyway?" sighed the old man. "I am practically deaf, and I can make out everything they're saying."

The petite woman sitting in front of the old man agreed,

and they started a conversation. Cristina only had eyes for her daughter. Mia had been such a blessing. Every day she had her was a wonderful day. Cristina leaned over and put the back of her hand on Mia's head.

"Does your head hurt, baby?"

"Mommy, I'm not a baby."

No, thought Cristina, her little one was no longer a baby. Gone were her baby's chubby legs and arms, her full cheeks. In their place was this growing child with scrawny legs and arms. Leo had named her "chunky monkey" when she was a baby because she had been soft and chubby. When Mia turned three, the baby fat had come off practically overnight.

"Where does she get her beautiful dark skin?" asked the petite lady.

This question, and it was asked a lot, always stumped Cristina. It would make her burn with guilt, and she could feel the heavy weight of her secret. People were being friendly and polite when they mentioned it, but even so, it always made Cristina uncomfortable.

"No, nope, you're not fooling anyone," Dora had once joked. "*Esta no es tuya.*" This one is not yours.

Cristina and Leo would always laugh nervously. If people only knew. Mia had inherited her mother's beautiful color. Mateo was as dark-skinned as Mexicans come, and Beatriz was fairly light. This mix had contributed to the russet color on Mia's little face. Recently, Mateo had started calling Mia "Little Isa." Cristina had had to act quickly. She gently discouraged the habit, coming up with playful ways of reminding everyone that she was Mia and not Little Isa. Mia was her own little person and nobody else.

The nosy petite woman was still staring at her, expecting an answer and Cristina blurted out, "Oh, she looks like my father. The spitting image."

"*Que cosas*," sighed the woman. "It's amazing how our children come out. I have four children and all four look like my husband. No one inherited my fair complexion."

Cristina nodded and stared at the woman's face. She had Mia's skin coloring, but her face was literally shellacked with a foundation and a powder several shades lighter.

"No more Legos," exclaimed Mia. "Mommy, my neck is still sweaty."

Cristina pulled Mia up on her lap and hugged her tight. She inhaled Mia's delicious little-girl smell and looked at her daughter's long, skinny legs. When had her baby gotten so big? And when would she ever feel free from the burden of what she knew? Would the knowledge and the feelings of betrayal ever leave her? Would Mia ever feel completely hers? Why did she have to choose between a baby and her only sister? She knew that Isa's distance from the family had everything to do with Mia and nothing to do with her career. And deep, deep in her heart, Cristina felt guilty about not doing the right thing. The day she had walked out of that hospital room with Mia, she could literally feel Isa's emotional maternal force field pulling her back. But she had chosen to ignore it. And she was paying the price.

"Mia Alvarez?" the receptionist called.

"Coming," answered Cristina, as she reached for her child's hand and squeezed it tight. This was her life now. Always uneasy and vigilant, sometimes feeling like a criminal, a child snatcher . . . always moving. Never fully at peace.

chapter 23—Isa

Isa moved to Seattle the same year that Mia started kindergarten. She felt that even after putting in so many hours of work, all her time and commitment, she was not being adequately mentored at Baulm, Tourney, and Deloit. She wanted to join a firm where more women held positions of power. She was tired of playing the game, behaving, nose to the grindstone, making no waves, yet still finding that it came down to the same good old boys network. The men would enjoy all the advantages that women would not. As men, they were part of the club, and they had more access to the kind of networking opportunities that allowed her male counterparts to flourish. As a single, non-parent female, she had given them all her time, even tried to take up golf and understand football.

Her only ally, an outspoken Asian American feminist, had tried to sue the firm. Like Isa, she had always received positive reviews, but promotions were slow to come. After a decade, Sue Ellen got sick and tired of watching her younger, less qualified male colleagues be given preferential treatment.

Unlike Sue Ellen, Isa didn't want to fight the firm. She was tired of watching brave women like Sue Ellen give up part or all of their lives to the struggle. She didn't have what they had—she didn't have that kind of fighting spirit. The indignity of the whole situation made her sick.

"You're a rare bird," Sue Ellen had told her one day at lunch.

"I'm a lonely bird," she had answered. "I have no one to fight for. I'm content with the money I make and the life I live."

"What about other women?" Sue Ellen asked. "Up-and -coming young women who, like us, thought, hey, get good grades, do well in law school, get a great job, and then become an equity partner."

"I'm not like you, Sue Ellen. I think that, like you, if they want it bad enough, they'll fight for it. Besides, have you noticed how complacent these young women have already become?"

"Yeah, and don't take offense, Isa, but I've always seen you as one of those apathetic feminists."

"Isn't that an oxymoron? Besides, I don't consider myself a feminist. Isn't part of being a feminist doing something? About sexism? I do nothing. I'm just a female lawyer."

"You're smart, driven, and you can take those old boys to task. You're just so passive sometimes."

"I choose to be. My life is complicated enough. I just like doing my own thing and being left alone. I don't see myself as a leader, not because I can't, but because it's just not me."

"You're a rare bird, Isa," Sue Ellen repeated.

There were endless minutes and hours, outside of normal billing hours, dedicated to organizing herself and staying organized. Running around like a hamster on the proverbial wheel was rewarding on so many levels, and absolutely lifesaving on all others. The more she worked, the less time she had to think about missing Mia, but her child was always on her mind.

Isa was never empty-handed. On airplanes, she would wear headphones regardless of what movie was playing. The person in the seat beside her could never ask where she was heading, and the young mother at the doctor's office could not ask her if she had kids. Isa never wasted time. She always carried reading material. She was never without files to read and briefs to write.

Of course, she did draw the line at using the infamous Bluetooth or discussing business on her cell in the line at Starbucks. Being busy, staying engaged, and looking occupied had absolutely nothing to do with acting like an obnoxious person who thinks that the minutiae of their day should be forced upon innocent bystanders.

Isa's days started with a piece of fruit, a double espresso and, if she could fit it in, thirty minutes on her treadmill. And she had learned, long ago, that yes, she was industrious out of fear, and yes, she was fully aware of this, and yes, she had made peace with it. Embraced it, even. Waking up at five meant that coming home might involve catching one or two hours of television and grabbing a bite to eat, then falling into bed, bone-tired.

Slowing down and being aware meant that thoughts would invade her consciousness and start playing the same broken record. Mia and then Mia and more Mia. Not thinking about Mia was like trying to meditate—she just couldn't do it. How do you think of nothing? Impossible. How could her real, live, flesh-and-blood child who was being raised by her sister and brother-in-law—the child that she held to her bosom for two complete days—be forgotten? Isa feared that slowing down, experiencing real solitude and awareness, meant that she would actually have to do something about these thoughts. And there was nothing that she could do. Absolutely nothing.

Now that Mia was starting school, she kept thinking of the new series of milestones that she would be missing. One day, her daughter would know, and she would probably ask, or at least wonder. *Did my real mother ever feel bad about missing my first day of school? Helping me pick out my first backpack?* Isa knew that these questions would be inevitable, if truth be told.

She didn't know why it took her so long, but one day the

idea came to her. She would write her daughter letters. She could write in real-time connection, even if it might be years before Mia actually read them. Because she would read them. She might be twenty, she might be thirty, but as God was her witness, her daughter would one day know.

⚓

When Isa informed her parents that she would be relocating to Seattle, they were upset. Why not Austin or Houston? Texas was big and had plenty of job opportunities, and it wasn't across the country. Isa didn't want to tell them that anywhere in the great state was too close for comfort, so she lied. She told them that she had applied all over Texas, but the job that came through happened to be in Seattle.

In Seattle, Isa met the person she considered her true soul mate, Dr. Evie Marie Sanders. After having thrown out her back for the second time, Isa had been told that she should see a chiropractor and get adjusted. When she asked her coworkers, they laughed and chided her. In their eyes, chiropractic care was nothing but remnants of bygone medical tomfoolery. Back home, Isa's mom used to see Doña Hermita, a *huesera*, a traditional bonesetter who used to manipulate her mother's body every six months, almost like a chiropractor. Isa had once been there when Dona Hermita had set one of her mother's dislocated joints. Isa had found the practice interesting but didn't care to try it. The lack of any medical certificates and the manipulation of human bones seemed like a risky marriage to her, and she wanted no part of it. But this didn't mean that she wasn't curious about it.

Evie's office was on the same street as hers, and when Isa passed it on the way to Hope's Café, two doors down, she loved how cozy and Zen Dr. Sanders's office looked. It was more than a doctor's office; it resembled a spa. Inside the lights were always dim and the walls were painted in a combination of soft and burnt orange hues. There was a water fountain in the corner of the room and brown wicker furniture with earth-toned cushions. To Isa, the office looked like a place where clients could walk in, curl up in a corner, and sleep. More importantly, outside below the sign was a placeholder with a card that read: FREE CONSULTATION. WALK-INS WELCOME. Isa had been relying on her doctor and had been taking muscle relaxers, pills that she could not take during the day, but which, when combined with alcohol in the evening, put her to sleep.

Evie loved to tell the story, and Isa loved to chime in and embellish or clarify. "The day that Isa came through my door, I was rushing and having a terrible, no-good day. My receptionist was out sick and my computer had crashed. I was considering canceling the day's appointments and closing up shop. Just as I was about to open the scheduling book, Isa walked through the door. She looked awful and could barely walk. I sprang up from the front desk and waved her back into the examining room."

"Sprang? That's an understatement," Isa would say. "She flew across the desk, so overtaken by my feminine wiles and exotic beauty."

"Pul-eese!" laughed Evie.

"Okay, seriously, no joke, Evie worked miracles on me that day. When I walked through her doors and she escorted me to the back, without so much as asking me to fill a history card or ask my name, I wanted to cry. I was so grateful. She seemed to know exactly where to touch, pop, and massage. After my first consultation and adjustment, she made a call and made sure that I could drive across town and see a masseuse for deep-tissue massage that very afternoon."

"My adjustments are now her crack. I keep telling her that her body is the vessel where she locks up all of her worries and anxieties. She is a workaholic and a worry-aholic."

Neither had known the other was gay. In that first session, Evie found out that Isa was a lawyer, that she was from Texas, and that she had just purchased her first condo. Isa started seeing Dr. Sanders twice a week at the beginning and assumed that she was a married woman with children, but one day, Isa spotted Evie in Belltown, getting out of her green Volvo at a flower shop. The car was neat and clean, so the pink triangle stood out and piqued Isa's attention. After that, Isa figured out a way to find out if the beautiful Dr. Sanders was, indeed, interested in women.

"I thought Isa was really beautiful . . . and she hates what I am going to say, but she had an 'exotic' appeal. Even in her plain black and navy suits she was striking, *muy caliente!*"

"Every time she uses the word *exotic*," laughed Isa, "I feel like a spotted jaguar pacing back and forth in a zoo cage."

"No, no, listen to this, everybody," Evie would add. "She came off as a very professional woman, but it was clear that she was withholding something."

"When I saw the sticker on the car, you all know the one," Isa would say, "I asked myself so many questions. Does she just support gay people? Or is she gay? If she is, is she seeing anyone? She might even be married. Then it dawned on me, I never even bothered to check for a wedding ring."

"Okay, wait," Evie would interject, "it gets better. After Isa sees my sticker, she goes out and buys herself a rainbow keychain—one that was half the size of her car."

"So not true!" Isa would shout over their friends' hysterical laughter.

"It was probably the only rainbow-colored anything this woman's ever bought in her entire life."

"I'm a private lesbian!" sang Isa, to the tune of Tina Turner's 'Private Dancer.'"

ود

When Isa met Evie, Isa felt, for the first time, that the universe had finally thrown some real, good, genuine love her way. Unlike other women, with whom Isa never felt a hundred percent comfortable, she felt like she had always known Evie. The first time Isa told Evie about Mia, Evie held her in her arms while she cried. She rocked her back and forth and told her it was all going to be okay. Evie also told her that she was going to help her move forward, not in a 'move on, get over it' kind of way, not in a closure kind of way, but to learn to live with her decision, to manage her emotions.

That concept had not really occurred to Isa. She had always felt that it was all or nothing. Happiness was reuniting with her daughter, at all costs, and unhappiness was always regretting what she had done and being in a perpetual "what if" mode.

In the beginning, they had talked long into the night, comforting each other. And for the first time, Isa didn't feel so alone. It was also the first time that she had understood how Cristina was able to cope with their secret. Cristina had a partner in crime, someone she could talk to, an emotional accomplice, someone who could talk her off the ledge and also encourage her to let go, to live a little. Cristina had Leo.

With Evie at her side, Isa learned to enjoy life again. She also learned to cut herself some slack. There would be good days; there would be bad days. And it was okay. Together they would take it day by day.

By the time that Mia was about to turn seven, Evie and Isa had moved in together. They had bought what they both jokingly referred to as an artificial Victorian house, since their new "green home" was a replica of a Victorian home in an eco-friendly neighborhood. Their home, done in different shades of pastel pinks and purple, to resemble a house they had once rented in Cape May, sat on a darling cul-de-sac. Their friends liked to joke that their streets were so well-manicured that their neighborhood looked like a giant movie set.

Their beautifully landscaped community came fully equipped with a man-made pond, a walking trail, and a community center that featured Kid Night and Indie Movie Night for the adults.

⚓

Through Evie, Isa met Edward and Rebecca, who had gone to chiropractic school with Evie. Evie was like an aunt to their children. They were also the same couple who had encouraged them to move into their eco-friendly neighborhood. Evie also introduced Isa to her close-knit circle of lesbian friends, even though Isa was afraid they would judge her for being closeted. They had all been quite understanding and had assured her that coming out was none of their business. All but one, Janine, who once rather caustically had said, "Well, Isa, you can't use the 'culture' excuse forever." It had been a rather awkward moment, since Isa, who was a little tipsy herself, had let it slip that it was easier for white women with smaller families, or no families, to come out. Isa didn't care much for her comments. She had concerns that outweighed how or when she would, if ever, reveal her sexual identity. As far as she was concerned, no one at work had asked, and she was not about to say anything.

chapter 24 – Cristina

Rio Chico, Texas 2012

"Mommy?" asked Mia.

"Yeah?" said Cristina, while she tossed dirty laundry into the washing machine.

"You know how last year I wanted a baby for my sixth birthday? Then again for Christmas?"

"Uh huh?"

Now, her daughter had Cristina's full attention. The topic of a baby sister or brother had first started coming up when Mia was three. Cristina thought it was just a phase, and it was. Then all of the sudden, last Christmas, there it was again on her Christmas list. Mia wanted not one baby, but two. Twins. She had asked Santa Claus for twins. The best Leo and Cristina had been able to come up with were two matching baby dolls and a twin stroller. Mia loved her gift and never brought up the idea of babies again. But her questions had prompted Cristina and Leo to tell Mia about Adelita and the other two babies and the fact that they would probably never have another baby again.

These discussions were conversations played out in bed, five minutes before Cristina and Leo dozed off, conversations and concerns easily forgotten in the morning. But something had happened the day before that made Cristina rethink the whole conversation, the bit about not being able to conceive. After years of being on the pill—because she just couldn't bring herself to have her tubes tied—Cristina had stopped taking them and was thinking of having the operation. Just get the whole thing over with. Then, even if she wanted to, she wouldn't be able to even try. They had Mia. Mia was all that they needed.

So, when the last pill ran out, she didn't get a refill, but she kept putting off the conversation with Leo and the inevitable doctor's appointment because she didn't think that she could get pregnant so soon. But all the signs were there: tender breasts, fatigue, and—though maybe it was all in her head—nausea. Cristina knew she should have gone out and bought a drug store pregnancy test, but part of her thought that, on a subconscious level, these real symptoms might be a false pregnancy. Maybe she still wanted a baby so much that she was feeling these things.

She had heard of women with false pregnancies, their symptoms very real and even manifesting stomach bloating that resembled the physical state. She knew she should just take the test and see the negative result for herself, but she wanted to hold onto the possibility. She would wait just a little longer before taking a test and calling her doctor.

ᴗ⚓

"Mama!" Mia had said, tugging on her T-shirt, "are you hearing me?"

"Oh, sweetie, sorry. Mommy was just thinking," she answered Mia. "I'm sorry, do you still want a baby sister or brother?"

"No way! That's what I wanted to talk to you about. Denny—she's in my class—she says she hates her baby sister, so I hate her, too."

"Well, that's not nice. Denny just needs to learn to share."

"No, Mom, Denny says that now that she has a baby sister, she has to do everything in the house, like all of the wash and all of the cleaning and sometimes dinner."

"Ay, Mia, I doubt that Denny's baby sister turned her into a child slave."

"What's a child slave?"

"Never mind, I just think that Denny misses being the only one. Do you like being the only one?"

"I love it. And I want to be the only one always."

"You will," Cristina assured her.

◆

That afternoon, Cristina left Mia with Leo. They were both sitting on the couch watching the Cartoon Network. Thank goodness for fathers, thought Cristina. She could do a lot of things with her daughter, but she didn't have the patience to sit and watch cartoons.

"Off to the store . . . hello, I'm leaving?"

"Oh, yeah," said Leo, who was riveted by *Johnny Test*.

"Do you want anything?"

"I want Oreos!" shouted Mia.

"Anything else?" asked Cristina.

"No, just get the real thing, not those crappy phony ones," Leo called back and then started to tickle Mia and wrestle her on the couch.

Cristina took such pleasure in these scenes of domestic tranquility, family life. There was a time when she thought that she would never have this, and thanks to her sister, she had a full life, and for that she was grateful. Cristina also wanted to start reconnecting with Isa. It had been seven years, with ups and downs. No one had yelled, but the tension between them was palpable. Beatriz had picked up on it, and when she had said that maybe Isa resented the fact that she was childless and unmarried, Cristina had said nothing.

The truth was that the conversations between the sisters were always short, nervous, obligatory exchanges where the only topics discussed were Mia and their parents. Deep down, Cristina felt responsible for her sister's inability to find a mate, and something told her that finding a soul mate and having a baby would only make things worse. So not only had Cristina taken her child away, she thought, but she was the one responsible for Isa's giving up on looking for Mr. Right.

⚓

Leo was outside watering the lawn, and Mia was doing cartwheels on the dry spots. Seeing her, Mia bolted toward her mother and asked for the Oreos. Cristina raised the plastic bag over her head. "Go inside and wash your hands first," she laughed. Inside, Cristina pulled the pregnancy test out of the bag and threw it into the junk drawer while she put the cookies out on a plate and poured milk for the three of them. She put everything out on a tray and walked out to their backyard patio. Back inside, she ran into Mia and said, "Tell Daddy the cookies are out back with the milk. I'm going to the bathroom, meet you out back, don't eat all of the cookies without me."

⚓

Cristina stared nervously at the pregnancy stick. She wanted to hold onto the possibility that her breasts were really tender and that it wasn't something that her body had pulled because she had willed it so badly.

"Mommy!" cried Mia on the other side of the door. "Daddy says that you better hurry up or we're going to finish all of the cookies."

"Coming!" said Cristina. "Mommy's coming."

chapter 25–Isa

Rio Chico, Texas, 2013

Maria Candelaria Alvarez was born on the first of November at 6:15 a.m. She was a big baby, weighing in at nine pounds. She was named after Leo's mother. Cristina called her Candy, because she wanted to eat her up and because it beat Candelaria, a name that she had agreed to out of respect for her husband's deceased mother.

Candy was the complete opposite of her sister Mia, with blonde hair and blue eyes, eyes that would later turn green like Cristina's. The day Candy was born, she was the only little girl in the maternity ward. But instead of referring to Candy as the "little girl" the nurses and staff called her "the *gringita*." All of the fuss about how beautiful and white she was, how fair, blonde, and blue-eyed, wasn't enough, so they added the extra qualifier. No one ever stopped to think that perhaps constantly declaring Candy the most "beautiful baby ever" within earshot of the other new parents was not only callous but also brazen.

Leo had gone home to get some rest, and Beatriz was going to be spending the day with Cristina until visiting hours were over. Isa was stuck in the Dallas airport, waiting to fly home and spend a whole week with Mia. It was the first time that she would be able to spend so much time with her.

The last nine months had been very difficult for Isa, after hearing that Cristina was pregnant. Thanks to Evie, she had worked on accepting her life as it was. While other women felt like they were improperly raising their children, she had bucked at the starting gate. She hadn't even had the guts to fight for her child.

Evie thought that Isa had moved on, until one evening during dinner prep, when Isa had her big idea.

"What if I did it in stages?"

"Did what in stages?"

"Got Mia back."

"Babe, you can't do this."

"No, I know, I will never have Mia to myself, but what about moving down there? Then I tell her that she has two moms." Evie momentarily stopped what she was doing and shifted uncomfortably in her seat.

"Or three?"

"Two, for now," Isa said quietly.

"Wow, okay. But you would have to tell your parents . . . and everybody, about us."

"Of course . . . someday."

"Someday, when?" Evie asked irritably.

"Evie, one thing at a time. We'll figure that out."

Evie stood, sighed, and looked straight at Isa. "Figure it out when? Do I get a say in the matter? As in, 'Hey, Evie, would you consider moving to Texas with me?'"

"Aw, come on, I finally find a solution to my biggest problem, and you make this all about you?"

Evie snapped, "I'm sorry, about *me*? Are you kidding? Did you just say that? It's *your* emotional fires that we're always putting out—me mostly—and you have the audacity to call *me* selfish?"

Isa rarely saw Evie shaken up.

"I'm sorry. I'm so stupid."

Evie took a deep breath and asked a question whose answer she was afraid to hear. "Isa, what if I decided that I wasn't coming? Would you still move?"

"I don't know. I don't know."

～

That night, Isa decided that she would visit her new niece and hang out with Mia, to get a feel for things before she decided anything. She promised Evie she wouldn't decide anything until after she came back to Seattle.

～

In the airport, Isa looked at the contents of her carryon and wondered if what she had was enough. She had ordered a personalized Big Sister T-shirt and a book about the arrival of new babies, and waiting at her mother's was the biggest present: a large Dora the Explorer house with every imaginable accessory. She was planning on distracting Mia with a whole new world of play. She had visions of lying on Mia's floor and assembling the large house and opening one package of frills after another. She would fill every hour of the week with quality bonding time and win her daughter's heart, show her how much she was loved.

One thing did worry her. When her mother had called her to give her the news, all she could talk about were the baby's looks.

"Isa, nothing is going to happen to Mia," Evie said. "Look at you and your sister. You're darker, she's lighter. So what? You survived. Did it kill you? You love each other despite those differences."

"Yes, despite all of the drama between us, I survived, but will Mia survive it? I had Dad to look to. I was his dark child. I took after him. I didn't feel alone. Mia won't have anyone."

"Yes, she will."

"Who?"

"You, silly goose—and her grandfather."

Evie had a point, she always did, but what would happen if Mia ever found out the truth? One more thing for the kid to add to her long list of grievances against the unfairness of life.

～⚓

Once in Texas, the minute that Isa set eyes on Mia, all her anxieties melted away. She took in every inch of her growing child. Mia was always excited to see her aunt "Tita," and it looked like it was going to be a promising week.

Cristina had to stay in the hospital for almost a week due to maternal fever complications, so Isa established a daily routine with Mia. She would drive her to school in the morning, then pick her up and go visit Cristina, Leo, and the baby in the hospital. The week flew by, and there was no time for awkwardness between sisters.

～⚓

Every night Cristina was in the hospital, Mia had asked her aunt to share her big, white, four-poster bed. The first night, after Mia had fallen asleep, Isa realized that it was the first time that she had slept next to her child since the week she was born.

～⚓

The next morning, Isa didn't want to move. She waited until Mia opened her eyes.

"Hey, sleepyhead. How did you sleep?"

"I was so warm. It's usually so cold in here."

"Maybe we should crank up the heat?"

"No, sleep with me again!"

Mia's request was like a big hug to her heart.

"Hey, want to go out for breakfast before school?" Isa had asked.

"McDonalds?"

"Okay, let's jump out of our warm little nest at the count of three—one, two, three!"

They threw the blankets off each other and set about their morning rituals. While brushing their teeth at the sink, Mia asked, "*Tía*, why do you live so far away?"

"Because my job is far away."

"Well, get a job here. Daddy can make you a teacher."

Isa had laughed and actually considered the idea. When a seven-year-old says it, it sounds so easy. Maybe she could really do this. She could start a life in Rio Chico. As soon as she registered this, her mind immediately went through everything that could go wrong—starting with her relationship with Evie. Would she be the stigmatized lesbian lawyer? And Evie, would she even get patients? There were plenty of closeted folk in Rio Chico, and people knew that. It was a "don't ask, don't tell" sort of understanding. But she would be out. Evie would never allow her to remain closeted. How else would you explain a roommate who resided with you permanently?

There was an alternative, and its name was McCullers, the next big city. McCullers wasn't New York, but it was still a city where you could remain anonymous—kind of. She could work in Rio Chico and live with Evie close to home. Inspired by the time shared with Mia and all of the memories they had created, Isa felt like she could do anything. She was moving. Why not? It would take some time to get her affairs in order. She would not tell Evie over the phone. She would wait to get home before going any further.

For the rest of the week, Isa spent her day with her parents until she picked Mia up from school. They had dinner out practically every night. Mia was having such a great time that she hardly had time to think of the new baby or her parents. She had gone out to the movies on a school night, and *Tía* Isa had taken her shopping for new shoes and books. So many books.

At the hospital, Cristina was smitten with the new addition. Mia would visit for twenty minutes a day, and there were never any tensions with Cristina, like there usually were. Isa liked to pretend that this was her life now—just she and Mia, visiting Cristina and the new baby, Candy.

When Isa brought Mia home from school and told her that her mother was home, Mia darted into the bedroom, tossing her book bag on the way and flung herself into Cristina's arms. From the door, Isa watched the joyful reunion. She watched Mia kick off her shoes and burrow under the comforter with Cristina, who hugged her daughter and smothered her with kisses.

Cristina started to ask Mia about her new dollhouse when Mia announced, "*Tía* Isa, you can go sleep with *Abuela* and *Abuelo* now. I'm sleeping with my mommy tonight."

Mother and daughter started talking and seemed to be in their own world while Isa snuck out of the room, willing herself not to cry.

chapter 26–Cristina

Rio Chico, Texas, 2014

Two. Of everything. Two separate meals to prepare, two separate loads of wash. Even two car seats, if a booster seat still counted as a car seat. Cristina and Leo loved that they were a family of four. There was something about the number four. Maybe it was the symmetry? The balance? Four felt right. Four felt complete. She loved that come dinnertime there were four of them at the table. Four in the car, and at night, four people who called their house a home. Candy, already a toddler, was healthy and happy. During outings, each parent could tend to one child. On this particular morning, Candy was sitting at the children's table in the kitchen chewing on a chicken nugget.

"Candy? Candy? Look here, look here!"

"*Hija*, stop talking to her, or she won't finish her food."

"She's making a mess," Mia said, while giggling.

"Mia, are you happy to be an older sister?"

"*Si, mami*, I am!"

Cristina watched the bonds that both girls were forming. For Mia, it was the closest thing to having a puppy. Her older daughter was a precocious child, the kind who was reading by herself at the age of four—short chapter books. Mia read to the baby, which was great because it had allowed Cristina to do other things. As soon as Candy was big enough to sit up, she had Mia climb into the crib with her and read her a book.

At the mall, Mia always asked to push the stroller, and the best part of her morning was when Cristina woke her by putting the baby on her bed and having Candy gently wake her up. Watching her two daughters reminded Cristina of the many times that she had shared places, times, and events with Isa.

⌣⤚

Isa was always in the back of her mind. The minute that she had learned about her pregnancy, a whole new weight had been added to her already heavy burden. One more thing to tip the scales in her favor.

In the beginning, Cristina was so focused on making sure that both girls received equal attention that she consciously made the decision not to breastfeed Candy. At the hospital, Candy had taken to nursing quite well, but every time the baby latched on, the bond, the physical connection was so strong she feared that she would love one baby more.

The girls meant everything to her and Leo. She took great pride in the fact that life had given her the opportunity to be kept busy. Busy with the goings-on of raising a family.

chapter 27–Isa

Seattle, Washington, 2016

Dear Mia,

Eleven years, six months, and twenty-one days ago, you came into this world—my world, your mother's and your father's world—and changed it forever. Mia, I am your mother. I have more than a hundred letters describing how I felt and what I couldn't say. I wanted you to know what I was thinking, what I was feeling during all these years when I didn't have you. I didn't want to get in the way. I have never wanted to interfere with the ties you have with your mother and father. Why am I sharing now? I feel that now that you are older and wiser, we could get to know each other better.

Mia, next month is Abuelo Mateo and Abuela Beatriz's big anniversary party, and I am thinking of your parents. With both a heavy and joyous heart, I wanted to tell you the truth. I have no idea what you will say or how you will react when you read this. I am so afraid. I am so nervous. Mia, I love you, please, please don't hate me. . .

❧

Immediately after writing the letter, Isa walked into the kitchen and lit it on fire. She watched the flames take over the cream-colored paper and leave nothing but ashes in the deep, stainless steel sink. Of all of the letters she had ever written to her daughter, only eleven had survived. She knew the only party who would benefit from the letters would be herself. She knew every letter was a burden that she shook off herself and heaved upon Mia.

But she did have an idea of where to start.

Isa had recently realized that she wanted to work for herself. After all these years, the idea finally appealed to her. It was as she was drafting her letter of resignation. Talking to Evie about what she had in savings, it occurred to her that if she was ever going to make the move to Texas, even if it were just to try it out, this was the time. Evie was onboard.

"You keep your business and we hold onto the house."

"And if it works out," said Evie with a smile, "I join you in South Texas and become a kept woman."

"You could do whatever you wanted to."

"But meanwhile," reassured Evie, "everything stays in place, just in case."

"It's this 'just-in-case' clause that kills me. What if Mia hates me? If she hates me so much she doesn't ever want to see me?"

"You can count on that being part of her reaction, but it will be the toughest part. How much worse can it get after that?"

"She hates you . . ."

Evie threw a cushion in Isa's face and cried, "She can't hate me. I'm super lovable, of course she will like me!"

⌣

Their thinking wasn't a result of just that conversation. Change, for both them, had been a long time coming. Isa was thinking of leaving her law firm and getting a job elsewhere. Evie had wanted to study acupuncture and work for someone else. She was tired of being everything at her job. There was so much to figure out, but they would cross the bridges when they were there. It was all going to happen. Meanwhile, Evie was *Googling* South Texas real estate and drooling over the possibilities.

Isa had different concerns. How would her sister and brother-in-law react initially? Would they be angry? Would they be understanding? Isa was oddly optimistic. Maybe they would even welcome the truth. Maybe they would feel relief. Mia would always love them. Always. It's her biological mother she would hate.

Maybe she was making a big deal out of nothing. There was that incredibly small chance that Mia would accept that she had a mother who looked like her, and if she wanted to meet her father, Isa would move heaven and earth to find William.

ᴥ

Isa and Cristina had had their ups and downs over the years, but in the past six months, they had worked together on a common goal. They had been e-mailing and phoning back and forth over preparations for their parents' big wedding-sized party for their forty-second anniversary. Initially, it was supposed to be for their fortieth, but something had always come up. It had been Evie's idea to have the big "talk" after the party.

"There will be a whole lot of drama, babe. Do not underestimate that for one minute. Like, you-might-not-want-to-send-in-that-resignation-letter-yet kind of drama," Evie had said.

Isa knew that Evie was right. She had stopped drinking three years ago and vowed never to go back. Would one drink, or two, help steel her nerves?

◡◖

"Absolutely *not!*" Evie had cried when Isa had suggested it.

"I shouldn't have told you!"

"But you did, and do you know why? Because you don't need a drink. Now, here, call her. Call her right now. Get it over with."

Evie walked out of the room and Isa took a deep breath. *I can do this. I can do this.* She made the call. And it didn't go well.

Cristina had answered the phone in her usual chipper manner, going on about the table linens and centerpieces for the party. When she sensed that Isa wasn't interested in party planning, she asked if something was wrong. There had been silence on the other end until Isa came right out and told her what she wanted to do. And before Isa could say anything, Cristina spoke. Her voice sounded firm and forceful.

"No. Not now."

"Then when?" Isa had answered caustically.

"Why would you choose now?"

"The timing works for me. I can see if living in Texas would work for all of us, Cristina."

"The timing works for you?"

"No, it's not just that—"

"Mia is turning twelve soon. She is a vulnerable preteen. Can't you wait until she is in college? Right now she freaks out over not having the right shoes or discovering a pimple on her forehead. You want to tell her now?"

"Cristina, you're not being fair—"

"She can't know right now, Isa. Not right now."

Cristina's anger caught Isa by surprise. For thirty seconds no one spoke. It seemed forever. They each waited the other out, until Isa hung up. She was indignant and outraged.

◡◖

She didn't realize it then, but she had started to hate Cristina immediately after it happened. They were sisters, yes, she knew. And she should have known better, but they were equally guilty. She was aware that Cristina felt remorseful about what they had done, but hands down, Isa had suffered the most. For years, she had been polite, circumspect, and professional like the lawyer she was. She had been forced to keep her distance. Physically and emotionally.

And it had taken her years to come to this decision. But enough was enough. No more thinking about this. The truth must be told. Empathy, sympathy, family ties, and obligation. Always putting others' needs before her own. No more. Next week, after the big party, it was going to happen. She would tell her parents first and then Mia, whether Cristina and Leo liked it or not. She could not, would not continue to harbor these feelings toward her only sister. It wasn't right, and she didn't like it. They would either take care of this problem and move on, or not be sisters at all. She wanted everyone to be a family again. Because she couldn't live with this any longer. She just couldn't.

chapter 28–**Mia**

Rio Chico, Texas, 2016
10:00 a.m. Saturday

"Mia! Mia!" called Cristina.

"What?" grumbled Mia.

Mia hated when her mother yelled from the kitchen or the living room. Annoyed, Mia walked toward her dresser, grabbed her music and earbuds, and plugged herself in. Eventually, her mother would come. She never got mad at her anyway. Plopping herself on her belly, face down over the side of her bed, Mia listened to her music and scrolled through Instagram posts of models in New York City.

Her aunt had promised to take her to New York someday, and she couldn't wait. One day, she would fly out to the big city, and her rich aunt would buy her the hippest outfits, and everyone who had ever doubted her coolness would be jealous. She would get an expensive haircut and maybe some Christian Dior lip gloss, like Ariana's. She would be the most sophisticated girl in her class. Her Aunt Isa lived in Seattle, but she was just as classy as any model. She wore elegant suits, sported glossy, salon-styled hair, and had stunning outfits.

When she was mad at her parents or hated everything about Rio Chico, Mia would envision moving to NY with her Aunt Isa.

She would picture herself as just another one of the wealthy kids who lived on the Upper East Side. At least that's how *Law and Order*, her dad's favorite show, made it look like. She would go to a nice private school like the girls on *Gossip Girl*. She would take the subway to school and meet her friends at some quaint café for hot cocoa and scones. She didn't even know what scones tasted like, but she had an idea and had read plenty about the buttery pastry.

It's not that she didn't like her own small town, it's just that Mia always felt like she belonged somewhere else. She felt worldlier than her peers. She looked up to her *Tía* Isa, who was a career woman. She was a lawyer and had been to New York more than a dozen times.

"Mia?" called Cristina, as she removed her daughter's earbuds. "I have been screaming my head off for over ten minutes!"

"Mom, I was listening to music, how was I supposed to hear you!"

"You answered me the first time," Cristina said, looking confused.

"Mom, I think you're hearing things."

Feeling guilty and looking remorseful, Cristina sat down next to her daughter and said, "We have to talk about the back-to-school party."

"What about it?" asked Mia, sitting up.

"You're not going to be able to go."

"What? But you said—" cried Mia incredulously.

"I thought we could swing it, but today is going to be crazy. There is just no way that we're going to make it work. Daddy's right, you'd be missing the church service."

"But Mom! This is the biggest party before school starts! It's not fair! You said I could!"

"Yes, against your father's wishes, I said that I could make it work, but it's too much and, Mia, you have to learn you can't always get your own way."

"This is so unfair! How can you change your mind the day of?" yelled Mia, who had started to cry.

This is how it felt to put her foot down. Awful. Crushing. Why was it so hard to tell her kid no? Why did she let her own daughter speak to her like that? She knew exactly why, and that made her feel worse. She allowed Mia's inappropriate behavior because of her guilty secret. She was terrified that one day Mia would find out the truth, and when she did, her daughter would only look back at those moments and declare them evidence . . . proof that she wasn't loved enough.

⚓

11:15 a.m. Saturday

Mia had cried into her pillow and knew that any moment now, her mother would knock on her door and tell her that she had worked everything out. When her parents didn't come, Mia had slammed her closet door a couple of times, rattled the mirror on the back of her door, and had even thrown a hardcover book against the wall. Nothing. They were serious this time. Mia now had the phone pressed to her ear.

"I guess it's not going to happen," said Jodie. "Bummer."

"Jodie, if I don't go to this party, Sara and Veronica are going to think I hate them," Mia said quietly.

"There'll be other parties. Besides, Sara and Veronica barely know we exist, remember?" said Jodie.

Jodie didn't beg her to plead with her parents. She even seemed bored and indifferent. After they had hung up, Mia wondered if maybe Jodie had been in the middle of something and would call back to commiserate. She would express how disappointed she was that Mia wasn't coming. Yes, that was it, Mia figured. Jodie would call back.

But she didn't. After fifteen minutes of staring at the phone,

Mia realized that, perhaps, no one would notice. No one would care. She was invisible. Mia sat up and looked at herself in the mirror. Looking back at her was a lanky, dark-skinned girl with jet-black, straight hair. Had Jodie already ditched her for Ariana? How had she not seen this coming? Ariana had started hanging out with them at the end of sixth grade. She assumed they were best friends, but now it was clear, very clear, that was not the case.

All Mia wanted to do was to fit in, to be a natural part of the cool-girl landscape, not just one of their lackeys. She wanted to be at the center of things, and at Gloria Anzaldua Middle School, the epicenter was with Sara and Veronica's group. Mia had been part of the right group of girls since kindergarten. She was never the most popular, not even close, but she was part of the herd. Her father was a high-school vice principal with bigger ambitions. He was just two years away from getting his doctorate and applying to be a principal. She didn't live in a sprawling house with a three-car garage and a swimming pool, like Sara did, but she did live in a respectable, gated neighborhood. She wasn't a hundred percent proud of her address—her house was easily the smallest and the least customized in the entire development—but it would do until her father received a promotion. Life, for Mia, was only going to get better, and when her family moved to a larger house, everyone would notice.

～❧

Sometimes Mia felt like she lived on the edge of . . . everything. Near, but not close enough. She wasn't pretty enough or rich enough. Just not enough. Jodie was pretty. So were Sara and Veronica. Ariana was plain, but her mother—Rio Chico's most popular orthodontist—made sure she was always wearing the trendiest outfits. Most importantly, what all these girls had in common was something that she did not. These girls came from families with deep roots in Rio Chico, and this counted for a lot.

"*De quien eres?*" Whose kid are you? Since Mia could remember, this was the first question people outside of her family would ask. Eventually, she would try to avoid it, since the exchange usually embarrassed both parties. She couldn't answer like Sara and say "Orlando and Samantha Gonzalez." A conversation about Orlando Gonzalez Sr., county commissioner, would ensue, and Mia would be left feeling irrelevant.

Mia's family was *de aya*, from over there—south of the border where all the *Méxicanos* lived—and she had always resented this divide. In a small South Texas border town like Rio Chico, you could only be three things: a Mexican with roots and connections to people who lived in the center of town, a non-Mexican outsider, or from *el otro lado*, from the other side. Mia was stuck in the middle between the first and third. Her grandparents had been born and raised just half an hour south of the Rio Grande and had settled in their humble *colonia* when they had immigrated in the early seventies. But her parents were both born here and raised in Rio Chico. They had both graduated from Rio Chico High School and her dad had gone to college and graduate school.

When Mia was young, she didn't notice what people wore, where they lived, or where they came from. She was a clever child with a wild imagination. Before she began obsessing about shoes or jeans, she'd hunted tigers in her backyard and pretended to spot herds of elephants in the distance. When it rained, she liked to take cover under the trampoline and pretend she was in the jungle.

In middle school, Mia turned into a self-conscious girl, one who was more concerned about her place in the world and how others perceived her. Leo missed the inquisitive side of his daughter and hardly recognized the girl who liked to come straight home and try on the next day's outfits instead of helping him with the yard work.

"I feel like she is letting go of who she really is," Leo would complain to Cristina.

"She's in middle school, and being social is important," Cristina would counter.

"It's not that, honey, it's just that I see these kids every day, and I feel like we're losing the old, adventure-driven Mia, the kid who was curious about the world."

"Her body is changing; she's becoming a young woman. It's natural for her to want to fit in."

"Why can't she fit in as herself?"

Cristina didn't have an answer for that. It was never what Leo wanted to hear. Leo was one of those guys whom people just followed; he had all the qualities of a natural-born leader. He was a poor kid who'd been raised by a single mother who had brought him up to be confident and to live his life with purpose. Leo was equal parts humility and assertiveness. These character traits made him the Pied Piper of the popular. Mia wasn't as confident as her father. She looked to others for guidance. She never, not even for a second, saw herself as a trendsetter or as someone anyone else would want to follow, and that killed Leo.

Too often Leo felt that his daughter would never change. He worried that they had raised a spoiled brat. Cristina was more optimistic. She believed that her daughter, and she herself, were works in progress.

chapter 29–Mia

Rio Chico, Texas, 2016
12:45 p.m. Saturday

Mia lay in bed crying, her eyes red and puffier than the sleeves on the ugly dress she was supposed to be wearing. Jodie had never called back. She was probably having a great time at Splash Town.

School was starting on Monday, and Mia wouldn't be part of anything. Whatever her friends would be laughing about today or learning about each other . . . she wouldn't be a part of it. She was a straight-A student and kept her room organized.

They were not content to just ruin her Saturday and her life, but now they wanted their girls to be more responsible. When her mother had not come back into the room, Mia had waited a reasonable amount of time and then come out to get something to eat. She hadn't felt like eating anything until something was heated up in the microwave, and the smell of food was everywhere. Her parents were arguing, and when she heard her name, she stopped to listen. She could see her mom, sitting at the breakfast table, smoothing wrinkles out of the tablecloth and trying to not sound confrontational. "She needs to focus on her school work," she said.

"And she will, Cristina, but meanwhile she will also wash dishes and fold laundry."

"Every night?"

"Dishes every night and folding only when there is laundry."

"I just think that's too much."

"All she has to do is scrape dishes and load the machine. Candy can help her fold clothes."

"What if Candy thinks it's unfair to her? She's only five."

"Cristina, this is why we're having this conversation. You always find an out for them. You had chores; I had chores. It's not child abuse. Did you hear Mia slam the door in there?"

"Times have changed."

Leo pulled the leftovers out of the microwave and leaned on the breakfast bar. He took a deep breath and started to eat his rice and beans. He looked up at his wife and asked, "Are you on board?"

"Yes. I am. You're right."

"Our girls deserve better. They need to grow up to be responsible adults."

❧

Mia could not believe her ears. Dishes every night? Neither she nor Candy were ever expected to so much as clear a dish from the table or tidy up couch cushions, much less do their parents' work. That was their job. Not hers.

"We should start having them do chores for a weekly allowance," she heard her dad say.

"Okay," her mom had agreed.

"It will teach them the value of money. They will have to buy their own candy at the movies, and no more getting them whatever they want at the store. If they want it, they can save up for it."

Upon hearing her father's words, Mia burst into the room, hips cocked to one side, right wrist on her bony hip, and geared up for battle, but her father interrupted her before she could say anything.

"Why, come on in, your highness. How can Mom and I serve you better?" Leo's voice was musical and mocking in tone.

Stung, Mia looked to her mom, expecting her to be supportive.

"Your father is right, kiddo," Cristina replied, a sullen response in comparison with her dad's more authoritative way.

"What have I done to deserve this? I stay out of trouble, unlike girls like Vanessa Villa, who never does what her parents tell her to do. I don't do drugs. I don't date. I make straight A's. Isn't that enough?"

"No, it's not enough," her dad said.

"We're doing this because we love you, honey."

"Well, don't love me so much!"

Mia stormed off back to her room, and Cristina started to go after her.

"Don't," Leo told her. "Let her sulk a little. Right now she won't understand what we're trying to do. It's our fault for not doing this sooner. She needs to learn to appreciate what she has and to recognize the value of things. She needs to know that it's not enough to just do well in school and stay away from huffing paint—"

"Paint?"

"Yeah, or drugs, glue, whatever. She needs to know that she's making good grades for herself and her future, not just to please us—and by extension, that not everything will be handed to her. If she thinks the honor roll is going to be her only gesture of goodwill, she has another thing coming."

"I agree. I've overindulged her, but this is going to be diffi-cult and painful."

⚓

Mia threw herself back onto her bed. She was pulling some stray threads from the edge of the comforter when her mother let herself in.

"It's Mom, babe," said Cristina as she walked in with a sandwich and Mia's favorite potato chips. "Hungry?"

"No," answered Mia quietly.

"I'm going to go to the reception hall and make sure everything is in order. Do you need anything from the store?"

"No," mumbled Mia, avoiding eye contact and trying to hold back her tears.

⚓

1:15 p.m. Saturday

"Is my drama queen still in her room?" asked Leo.

"Yes," sighed Cristina. "I feel so guilty. You know, there is still time for her to make the party, and everything is set at the hall. Should I drive her over and find someone to pick her up?"

"No. Don't even think about it."

chapter 30—Mia

"Mia?" called Cristina. "Time to get dressed."

"Coming," Mia drawled as she dragged herself off the bed.

"Are you still angry?" Cristina asked as she poked her head into the room.

Mia wouldn't look up at her mother, so when Cristina knelt down beside the bed and saw how red her daughter's eyes still were, she stood up, walked out, and came back with a damp hand towel to wipe Mia's tear-streaked face.

⸙

5:45 p.m. Saturday

Mia's empathy towards her mother had lasted for all of twenty minutes. Just when she was starting to get over the whole party thing, Jodie called her from her mother's cell phone to let her know that a group of them were headed to a pizza place after the party. Mia was furious all over again.

Secretly, Mia was glad that her eyes were still red. Her angry, irritated eyes would tell a story, one that would make her parents feel sorry for her. All dressed up, she opened her top drawer and pulled out her hairbrush.

Mia stepped over the threshold of her bedroom and noticed there was no one in the hall. *Good*, she thought. She was going to sneak into the garage, climb into her dad's truck, and wait for everyone there. No sooner had she made it down the hall, when Leo rushed towards her, grabbed her by one arm, and put his other hand on her waist. He twirled her around, while Candy, who was sitting on the couch, clapped her hands.

"Look at my little girl!" Leo exclaimed, while Mia tried to wriggle out of his embrace. "Where did my baby go? When did she turn into this lovely young woman who is going to leave me one day?"

"Where is she going?" Candy had asked, looking worried all of a sudden.

"Who knows?" said Leo. "But some handsome man is going to steal her away from us one day."

"Leave me alone, Dad," Mia said as she pulled away and tugged at her tights. "Where is Mom? I thought she was in a hurry?"

"Are you going to dance with your old man tonight?"

"I don't dance."

Leo pretended Mia had shot an arrow straight through his heart. Candy jumped off the couch and ran back towards her parents' bedroom, while Leo and Mia waited in the living room. "We have a big party to attend, ladies, so let's get a move on," Leo called down the hall, as he jiggled the car keys in his pocket.

Mia walked over to the mirror by the kitchen to check if her tights looked saggy. She hated the image staring back at her. She looked like skinny on a stick. Her only consolation was that she wasn't wearing anything like Candy was. Candy's ensemble was a real dork fest. Cristina had made Candy bows from the dress material and glue-gunned them to her black patent-leather shoes. And to tie the whole outfit together, *Abuela* had given Candy a tiny, beaded purse that she had bought at the dollar store.

Mia was busy being critical of Candy's dress, when Cristina walked into the living room looking absolutely stunning. Her mother looked like someone who could easily get the lead in a *telenovela*. Mia wanted to say something, but held back, remembering that she was furious.

"Mia, you look beautiful! Let me see the new shoes," Cristina said.

She didn't feel beautiful, and she hated when people told her that she did. She started walking toward the garage door. She wanted to get into her dad's new double cab truck and get the stupid party over with. In the garage, she heard the door start to open and waited for her father to unlock the truck. She hoisted herself up and, scrunching the bottom of her dress to ensure maximum wrinkling, sat down staring straight ahead. In the front seat, her mother tried to delicately get the seat belt on without wrinkling her dress, before she gave up and just left it undone.

❧

"Okay, I think we're all set," Cristina announced from the front seat. Leo slipped in one of his favorite Tejano CDs into the stereo and mentioned something about the band that would be playing that night. He was in a merry mood. And most of the mood was due to the fact that he was driving his new Chevy Silverado. Mia sat in the back and noticed that her stomach was rumbling. She thought of the traditional wedding food and felt sick. She hated it. Nothing ever changed. It was always *carne guisada*, rice, potato salad, two slices of plain white bread, and watered-down iced tea. Stiffly she sat in the back, fuming and mentally rehashing all the ways she had been wronged.

"*Listos*? Everybody ready?" asked Leo, as he turned up the radio, leaned backward, adjusted the rearview mirror, and pulled out of the driveway. Cristina asked Mia something, but Mia pretended not to hear. Cristina disregarded her daughter's snub; she was too excited about the party to indulge Mia's crabbiness. Leo drove them out of the neighborhood and turned the truck onto the ramp, slowly merging with the rest of the traffic on the busy highway, while in the back, Mia gave a very deliberate and heavy sigh. She crossed her arms over her chest and rolled her eyes.

"You know who is going to be there, Mia?" asked Cristina, trying to make small talk and lighten her daughter's mood.

When Mia didn't answer, Cristina talked about her friend Andrea and her daughter Sofia, who was one year ahead of Mia in school. "Maybe you can ask Sofia to sit at our table and you two can hang out tonight?" Mia didn't even bother to answer. She didn't care. She would be indifferent all night if she had to be. Cristina stopped talking, and that's when Leo suddenly turned down the music, and everything became eerily quiet. Mia froze. She knew that she had gone too far; now her father was angry, and he was really going to let her have it. Bracing herself for the worst, she gradually uncrossed her arms, bit her lip, and straightened up.

But before Leo could utter a word, his lovely wife farted in the front seat. Alone, the act would not have been that funny, but there was a long history of fart-related lore in the family. The first was that Cristina had broken her own rule: never fart in front of others. The second had to do with an incident that had never been forgotten. When Mia was only four years old, she had been waiting in line with her mother at Burger King, eagerly anticipating her meal, but unfortunately at eye level with a rather large woman's bottom, when the woman farted in Mia's little face. The fart had rattled the woman so much that it had caused her to back up against Mia's face. Every time Cristina told the story, she would finish by saying, "Poor Mia never had a chance, to have something like that just happen in your face. It's like the woman had farted into the rim of the Grand Canyon. It was so loud that she ran out of the restaurant." Mia had cried, "I don't want a hamburger anymore. I don't want it." Customers who had witnessed the spectacle went into fits of hysterical laughter.

Cristina had been on a cabbage diet for the last two weeks, and now that cabbage had caught up with her big time. Genuinely concerned, Candy asked, "Mommy, did you poop your new dress?" Mia couldn't help but snicker, and then Cristina and Leo joined in. Pretty soon Leo was laughing so hard he was wheezing and wiping tears away from his eyes. And every time Cristina tried to talk, she sounded like a honking goose, which led to even more laughter. For a whole minute and then some, the family was united by one wet and disgusting fart. A lack of rectitude and propriety had unified them, and with it the kind of laughing that takes your breath away and makes your sides ache.

Seizing the moment, Cristina turned toward the back seat, squeezed Mia's thigh, and gave her the "are we good?" look. Mia smiled and wished that her mother's hand would just stay there. In that one small gesture, she realized how much she truly loved her mother, her father, and her sister. She loved that she had a family, a whole family, a complete one. Jodie's parents had been divorced forever, and even Ariana's parents were separated. Who cared about a stupid party, when she had family? And chocolate? Mia had convinced her *Tía* Isa that there should be a chocolate fountain at the party, so there was something to look forward to after all.

In the front seat, Leo turned the music up and started drumming his fingers on the steering wheel as he stared ahead with his eyes on the road. Mia looked down at her new shoes—the only part of the new outfit that she really appreciated. Candy was toying with her little beaded purse, desperately trying to squeeze a strawberry-flavored ChapStick and her favorite Beanie Baby into a purse the size of a small tomato.

From the back seat, Mia watched her mother flip open her mirror visor. She was happily reapplying some foundation on her tear-stained cheeks, when all of a sudden, Leo steered sharply to the wrong side of the road. They could all hear the sound of metal dragging and scraping against the concrete barrier as the truck struggled to come to a complete stop.

"Everybody okay?" asked Leo. He'd narrowly avoided an oncoming car. The Silverado was on the wrong side of the road, but they were safe. Collectively, they all breathed a sigh of relief, but that momentary sigh was followed by a deafening crash.

꿋

Mia woke up to the bright red-and-blue flashing lights of several police cruisers and more than one ambulance. She felt something heavy on her chest, an immense pressure, followed by pain. Someone was trying to wake her. When the man, a paramedic, noticed that she had regained consciousness, he started to cut off her seat belt and gently carry her out. Frantically, Mia looked around and cried out for her mother, but she did not see her. She was not in the car. Neither was her father nor Candy. She opened her mouth, formed a string of words, and mentally cast them out, "Mom! *Mami!* M-aaaaa-m-iiiii!!!," but it was obvious that nothing was coming out of her mouth. Nothing. Not one word. It hurt so much. She screamed again. Nothing. Her cries were stuck. Wedged between her throat and her dry lips.

Jesus, she thought.

But could not speak. Smothered by her worst fears, the words continued to cower in her throat. Hiding spinelessly. Refusing to budge. Failing her. She turned to face the paramedic. Her eyes pleading with him. Her mind racing ahead. Frantically making deals with God. *Please let my family be okay, please let my family be okay* . . . but the anguished look on the man's face told her everything.

Then, she heard it.

A blood-curdling scream.

And she realized that it was her own.

chapter 31—Beatriz

Rio Chico, Texas, 2016

No one should have to bury their daughter, thought Beatriz, as she sat at the edge of Cristina and Leo's enormous, king-sized bed. She slowly kicked off her shoes and ran her toes back and forth on the beige carpet. She did not want to be in her daughter's house, but she had no choice. In tears, and shaking with profound grief, Beatriz sobbed, "Why, God? Why put my little girl through so much? She had so many years left."

Mateo had driven Beatriz to the house because Mia and Candy needed more clothes and because Isa had asked her to collect all of Cristina and Leo's legal documents. The aging woman turned around and slowly but gently rearranged the mountain of small, decorative pillows at the head of the bed. When one of the pillows accidentally tumbled onto the floor, she bent down to retrieve it, stiffening and holding her back. Tucked under the folds of the dust ruffle, she spotted the light, blue material sticking out from under the bed. It was Cristina's nightgown. Beatriz picked it up, cried loudly and then buried her face in it, finding the familiar scents of her daughter's shampoo and favorite perfume.

Dora burst into the bedroom. Dora had come along, not wanting to leave her best friend alone, especially in the house.

"Beatriz? *Que te pasa?*" Dora asked as she walked up to her, embraced her, and gently stroked her hair. "Oh, you poor thing. Cry it out, *amiga*," she continued. "Let it all out. It's okay."

Grabbing a tissue from her daughter's nightstand, Beatriz sniffled. "She was my best friend, Dora. My Cristina."

"*Llora, llora.* There is nothing to do but to cry."

❧

Mia and Candy had stayed home for the first two weeks after the accident. Mia had escaped the wreckage with a sore leg and a few scratches, while Candy had scratches on her face. For Beatriz, the last fourteen days had all been one big blur of activity. There was tending to the technical details of a double funeral, making room for and managing the needs of three extra people in her home, and up until three days ago, seeing to the needs of the visitors who would stop by to offer their condolences. Through it all, Isa had been a lifesaver. She had spoken with all of the authorities, made funeral arrangements, and even managed to keep the kids distracted by taking them out to eat every other meal.

Beatriz was in awe of her older daughter's strength. Isa, the husbandless and childless daughter, had swooped in and single-handedly taken care of everyone's needs. Mateo, who was usually quiet, had become more distant than ever. He spent most of his time at the junkyard, pretending nothing had happened. And Beatriz didn't have it in her to scold him for his silence either; his swollen eyelids and blackened eye-sockets betrayed his deep sorrow and grief.

When Isa wasn't on the phone or examining official forms and documents, she was driving the girls to a therapist in McCullers and keeping them busy. She distracted them with shopping trips for extra school supplies and clothes. Beatriz knew that sooner or later, Cristina and Leo's death would hit

Isa like a tsunami. Isa had flown back to Seattle the morning before, until she could figure out her next move, and Beatriz worried that she wouldn't be with her when reality set in.

"*Mami*," she had reassured Beatriz. "I'm going to be right back. I need to go home and figure out what I'm going to do. You're not alone in this."

The truth was Beatriz was lucky if she made it through the day without leaving the stove on or putting milk back into a cupboard instead of the fridge. She was still walking around feeling a little dazed and confused. She was keeping up with the house out of habit. Her body was on domestic cruise control, seeing to the same daily routine she had managed for years. The problem, this time around, was that she had to adjust to the needs of a twelve-year-old and a five-year-old. She was anxious about the girls going back to school. As long as they were around, she had to be strong and available. Dishes had to be prepared and then washed. Beatriz had to be up to take care of her granddaughters' needs, and this was a blessing. Her biggest fear was drawing the shades and crawling into her bed, succumbing to depression.

Isa had left them plenty of money, and she had also taken with her all the paperwork and contact information necessary to tend to Cristina and Leo's affairs. The only new thing that Beatriz and Mateo had learned about their daughter and son-in-law was that the bank would be repossessing the house and Cristina's car. Beatriz and Mateo had suspected some debt, but never imagined how bad.

Leo's family had showed up at the funeral, paid their respects, and walked right out. No one had asked what they could do to help, or what would happen to the children. Even though Beatriz was initially insulted, Isa reminded her that Leo's family's indifference was to their advantage. "*Ama*, would you want them to fight for custody of the children?" Isa knew that this wasn't even a remote possibility; the children would end up in her custody, she would see to that.

༈

Isa had come back into their lives under the saddest of circumstances. Over the years, Beatriz had watched her older daughter grow increasingly distant. Something had changed, and she had never been able find out what or why. Whenever she asked Isa if anything was the matter, Isa would assure her that everything was fine. "*Mami*," Isa would reply, "I'm just married to my career right now." When Mia was a baby, Isa visited twice a year. The family could always count on seeing her over Christmas and one week during the summer. Sometimes Isa showed up unexpectedly if she was doing business in Texas.

In the beginning, the rift between sisters had caused Beatriz endless heartache. Whenever Beatriz asked Cristina about this, Cristina always reassured her that everything was okay.

"*Ama*, we talk all the time," Cristina would lie. "Two to three times a month. Isa is just so busy."

She should not have been surprised. Beatriz's own relationship with her siblings had changed just as much, if not more. Where she once attended large family gatherings with her siblings in Mexico, surrounded by a growing army of nieces and nephews, now she was lucky if she saw her brother and sisters once or twice a year. As soon as the kids were married and the grandchildren came along, schedules and distance had all colluded to keep everyone as far apart from each other as possible. She had hoped that her two daughters would not allow the same to happen, but it had. Isa was now the only one left.

Beatriz hadn't given much thought to what would happen to the kids, but assumed that she would raise them. Isa's talk about taking over was pure nonsense. She couldn't see Isa living anywhere besides away from Rio Chico. She also didn't want her only living child to sacrifice her entire life to raising some-one else's children. If Isa was having a difficult time finding a man now, it would be twice as hard with children in tow.

Beatriz found it easier to deal with Candy than Mia. She had always been able to read the younger child best. Candy was still young. She allowed adults to hold her and comfort her. The thing that frightened Candy these days was thoughts of her own death. Many of the well-meaning visitors kept telling her that God had taken her parents and that they were up in heaven, waiting for her. This meant that some nights, the poor kid was terrified of falling asleep and being taken in the middle of the night.

Candy could also go for hours at a time acting like noth-ing had ever happened, until she awoke with night terrors. It was Beatriz's job to swoop in and gather her granddaughter in her lap, hold her tight against her heavy bosom, and rock her back and forth until, eventually, Candy calmed down. The lit-tle one's crying would also upset Mia, who would wake up from sleep, only to be reminded of what had happened.

Yet, as sad as it all was, had her two granddaughters not survived, Beatriz would have just stayed in her bed. Hiding from life. Wanting nothing from it.

The morning the girls went back to school, Beatriz woke up extra early to make an elaborate breakfast of homemade flour tortillas, fried eggs, and hash browns cooked with sautéed onions. The radio sat on the breakfast bar and, after passing it by once and then twice, Beatriz figured that two weeks of *guar-dando luto* was enough. Gone were the days when mourning meant that radio and television were off limits for long periods of time. She needed a distraction and she needed it now. She called out Candy's name and didn't hear any reply. The little one was not an early riser. Walking into their bedroom, Beatriz leaned over her and called her name, "Candy? Candy?"

"*Buenos días*," continued Beatriz, as she sat on the edge of Candy's bed and gently tapped her shoulder.

"*Wela*, I'm so sleepy. I don't want to go to school."

"You have a new teacher. Don't you want to meet her?"

"No. I want to stay with you."

"Don't you want to put on your new shoes and try out your new backpack?"

For Candy, the idea of putting on all of her new stuff was suddenly very appealing, and she quickly scrambled out of bed. While Candy threw off her red Clifford pajamas, Beatriz ran back and forth between the kitchen and the bedroom. She took a warm hand towel, wet it, and cleaned the sleep out of Candy's eyes. She found the pink box where Cristina kept all of the child's brushes, barrettes, and ponytail bands. "Okay, *mija*, pick out the color you want, and I'm going to come back and fix your hair, okay?"

Mia walked into the bedroom with a towel on her head.

"Are you going to go to school with wet hair?"

"No, I brought the hairdryer."

"Do you know Adriana? Karo's daughter? I think she will be on your bus."

"I know who she is, *Wela*, but she is in high school."

"In high school? That little thing? Why, she is almost as small as Candy is."

"Yeah, she's really short."

This was probably all that Beatriz would get from Mia this morning. She was hoping that she would meet some nice girl to be friends with in the neighborhood. She seemed so lonely.

⚓

Beatriz was happy for the kids. Going back to school would give them other things to think about. Soon, she would see her kitchen table piled high with books and craft projects, just like when Isa and Cristina were children.

The morning had gone on without incident. Candy had been her usual sprightly self and Mia was her usual indifferent self. Beatriz recalled a conversation with Cristina, not even three weeks before the accident. They had discussed Mia's unresponsive attitude, and Cristina had asked if it was normal for kids at that age.

"Was I like that, *Ama*?"

"No, not really. But I will tell you who was."

"Isa?"

"At her age, you started to become more self-assured. Your sister, on the other hand, became a bit withdrawn, not too much, but just enough for me to notice it."

"When did Isa outgrow it?" Cristina asked.

"It won't last long. Don't worry. *Ay hija*, it's in the blood. Mia is like your sister, who is like your *Tía* Cuca, on your father's side. They can be full of joy on the inside, but they are wired to be *serias*, very serious. That's why being a lawyer suits Isa so well. She is so serious-minded."

"It's just that Mia used to have a lighter side, but sixth grade seemed to change everything. I am really worried about her."

"Don't worry, she's probably just trying to figure things out. You kids overanalyze everything. You even want to manage their emotions. What are you going to leave for them to do, ah?"

⚓

When Mia boarded her bus, Beatriz felt like she was watching Isa. But Mia wasn't Isa, she was Mia. She was going to have to be very careful, vigilant about not treating her like she was Isa. Mia might look a lot like her *Tía* Isa, but she was her own person, with her own path, her own journey. And she was going to have a very difficult one. Candy, on the other hand, was so much like Cristina, mostly calm, bubbly, and loving. She was easy to warm up to. Mia seemed to be at that stage where contact with adults made her recoil. And it pained Beatriz not to be able to take her oldest granddaughter in her arms. But how could she? Mia was already as tall as her mother had been; her chest was in the early stages of blossoming. The kid was undergoing the most important growing phase of her life, and Beatriz wondered if the trauma of both her parents' death would stunt her growth.

Back inside the house, Beatriz was greeted with the low hum of the radio, barely discernable. She looked at the mound of dirty dishes and remembered that today was laundry day. There were beds to be made, plants to be watered, and dinner to be considered. She was mentally ticking the list of everything that needed doing when the phone rang.

"*Ama?*"

"Isa?"

"*Si, mami.*"

"*Hija? Todo bien?* Everything okay?"

"Yes and no, Mom. Are the girls still there?"

"No, Candy's bus just left. Mia's left before that."

"How did their morning go? Did they bring up . . ." but Isa choked up and couldn't finish the sentence.

"*No, gracias a Dios.*"

"I hate that I can't be there. But I will be there soon. And, *Mami*, I'm moving back home. I meant what I said. I will raise those girls like they were my own."

"No, *hija*. You have your life. I've raised children before, I can do it again. I just wish that I wasn't so old and useless."

"*Ama*, you're not useless."

"Just old, right?"

"*Ama*, right now, honestly, I don't know how I am going to make it all work out, but I will. I promise."

"Isa?"

"*Si, Mami.*"

"You wouldn't take them away? You would move here, right? You wouldn't do that to your father and me?"

"*No, Mami.* I wouldn't do that."

"Well, *hija*, take all the time that you need then."

"*Mami*, another thing . . . I couldn't save the house. It belongs to the bank now. I mean, we can still go in and out for a while, but eventually . . ."

Beatriz hadn't even wanted to think about the house. She only knew that they had time. Time to wait before vacating, but should the children be allowed back? Did they need to see it one last time? Or would that bring back too many memories? What did she need to keep? Questions assailed her mind, and she felt leaden with worry. She turned around and walked into her bedroom. She closed the curtains, kicked off her shoes, and buried herself under the sheets. She turned into the pillow and wept. She wept because she had what seemed like a whole eternity until the girls returned; even Mateo wouldn't be coming home for lunch. She was alone, and she hated the silence. She wept because she was afraid that once she fell asleep, she would have to wake up to the same reality.

But before succumbing to the kind of sleep that only depression can induce, she made a deal with herself. She would go on. She would take things one step at a time.

༄

Beatriz woke up to the sound of children in the street. The clock on her nightstand told her she was late. She stood, a little dazed and disoriented.

"Hi, *Wela*! I walked from the bus stop all by myself."

"Did you have a good time?"

"*Sí*, look it? Look?" and Candy pulled her backpack off her shoulders and started to unload it right in the living room.

The look on her cherubic granddaughter's face softened Beatriz's features and reminded her that everything was okay. Despite having lost both parents, this child had boarded a bus with kids who were unfamiliar, made it through a whole day of school, and faced her new teacher. If Candy could get on with life, so could she.

chapter 32—Isa

It felt totally wrong, but what could she do? In her own living room and in the comfort of the familiar surroundings of Seattle, her mind kept drifting back to the day of Cristina and Leo's funeral.

She could visualize Cristina's casket being lowered into the ground, and her chest would tighten.

The cemetery where Cristina and Leo were buried looked nothing like the bucolic cemeteries people like to envision from the movies. There were portions of the Santa Maria Cemetery so overgrown that the gravestones could not be read. Much of the grass had grown dormant and turned brown. Isa had even taken the time to pick up trash.

Tough Texas weeds stubbornly grew among the graves. Isa had been outraged at the lack of care. Sun-colored ribbons littered the graves, and fake flowers, once bright and shiny, were partially buried in the dirt. Cristina had loved beautiful things. Yet, her new home seemed so undignified and disrespectful. Worse yet, the casket-lowering devices looked old and compromised. Isa was glad that neither Cristina nor Leo had been aware of the mismatched casket-lowering straps and the crank handle wrapped in neon-orange duct tape.

As Cristina's coffin was lowered into the ground, Isa felt like she was having a heart attack. In addition to a tightening in her throat, she became unsteady and nauseous. Her heart was pounding, and she remembered feeling like her ears were going to explode under the pressure.

In contrast, Isa had been surprised by how composed both of her parents had been at the funeral. Beatriz had done her share of crying, and she figured that her father had done the same, only privately. At the graves, she saw Beatriz and Mateo standing side by side, flanking the girls like two stoic statues. Isa's mind was flooded with all kinds of should-haves and would-haves: with the secret Mia needed to know. She had watched the ropes lowering the casket. As she bent down to throw dirt on her sister's coffin, she fainted.

She had wanted to be the picture of strength for her family, show them that she was sturdy and solid, not the bag of bones that had collapsed on the green Astroturf.

On the plane ride home, Isa had written a checklist. There was so much on her plate at work. All her old plans would be put on hold. She could not quit now. She also knew that if she told her boss she was thinking of leaving, they would probably replace her faster than she could find another job. She had dependents; she had to be more responsible.

The second day that she was back from Texas, Isa worried incessantly over the girls—what and how they were doing.

"I feel like everything is happening without me," Isa exclaimed, closing her laptop and standing up to get a glass of water.

"Babe, chill. We'll figure it all out," Evie reassured her.

"Every day I'm away from them is another day lost. I'm supposed to help them get through all of this, and where am I? More than a thousand miles away."

"Well, you could quit your job and move to Texas tomorrow,

and then you could show up and say, 'Hey girls, I'm here for good, but now I'm homeless and jobless.'"

"Evie, I know. I know. I can't just quit. But what do I do? My parents have already made it very clear that if I bring the girls out here, they would never forgive me."

"I think that they would get used to it. Besides, we would visit, you know, take the girls down to visit at least twice a year."

Isa became very quiet, as she put her glass down on the counter. Evie came up behind her, wrapped her arms around her waist, and gently kissed the back of Isa's head. "I'm not trying to pressure you, but eventually you will have to tell them."

༄

Not too long ago, Isa had felt so courageous and resolute. She had felt the momentary thrill of imagining a life completely devoid of secrets. Now, she wasn't so sure. How would the girls react to knowing who she really was? Would they hate her and beg to go back to Texas with their grandparents? What if one of the many homophobic Rio Chico judges granted their grandparents custody because of her sexuality? Giving the girls up was not an option. But maybe giving Evie up was. Her only choice.

༄

Back in Texas, Isa had played the doting aunt. She had done everything she could to distract the children from death. She didn't want them to sit in the house and feel that life was over. They were still children, and though their parents were gone, it was still okay to go out for pizza and even watch a movie. Isa had made it a point to take them out for at least one meal a day. Eating out in public was also intimately familiar and reassuring. Everyone had a role to play. Starting with whose turn it was to pick a restaurant. You had to wait for the hostess to seat you, and if there were coloring mats for kids, they all participated.

The grandparents rarely came along. And in a small town, there was always someone that they knew. It could be one of Mia's teachers, an old classmate of Isa, or even a relative. For the time it took to anticipate their orders, they could forget about reality.

Isa had also driven the girls thirty-five miles away where she had found a family therapist. Mateo had joined them for one of the sessions so he would know where to take the girls once she was gone.

◆

At her parent's house, Isa slept on the living room couch. Occasionally, she would go to check in on the girls and see that both had fallen asleep with the television on. The night that Isa left, she realized that she hadn't done anything to make the back room comfortable.

When she had said goodbye the night before she left, she'd thought of purchasing some of those plastic drawer bins for the girls' clothes, a small desk for Mia's laptop, and a nice rug to go between the beds.

As soon as Isa could, she would sit down with the girls and tell them her long-term plans. They would be together. They would all have a new home.

◆

Isa and Evie were working on dinner. Isa had promised to be home by seven on Friday night. Mrs. Ritter, their nosy next-door neighbor, liked to spy on them at all hours. Both women were hoping that Mrs. Ritter was just a curmudgeon, but their suspicions were confirmed one late afternoon when Mrs. Ritter's Cadillac came home brandishing two bumper stickers. One read "Adam and Eve, not Adam and Steve," and the other just read "Genesis 19-7."

"Google it!" cried Evie, looking out the window.

"I did. Something about Lot going to the door and saying, 'Please my brothers, do not act wickedly.'"

The pair had joked about getting Mrs. Ritter a rainbow flag decal for her car. They were always civil to her, never rude. When Isa came back from Texas, Evie reported that while Isa was gone, Mrs. Ritter actually had the nerve to ask about Isa's whereabouts when she saw that her car had not moved in days. "Is everything okay with her?" Isa loved to hear Evie impersonate Mrs. Ritter. It was during a discussion about Mrs. Ritter that Evie suggested that they live as "roommates" in Texas.

"How would we explain sharing a bedroom?"

"I know, that was stupid." With a sigh, Evie continued, "I knew that this was going to happen someday."

"What?"

"Change. Reality bursting our little domestic bubble. Maybe this is the universe's way of forcing you to tell the truth. Just come out with it all."

"Evie, I can't just do that. I'm going to be the mother of two girls."

"So am I."

"Not right away," Isa said, looking out the window.

Evie had been chopping vegetables for a stir-fry and had just put on some water for the rice. Securing the lid on the pot, Evie turned down the burners on the vintage stove and sat down, across from Isa.

"What are you saying?"

Isa traced the tiles on the kitchen table with her index fingers and didn't dare look up. "That maybe at first it would just be me in Texas."

"Yeah, and for how long, Isa? A month? A year? A whole decade?"

"Oh, Evie, please."

"No, don't. I'm so sick of this shit. Are you leaving then?

Are you moving to Texas? Is that it? And I am supposed to wait in the wings, waiting for my signal to join you, which may be never?"

"Evie, no. I haven't made any decisions. I have so much on my plate right now."

"Okay, so let's talk about it. Tell me that moving to Texas together is on the table. Just be straight with them already."

"I can't tell them about me—about us—yet. It's too soon."

Evie could barely speak to her, or look her in the eye. She walked toward the stove, turned off the burners, grabbed the bowl of chopped vegetables and hurled them into the trashcan. "I think you should move out."

"What?" asked a confused Isa.

"You heard me, get your stuff and go."

"Evie?"

"If we are going to break up, I want us to do it now. I want you to see and feel what your new freedom is going to cost you. I am your life partner, the person you come home to every day. You cry, I cry with you. You hurt, I hurt with you. But apparently you can do this all by yourself."

"Evie, I don't want to break up!"

"Well, neither do I, but I'm tired. Tired of picking up everyone else's broken pieces. It's not your mother or your sister who has ever consoled you, held you, made it all bearable. It's always been me. And now, you can continue to lay your head on my shoulder, all the while, barely giving me a heads-up, 'Oh, by the way, Evie, when all of this is sorted out, I'll be gone for a year or two or five. Good luck with that.'"

"It won't be that long."

"Isa, we had this conversation years ago. Years ago . . . I really thought you would be ready by now."

Isa stood, reached for a tissue and begged, "Evie, don't say that."

"In Texas, you will have *them*. That hole you've been yearning to fill all your life will be filled. You won't need me, and I don't do standby."

"I'm tired, can we sleep on this?"

"No, please go . . . I'll be at Edward and Rebecca's until tomorrow. I don't want to see you here when I get back."

Isa felt run down and exhausted. She threw herself on the couch and cried into the pillow. Nothing was easy, even when the hardest decisions seemed to be made for you.

chapter 33—Mia

Rio Chico, Texas, 2016

Mia was mad at herself for being embarrassed about having to ride the bus. She had never been one of those kids. The kids who did ride the bus, the kids who lived in her grandparents' neighborhood, didn't like her or her "type." Besides, everyone knew what had happened to her parents, and she didn't want to cry and have them feel sorry for her.

☙

Mia was in the middle school's lobby by 7:30 a.m. She walked past her usual hangout spot—right underneath the high glass shelves that housed the basketball trophies—and kept walking toward the principal's office, turning into a narrow corridor where the hall tapered off into a secluded dead end. Mia made herself comfortable, sitting on the floor of the abandoned telephone booth. No one had called her last night to ask how she was doing. Maybe they were looking for her now, maybe they weren't.

Opening up her backpack, Mia started rummaging around for a pencil and a piece of paper. She was going to make a list. She was going to make a list of the things that she needed to do, as the therapist had suggested.

"Hi, I'm Tere," said a girl with black-and-white-striped jeans and bright red sneakers.

"Um, I'm Mia."

"I know who you are. I am really sorry to hear about your parents."

"Are you new here?" asked Mia.

"Well, I've been here since last May, so yeah, kind of new."

"Where did you move from?"

"Moved here from LA. and have been bored out of my mind in this lame-ass ghost town."

Mia looked at Tere, while she continued to ramble on and on about the cafeteria food. Mia was still trying to process Tere's presence. Then she noticed that Tere had actually stopped talking and was asking her something.

"Want to have lunch together sometime?"

"Oh, yeah. That would be great."

⚓

During Spanish, Mia thought of how Candy had been babied by both her parents, and at *Abuelas'* she was practically treated like an infant. If she wanted waffles, instead of *Wela*'s eggs for breakfast, her grandparents went out and bought them. If she wanted candy before dinner, *Wela* looked into her goody drawer and gave her whatever was in there. Was this going to continue?

Candy had started crawling into bed with her, and Mia was slowly adjusting to this. Candy would often cry about missing her parents, and Mia felt like she had to be the strong one.

Sometimes Mia hadn't been able to calm her down. She didn't want to wake up her grandparents, so she just rocked Candy until they both fell asleep.

She felt an incredible urge to run out of class and walk the eight blocks to Candy's elementary school. She wanted to take her baby sister by the hand and take her home. But where was home? Now that Candy was an orphan, she could no longer be a spoiled brat—which is how Mia had always perceived her. After all, who would call an orphaned five-year-old a spoiled brat?

ъ⌐

Since leaving school was not an option, she snuck into the auditorium. There were brightly colored posters and markers on the floor in the center of the auditorium's stage. Someone was in the middle of a project. The materials made Mia think of all of the activities her parents had helped her with at Candy's age. The brightly colored index cards that doubled as sight word cards. The math games. Who was going to be there for Candy? Her grandparents didn't even speak English. It might be a whole year before *Tía* Isa was able to come back for good. It was all up to her now. And it suddenly felt so urgent and overwhelming. What if she did a lousy job? What if she got so busy helping Candy that she couldn't keep up with her own work?

Mia was just about to sit somewhere and hide for a while when she heard footsteps and voices.

"Gerardo, please make sure that the podium is set up for tomorrow morning's assembly."

"Should I have an additional microphone ready?" asked another voice.

"No, just one."

It was the assistant principal and one of the male janitors. Mia felt like she had been caught doing something wrong and slowly stood up.

"Hi, sweetie," said Mrs. Garzon.

"Hi, Mrs. Garzon."

"Are you okay? Are you feeling well?"

"Yes, yes, I'm okay."

"Do you want to talk?"

"No, no, I'm good."

"Okay, then, I'll walk you back to class."

When Mrs. Garzon put her arm around Mia's shoulders, Mia couldn't help it, she broke down sobbing. Mrs. Garzon led her back to her office and gave her a tissue and handed her a small orange-flavored Gatorade. After Mrs. Garzon talked to her for a good twenty minutes, she excused herself for ten. When she came back, she brought Jodie and Ariana. Both girls ran to Mia's side and hugged her. They told her they were sorry they hadn't called, but that they just didn't know what to say or how to say it.

"Okay, ladies, it's almost lunch time. Tell you what, you two walk Mia to the bathroom. Mia, splash a little water on your face, and I'll write you guys a note. You can go straight to lunch, okay?"

Jodie and Ariana protectively grabbed hold of Mia's arms; they walked her down the hall towards the bathroom as if she were some kind of invalid, but Mia didn't care. Their presence was comforting. Maybe they had needed an extra push from someone important, or maybe they would eventually have sought her out on their own. At lunch, the usual group that hovered around Jodie and Ariana all sat next to the trio. When Mia wasn't in earshot, either Jodie or Ariana would explain to one of the other girls what was happening. They felt special and privileged to have been summoned by Mrs. Garzon to help.

Mia was a little overwhelmed with all the attention that she was getting. Everyone wanted to do something for her. "Do you want a napkin?" "Do you need help getting caught up in science?" The thoughtful offers kept coming, though only when Jodie or Ariana were around to hear them. When Mia spotted Tere in the lunch line, she asked Jodie if she could invite her.

"I met her this morning, her name is Tere, and she's really nice. Can she sit with us?"

"Of course," answered Jodie, as she sent Ariana to go get Tere. "I had her in English last year, she's kind of cool."

A whole week went by, and Mia felt privileged. She felt lucky to have old and new friends. Her old gang had even welcomed Tere. On this one particular day, Tere was a little quiet and distant.

"What's wrong?" Mia asked.

"Your friends, they are so fake."

"Fake how?"

"Well, for starters, acting like they own the whole place and saying mean things."

For the first time, Mia felt a little bit conflicted about hanging out with Jodie and the gang. And not for the reasons that Tere had mentioned. During gym, Jodie was talking about Tere behind her back, being critical of Tere and saying that she was too full of herself. Mia didn't say anything, but she felt that by staying silent, she had betrayed Tere. She was torn. Why couldn't Tere understand that these girls were her crew? They had been together, for better or for worse, since elementary school. She didn't want to choose. She didn't want to have to think. Especially now, when her life made no sense. No sense at all.

chapter 34–Beatriz

Rio Chico, Texas, 2016

Lavish celebrations were the kind of thing that other people did, like wearing a toupee or having the Virgin Mary or Jesus spray-painted on a vehicle. Her daughters had gone to great lengths to make the party a success, Cristina close by and Isa via long distance, to see that a hall was rented, a band hired, and meals catered. Who could have anticipated the tragedy? Beatriz knew that her life would never be the same again. When news about the accident had reached everyone at the party, Beatriz was hoping that it was one big mistake. Maybe, maybe the state trooper had been mistaken, maybe her daughter was just still unconscious. There was, in her frozen and terrified state of mind, a sliver of hope—as irrational as that was—the possibility that everyone was wrong.

Over the past few weeks, Beatriz had played and replayed these events in her mind. Still not believing it had all happened to her.

&

Candy quickly made friends with the kids on the street. She didn't care if her friends' parents were undocumented or lived in a one-bedroom home. In her world, there was more to explore and see. She investigated the rough nooks and crannies at her *abuelos'* house, never really caring about the exposed holes where once wires and hoses had been snuck in. It's not that she didn't get sad; sometimes, her parents' death would hit her hard. Candy would start asking for them and cry. There were nights when the little one woke up in her sleep screaming.

~•~

Now that Cristina was gone, Beatriz was on the phone with Isa every evening. Isa would ask her a hundred and one questions. What were the girls up to? What were they eating? Did they need more money?

"*Ama*, make sure to always have a bowl of fruit out on the kitchen table for them."

"I put out apples, they won't eat them."

"*Ama*, they can't eat all of those sweets. You promised."

"I know, *mija*, but the fruit just sits there and rots. They don't like it."

Beatriz felt guilty.

What worried her was Mia staying in her room all day long, holed up watching television, or doing homework at the kitchen table. Mia wasn't much for conversation either; she wasn't rude or impolite, but the message was loud and clear: *leave me alone.*

Beatriz was giving her space. At least she was doing her homework—in fact that is all that Mia did. She always had a book in her hand. Isa made regular contact with the school counselor, and the report was that school was fine and her teachers had not related anything unusual. Beatriz found those words very reassuring. Isa was obsessed with the girl's weekly meetings with a therapist, but Beatriz thought that what Mia was going through seemed normal for a kid who had just lost both of her parents. What did she expect? For Mia to be happy? She was already so proud of Mia for taking more of an interest in consoling and comforting Candy, but she was weary of Mia feeling like it was her whole identity.

⁓

Beatriz, however, was intrigued by something Dora had said, that Beatriz actually thought made sense. Her friend had suggested that Beatriz continue her usual neighborly rounds but take the girls with her.

"*Llevatelas*. Take them with you. Show them that life goes on. Introduce them to people, their new neighbors."

Beatriz liked the idea very much. The *colonia* was full of families with interesting stories. Individuals with ambitions much bigger than Mia's and sadness just as profound. She needed to expose her older granddaughter to the before and after of other people's hardships and show her that life was a process. She wanted her to meet friends of hers who had found happiness after tragedies and who had moved on with their lives.

chapter 35—Isa

Seattle, Washington, 2016

When Evie kicked her out, to her surprise, Isa felt relieved, but at the same time hopeful that her partner would take her back.

She just couldn't deal with Evie right now, but felt they would eventually reconcile. Sometimes the only choice you had was a bad choice, and this was one of them. It was risky. For Isa, reality was shifting; this was her world as it existed, not the one she was fantasizing about. She had to go for it. Reach. She needed to be with her daughter and her niece and root herself in their world if she ever wanted to gain any kind of emotional stability.

She could only tackle one thing at a time. She had packed up some clothes, all the paperwork that she needed, and she left Evie a note saying: "I love you. And I'm coming back for you. I promise."

⌐⌐

Isa checked herself into a Home Suites for a month. She needed her own space. And this neutral room was just the place. It was a blank slate, a clean slate. A whole new canvas where she could draw and sketch out the new life that awaited her. She filled drawers, lined up her work shoes by the bedroom door, and cleared the desk of all of the objects that didn't need to be there. Gone were the free stationary, complimentary pens, takeout menus, and directory of services.

Tonight Isa was going to attack all of her work matters and get through unfinished paperwork without worrying about having dinner with Evie, sitting with Evie for a bit of television, or going to bed before Evie was asleep. Isa was feeling a mad adrenaline rush. She felt alive again. Ultimately, she wanted to fly back to Texas as soon as it was possible. Meanwhile, she wanted to focus on the girls, and one call a night seemed to be working out just fine. Slowly Mia was allowing Isa into her world and sharing more and more details of her life. Beatriz had told her that Mia was reading to Candy in the evenings.

There was no doubt that for Candy, her older sister represented a constant in her life, and as long as Mia was at her side, even the most unfamiliar of landscapes had a sense of permanence. Still, Isa didn't want to burden Mia with the responsibility of being the one to comfort, when Mia needed so much comforting herself.

꒰ꔛ

Isa tried calling Evie, but she was not picking up at home or at the office. Her receptionist kept offering to take a message. Evie would come to her senses. She had to.

꒰ꔛ

Two weeks after Isa had settled in her new place, missing Evie, she received a frantic call from Mia. Isa had been in the car running some errands between meetings. Her caller ID indicated it was Gloria Anzaldua Middle School, and she immediately pulled over. Her chest tightened, and she felt like her heart was going to explode. Had something happened to Mia?

"Hello?" answered Isa, frantically. "This is she. Is everything okay? Is Mia okay?"

"Yes, I'm so sorry if we frightened you. This is Mrs. Garzon, from Mia's school. We met at your mother's house?"

"Oh, yes, Mrs. Garzon. Yes. Is she okay?"

"She is perfect. She just wanted to talk to you. Take your time, no worries."

What on earth was Mia calling about? And why was she calling from school? Isa turned the car off and pulled her seat back. She took a deep breath and waited.

"Mia? What's wrong?"

"*Tía* Isa, I'm sorry . . ."

"Are you okay?"

"Yeah. Well, I just needed to talk to someone. Mrs. Garzon pulled me out of class, just to see how I was doing, and I just started to cry. When she asked who I wanted to talk to, I said you."

A sharp knot caught in Isa's throat. Her daughter, her flesh and blood, was on the phone and had asked to talk to her. How many years had she waited for this?

"Mia, honey, I'm here for you, always will be. And I am doing everything that I can to figure out how to get back to Texas."

"Will you still be a lawyer?"

"It's all I know how to be, but you never know . . . maybe I'll surprise you and get some other kind of job."

"Where would we live?"

"I guess that I would first move in with you guys, until we find something."

"Would we live in *Los Polvos*?"

"Not if I can help it," laughed Isa.

"Last night, Grandma said that she wanted me to go out and visit the neighbors with her and Candy."

267

"I think that's her way of bonding with you; just go along with it."

"*Tía*, that sounds so embarrassing, not to mention awkward. People are going to think that I am crazy, or worse yet, a loser, with nothing else to do but hang out with my *abuela*."

"Mia, no one will think that you are a loser, but I do see how you can feel awkward. Can you promise me one thing?"

"What?"

"Just try it? Keep her company. She is hurting too."

"I'll try," Mia whispered.

Evie still wasn't picking up the phone. Isa left her messages anyway. Nothing was going to bring her down. She hadn't been able to make it back to Texas yet, but she was confident that she would soon. Isa felt guilty because she was so busy at work that she hadn't had much time to really miss Evie. She sent her flowers and left her messages. She knew Evie, and she knew that Evie would not give up on her. Or would she?

chapter 36 – Mia

Rio Chico, Texas, 2016

Mrs. Ellert, Mia's English teacher, had her back to the students as she frantically wrote the definition for the word "idiom" on the chalkboard. Mrs. Ellert moved fast, as if she were perpetually caffeinated. After she finished writing, she brushed off the chalk dust on her beige jacket.

"An idiom," she bellowed, as she confidently paced down the aisle, "is a phrase whose meaning cannot be determined by the literal definition of the phrase itself, but refers instead to a figurative meaning that is known only through common use."

"Mrs. Ellert, can you please repeat that in English?" groaned Mauricio, the class clown. His buddy Mario reached across the aisle and held his palm out for Mauricio, a big high five being in order. Mauricio slouched back down into his seat, while the class collectively snickered. Grinning at the boys' celebratory hand gesture, Mrs. Ellert moved back towards the board and resumed writing.

"That's fair, Mauricio. My bad." Mrs. Ellert thought that she was cool, that students liked her, but Mia cringed anytime she said something corny, like "my bad." Mrs. Ellert was new at the middle school and also one of the few white teachers in a sea of brown faces. Mia thought she was smart and liked her approach to teaching; she was also secretly hoping that she was nothing like Mr. Hellemen.

Mr. Hellemen had been the computer teacher last year, and he'd made it really clear that he didn't like Mexican kids. The students felt like he treated them as if they had absolutely no potential. He was mean, grumpy, and just plain racist. Mia had been in his classroom when the students had decided that they'd had enough of his condescending attitude, so they decided to give him a hard time.

This had been instigated after a racially charged incident the day before, when Mr. Hellemen had lectured the class about "their" culture's total disregard for education and how "your people" should break the cycle. With much bravado, a couple of the boys decided to do something about it.

The day after, the boys instructed everyone in the classroom to just sit in front of their computers and say nothing. Do nothing. If Mr. Hellemen threatened to get the principal, they would tell the principal what he had said about them. Some of the students were scared. They were the good students who were always concerned about their grade point average—the ones who usually paid extra attention to Mr. Hellemen (even when he treated them with disdain) and who had the highest grades. Other students were nervous and sort of undecided. What if they were expelled or flunked? Or suspended? Officially, everyone was still on the fence when Mr. Hellemen walked into the classroom. Not knowing what to do, everyone froze.

"Well, well, this is a surprise. Everybody seated at their desk. Quiet and ready to learn," said Mr. Hellemen, really pleased with himself. Mia was frozen in her seat. Out of the corner of her eye she could see Abelardo, the smartest guy in the class, and she was trying to gauge what he was going to do. Because whatever he did, she planned on doing. When Mr.

Hellemen turned his back to the classroom, she looked around and realized that the plan was still on.

"Are we doing it?" someone had whispered nearby. Like a proud peacock, Mr. Hellemen, who always wore neatly starched khakis and bright Ralph Lauren polo shirts, made the decision for them. He walked toward Candarito Gomez and, looking him up and down, started in on the poor guy.

"You see, this is what I am talking about, class. How much did these cowboy boots cost, Candarito? About two hundred dollars? The belt? Another hundred? I heard that these are expensive too. If your parents spent the same money on buying computers that they did on dressing you like *narco capos*, you all would be better off."

That did it. Everyone had the "oh, no, he didn't" look, and it was on. Mr. Hellemen asked everyone to turn on their computers and no one moved a muscle.

It was a small town, and most people knew Candarito and his family. Everyone knew that he had worked very hard for both his boots and his fancy *cinto piteado*. Everyone knew that Candarito's parents owned the mobile taco cart in the center of town. There was an abandoned lot next to the Radio Shack and Cash Your Check where his parents usually set it up. They sold the best tacos in town. Candarito worked there every day, including Saturday and Sunday. His family's taco mobile was even open during the holidays. When the local fast food places were closed, they always stayed open. He had probably worked his butt off for his ostrich boots, earning them fair and square—his flashy cowboy belt too—but Mr. Hellemen wouldn't know the difference between a drug dealer's child and one whose parents owned a food truck.

A whole minute might have passed but it felt like an eternity. "You people don't want to learn, and I am not going to force you." He wrote the assignment on the board and stayed at his desk for the rest of the period—pretending to be busy with something.

⌐⌐

That was a big victory for everyone, and Mr. Hellemen never talked about Candarito again. Mia liked the new white teacher. She could tell she was different, in a good way. Not like Mr. Hellemen. Mrs. Ellert, a petite blonde, would call on everyone and make everyone feel valued and capable. She also wore pretty dresses with shoes that always matched. Mia had been examining the suede buckles on her platform heels when Mrs. Ellert asked for everyone's attention.

"Okay, class, look at the board and repeat after me," she said, as she pointed toward the chalkboard with her ruler. "Idioms are phrases or expressions that have hidden meanings. The expressions don't mean exactly what the words say. Is that better, Mauricio?" she said as she playfully winked at him. "Before we leave class, your assignment is to come up with one idiom. Then we will share it," she said. "Better yet, I want everyone to write the definition of the word *idiom* and then come up with one idiom that is significant to you. Your homework tonight is to go online and find at least ten idioms." She turned her back to the class, and the boys groaned. "Meanwhile, try your best to come up with one right now and then share it," she said and headed toward her desk.

Mia stared at the empty page, and then it came to her. Without thinking, she just wrote, *Con el Jesus en la Boca*. As soon as she saw the complete idiom, her throat constricted, as if her vocal chords had been cut. She hated when this happened.

"Mia, have you thought about your idiom?" asked Mrs. Ellert. Mia nodded, but then froze. She had written her idiom down in Spanish. How do you translate this into English? But now that Mrs. Ellert was slowly making her way to her, she started to panic. Why had she written it in Spanish? Immediately, it occurred to Mia that there was a saying in English that meant the same, but what was it? She quickly scribbled a note over her Spanish idiom and slipped it to Sammy, who gave it to Jodie. Mia felt that Jodie would come through, help her out. But as soon as Jodie read the request, she actually laughed, and making sure that everyone could hear, said, "How would I know? I can barely speak Spanish, let alone read it!"

Mia wanted to die. What was she thinking? Jodie came from one of those old Mexican-American families who prided themselves on how little Spanish they knew. It showed how much more "American" they were. It was one of the many ways that some of the families in town distinguished themselves from new immigrants, those who were "less American." *Whatever happened to my orphan immunity?* Mia wondered. Jodie had thrown her under the bus. And she was crushed.

Mia had hit this brick wall again and again. And she was tired of it. Then it struck her. She didn't need them. Not at all. They added nothing to her life. Absolutely nothing. And she had Tere.

So when Jodie passed the note back to her, Mia didn't even bother to look her in the eyes. She didn't care, not anymore. There was no shame in speaking Spanish, and there was no indignity in knowing how to read or write it. Tere was right; these girls were not real friends.

❦

No sooner had Mia gotten her piece of paper back from Jodie, when Mrs. Ellert walked right up to her and gave her a gentle pat on the head. Mia handed her the idiom. Smiling, Mrs. Ellert announced, "Now, this is something. Mia, do you mind if I read this out loud?" Mia nervously nodded but feared the absolute worst. She braced herself for major humiliation, when all of a sudden, she heard Mrs. Ellert read the phrase in a very clear, crisp, and concise Spanish.

"*Me quede con el Jesus en la boca.* Now, the literal translation of this idiom is 'I was left with Jesus in the mouth.' But that is not what Mia means. Is it? The closest idiom in the English language is, 'With one's heart in one's mouth.' Now, this saying does not mean that your heart is in your mouth. Rather, it means that the person using it is worried, anxious, or very fearful of something. Great job, Mia."

Mia felt an immense sense of relief, but she was conflicted too. She liked pleasing Mrs. Ellert, but she didn't want anyone to think that she was weird, or worse yet, a show-off. Mauricio, who always blurted out what he was thinking, said, "I've heard that one before. My mother is always saying stuff like that." Mauricio, being biracial, half-white, half-Mexican, was exempt from the classroom's collective judgment. If he spoke Spanish or spoke of his Mexican side, it made him look good, scored him cool points. Mia secretly wondered if Mauricio was just trying to help her out.

⚓

The rest of the class period was quiet, as students worked silently and independently, but Mia couldn't help but think of her mother. Mia had heard this idiom more than once, from both her mother and grandmother.

When Candy was only a year and a half old, Cristina had taken her outside. The heat in South Texas was, as usual, dreadful, and every day she would give the baby a refreshing bath in the kiddy pool that they kept on the back porch. Cristina had filled the kiddy pool up to the hard, plastic rim and sat Candy down in the water. When the phone rang, she figured that she could answer it and keep an eye on the baby since the old wall phone hung right by the back door. The kiddy pool was just a couple of feet from the front door, so she picked up the phone and poked her head over the doorsill, thinking that she could answer the phone and still keep an eye on the baby.

Cristina couldn't remember who she was talking with or what the conversation was even about, but she must have lost track of time and did not know how long she had been talking—thirty seconds, a minute?—when she turned around and discovered Candy lying face up in the water, flopping around like a fish. She remembered dropping the phone and screaming. The sight of her little girl in that position shocked her so much that all she remembers was saying, "Jesus." Fortunately, Candy was fine, but Cristina never got over the incident. And she was always talking about it, as if talking about it would make the whole ordeal disappear.

For days all that Cristina could think about was "what if?" What if Candy had drowned because of her carelessness? What if she had caused her child permanent brain damage? Every time Cristina left Mia in charge of Candy, she repeated the infamous incident. She always ended the story with the phrase, *"Me quede con el Jesus en la boca."*

ক

That night, Mia asked *Abuelo* Mateo if he could drive her to a friend's house or the public library, since they didn't have any Internet, when Beatriz suggested that they visit Manuel and Alicia.

"No, *Wela*, please," Mia had pleaded.

"Ay, don't tell me that you're embarrassed. Alicia is very smart, she is going to college, and they have the Internet box."

"Wela, it's not a box."

"Whatever it is, a cable, they have it."

ক

After dinner that night, Beatriz and her two granddaughters walked into the darkness outside, guided by the flickering street lamps, past the *tiendita*, and Calle Caballo. They came upon a large empty lot with a foundation and building materials all around it and towards the back a small Winnebago. It wasn't exactly a mobile home, but a smaller affair, one of those traveling trailers that had been converted into someone's home. Beatriz knocked on the door and Alicia answered.

"*Pasen, pasen. . .*"

"*Gracias,* Alicia."

Candy had been there before, so she scrambled up to the loft where two little girls closer to her age were watching *The Lion King* on a small DVD player. Alicia pointed to a small little table and continued talking to them while simultaneously turning hot tortillas and stirring something really delicious in a shiny red frying pan.

"This is your house, Beatriz. I am so glad that we can help."

Mia couldn't believe that a family of four could live in such tight quarters. And where did they even have space for a computer? Every square inch of the trailer was home to an object that normally would have been stashed in a closet. Clean laundry was neatly folded on top of a large crockpot in the corner. The ironing board had been folded and it was leaning against a battered blue suitcase that was bulging with books. The trailer was quite orderly and tidy.

It was obvious that the little loft was both bed and bedroom for the two little girls. And just when Mia was wondering where the parents slept, Alicia spoke, as if reading her mind. "It's a small space, isn't it? Come, follow me, I'll get you all set up," she said as she gestured for Mia to follow her.

"It's not too small," lied Mia, embarrassed that she had probably been caught gawking.

"It's just temporary. We're building our house, slowly but surely. Why pay apartment rent when we can live here, right?"

Mia felt bad that Alicia, a grown woman, had felt that she had to explain herself, and was very relieved when Alicia led her to the small bedroom off the tiny space that was both kitchen and living area. She pointed to the laptop sitting in the middle of the bed. It was a shiny MacBook, not too shabby.

"We don't have a printer or anything, but the Internet is very reliable."

"Thank you."

"I went to college and dropped out. Now, I'm back and taking classes online. Manuel got me the laptop so I could finish my associate's."

Mia didn't know what an associate's was, but she was relieved when Alicia went back to the kitchen—only a foot away—and resumed her conversation with *Abuela*. The bedroom was very cozy. There was a real door that divided the bedroom from a tiny bathroom with a built-in shower stall. Mia sat at the edge of the neatly made bed and started searching for idioms.

★

When it was time to go, Candy had to be coaxed out of the loft. She wanted to stay. Alicia rolled up a tortilla with rice and beans and offered it to Candy while kissing *Abuela* on the cheek and saying goodbye. The trio walked out into the warm night, and Mia thought about how much richer her grandparents seemed than this couple. Then again, she would also trade places with those two little girls, who still had their parents. Alicia had asked her to come back anytime to use the Internet, and Mia offered to help the girls with their homework. Later she felt ashamed, because Alicia spoke excellent English and was in college. She was perfectly able to help out her own children. Had she offended her?

The next day, during lunch, Mia was talking about Alicia and the trailer. Her intention had never been to make fun of them at all. That's what Jodie did.

"How can you go to the bathroom so close to your kitchen, eww!"

"Well, maybe that way she can multitask, like cook from the toilet," someone else had chimed in.

Their words stung. Mia felt like she was betraying Alicia and her family. She didn't know how to make it stop.

"So, was there at least a door to the parents' bedroom? I mean, could the kids actually see the parents, you know?" The girls had all yelled "yuck" in unison and pretended to be horrified. Mia finished swallowing a bit of her burrito and cleared some things up. "No, the bedroom is an actual room. The kids can't see anything, but they have a view of the kitchen and the dining room."

"What is wrong with people, dude, if you can't afford a house, why have kids, right?" Ariana had remarked.

"Yeah, so irresponsible."

Then Tere, who had been listening and had had enough, picked up her tray and said, as she walked away, "You know, a lot of people live in trailers. Don't act like you don't know. You probably have a relative living in one." When Tere was out of earshot, Ariana spoke up.

"What's with her?"

"She probably lives in a trailer herself," said Jodie, and everyone laughed. Mia watched Tere walk away and wanted desperately to join her, but she felt glued to her seat. She sat there wishing that Tere's bravery would rub off on her.

The next day, Tere did not sit with the group, and Mia found her sitting two tables down from theirs.

"Hey, why are you sitting all the way over here?"

"You know why, Mia. Doesn't it make you feel uncomfortable that they make fun of poor people? That's your neighborhood."

"No, that's my grandparents' neighborhood, when my Aunt Isa—"

"Yes, when your Aunt Isa, the lawyer, comes to save you from your awful neighborhood, she will buy a big house, drive a fancy car, and then what?"

"Tere, what's wrong with you? I don't feel that way at all."

"My mother still lives in a trailer park."

"So what? You hate your mother."

"So, she is still my mother. Mia, you are so clueless. No, wait, hold that, you are not clueless, you're shallow and superficial. Can't you see that they just tolerate you? Out of pity? And you worship them like goddesses. You are so smart, but so dumb too. The only person that you ever think about is yourself. It's all about you. And now, you think that you are better than everybody. You bitch about your little sister, your poor grandparents—you're a whiny, spoiled brat."

Mia watched Tere pile her trash on her tray. She didn't know what to feel. Should she feel relief? The girls didn't like her too much anyway. But out of all of them, Tere had become someone Mia could rely on. Really trust. Mia felt the little world that she had finally built for herself slowly begin to crumble.

❧

That afternoon, when Tere didn't wait with her for the bus, Mia felt so alone. Mia saw that Tere didn't come out of the school building until her bus had pulled up. She was avoiding her, and as Mia watched her friend—former friend—board the bus, she felt like the worst person in the world.

◆

Standing there, Mia didn't feel like going to her grandparents' house. She wanted to go to her real home. She wanted to crawl inside her house and stay there forever. Maybe she could close her eyes and pretend that her parents were in another room, that everything was like it had been before. Or maybe she would just take a quick look around and then ask their old neighbor Joanna for a ride back home. She had plenty of time. The bus route to *Abuela*'s took forever anyway. Bus 54 was one of the last buses and her *colonia* was one of the last stops. She could have Joanna drop her off at the *tiendita*. No one would ever know. It was perfect. All she wanted to do was to walk around her old house.

Mia spotted the kids who lived in her old neighborhood and joined the line, waiting for the doors to open. As soon as she marched in, she realized there was no going back. She was going home, and it was both scary and exciting. Secretly thrilling. Not thinking, she sat in the first seat that seemed available. She hadn't even settled in before she felt someone hovering over her.

"That's my seat," said a tall girl with too much makeup.

"Sorry," Mia answered, as she stood to move.

"Forget it, just don't sit there again."

The old Mia would have been terrified. She hated confrontations and angering anyone, especially an older student. Any other day, she would have gone home and felt terrible about what happened. Today, it was clear that she had just sat in someone else's seat. She had bigger concerns.

Now, as her bus did its routine stops along her old neighborhood, she was comforted by the familiar homes and manicured lawns. Nothing had changed.

The therapist had asked Mia if there was anything she could

think of that would help her with what she kept referring to as "closure," as if anyone could ever close the door on their parents' death. But now Mia thought that maybe saying goodbye to her old home would help. She felt she had never said goodbye to her old house. When she had seen her parents lying in their coffins, they didn't seem real. And as soon as she started bawling her eyes out, *Tía* Isa had pulled her away, thinking that maybe she should never have been there in the first place. Right now all she wanted was to be home. Feel their presence, feel blanketed by everything that had once been hers, theirs.

She knew that the house was going to be sold and that anything left inside would be removed and put into storage. She had heard her grandparents talk to Isa on the phone about the house. Before she started school, the only thing Mia knew was that they still had phone service, because she called her house several times before the phone was eventually disconnected. Occasionally, Mia would find comfort in hearing her mother's voice on the answering machine, and in the background she could hear her father asking, "What's for dinner, honey?"

Her mother had meant to rerecord the message, but never did.

"Hi. You have reached the Alvarez residence. We can't take your call right now, but if you leave a message, we will get back to you as soon as we can—Honey, what's for dinner?"

Mia had left many messages. She left messages even when the machine was full. They always made her feel better, connected. They were very short at first because Mia always choked up. That terrible knot would just take residence in her throat and then she would have to hang up.

"Mom, Daddy . . . it's me . . . Mia . . ."

Then, she gradually left others.

"Hi, Mom, hi, Dad. I miss you. We miss you." Choke.

"Mom, Dad . . . pick up . . . please pick up."

Calling was always torture for Mia, but she couldn't help it. Somehow, listening to her parents made her feel, for a moment, as if a small part of them were still in this world with her. It's as if they were right there. The day the phone had been disconnected, Mia had cried the same way she'd cried on the day of the funeral. She had gone back to the bedroom, turned her radio on high, and cried into her pillow.

ᴗ⋆

When Mia stepped off the bus, she was shocked at how terrible the yard looked. No one had mowed it in weeks. There were weeds everywhere, and the wind had blown trash from all corners of the neighborhood into their driveway. The grass was tall and overgrown. Mia was glad her father wasn't around to see the mess. The water must have been turned off, because judging from the dry patches of grass, the sprinklers had stopped coming on in the evening.

Mia opened the mailbox and noticed that it was full of grocery store flyers and other junk mail. She went toward the side yard, opened the latch on the wooden gate, and found herself in her old back yard. She dropped her backpack on the dry grass and looked around for something to stand on.

She dragged Candy's old plastic picnic table against the wall that led to her parents' master bedroom bath. Sure enough, the small window was unlocked. Her parents never locked it, and they had made her go in through the window more than once when someone had forgotten the keys. As soon as she was in, Mia could smell her father's aftershave, or so she imagined. She was home.

Soon, Mia was walking around the house, caressing picture frames and looking for reminders of her old life. Her mother's favorite pictures still hung on the walls, and her dad's La-Z-Boy was still in the same place. Wouldn't the bank have made them take their stuff out? Some days Mia still couldn't believe that her parents were gone. At school, she would often fantasize about her mother being home, rearranging the living room furniture or fixing her and Candy a healthy fruit salad. All this time at her grandparents' house, she would pretend that her parents were still walking around the house, like nothing had ever happened.

But she couldn't pretend anymore. There was already a fine layer of dust on the surfaces that her mother had so diligently polished. Pieces of furniture were crowded together next to boxes half-filled with packing popcorn. Who was doing the packing? It wasn't *Tía* Isa or her grandparents. And where was it all going? What was going to happen to her parents' things? Would she never see another one of her mother's garments or hold one of her father's tools?

In her parents' bedroom, she could tell that someone had already started to pack clothes away. There were large boxes half-filled with clothes and knickknacks, but the bed had remained untouched. She fell right on top of it and tried to smell her parents, but she couldn't. The only scent she was picking up was her grandmother's, which was a mix of white bread and perfumed talcum powder. She lay there, watching the particles of dust float above her.

She pulled the covers over her head, wanting to go to sleep and never wake up. She wanted to make her parents reappear, to remember her mother's last touch. All she had to do was rub the spot on her boney left knee, where her mother had squeezed her last, to feel better. On her parents' bed, Mia felt like her heart was ripping apart. Nothing mattered at her house, nothing. Not Tere, not Jodie and the girls, not her teachers, not her terrible new bedroom, nothing. Not even her baby sister.

Sleep overcame her, but she didn't dream. She had fallen asleep taking a mental inventory: the living room, the basket of clothes on top of the washer, and her old toothbrush still encrusted with toothpaste. These were all connections to her past life, and now they would soon be all gone.

\~ ⚓

Mia curled up like their old cat and fell asleep, not waking until she was startled by the sound of a truck pulling up in the driveway. She hid in the closet, shaking. Who had just walked into her house and what were they doing there?

chapter 37—Beatriz

When Mia didn't get off her bus that afternoon, Beatriz didn't worry too much. The week before, she had stayed at school to work on a project, and another parent had given her a ride home. Had she told her this week and had she forgotten? Mateo had urged her not to worry. Kids were always staying after school for things. Maybe she was coming home on the late bus.

"Let's give it a couple of hours more," he had suggested. After two interminable hours, Beatriz asked Mateo to go out and drive around the neighborhood, while she ran over to Alicia's house and asked her to call the school. No one at school knew anything, and Beatriz had been encouraged to call all of Mia's friends.

"*Dios*," Beatriz told Dora, "I don't even know who her friends are. How would I know?"

"Ask the little one?"

"Candy might know a name or two, but she wouldn't know any phone numbers; she doesn't even know her own."

"Somebody on her bus must know. Who is in her grade? Think."

Beatriz left Dora at the house, in case Mia showed up, then

she dropped Candy off with their most trusted neighbors, Alma and Corita. Alma was a single mother and Corita was her young teenager daughter with special needs. Corita had developed a special friendship with Candy ever since the girls had moved in. Beatriz walked back to Alicia's house. Alicia would canvas the neighborhood with her; Alicia knew everyone.

"Let's ask Lupito, the Suarez's older kid," said Alicia.

"The skinny kid one with buckets of hair gel on his head?" asked Beatriz.

"Yup, that one. He is probably in Mia's grade."

When Beatriz asked him about her granddaughter, Lupito didn't even know who they were talking about.

"Who?"

"*La seria*," his mother reminded him. "The shy one," she repeated as she stared at her son, hoping that he had the answers.

"Oh, the new girl?"

"*Si*, the new girl. Was she on the bus today?"

"I don't know."

"What do you mean, you don't know?"

"I don't. Ask San Juanita, she might know."

Alicia led Beatriz out of the Suarez home and together they drove down to the light green house where the boy had said San Juanita lived. When they knocked on the heavy screen door, both the television and the radio were so loud that they didn't think anyone would hear them. Emboldened by her desperation, Beatriz pushed open the door and walked right into the living room. A small boy was lying on the couch, mesmerized by his handheld video game. Seeing the large, strange woman, he barely flinched and just screamed out for his mom. "*Ama*! Ma! Someone's looking for you! Ma! Ma!"

A petite woman with fine brown hair walked out of one of the bedrooms, holding a broom. "*Si*?" she asked. After Alicia and Beatriz explained, the woman summoned her oldest, San

Juanita, but San Juanita didn't know anything either. All she could tell them was that Mia didn't hang out with anyone who rode the bus, and that she couldn't remember if she had seen her today.

⁓

Back home, Alma was desperately trying to console Candy. Beatriz had begged her not to tell her anything, but Corita had overheard Alma and Beatriz talking and repeated what had happened to the five-year-old. Corita, genuinely distraught and sad, told Candy that she would be more than happy to be her new older sister, now that her sister had been kidnapped by a stranger.

By the time Beatriz had finished talking to Alma and was ready to take Candy home, her little granddaughter was inconsolable. She tried to explain to the child that no one had been kidnapped, but Candy could not be consoled. Alma apologized for her daughter, but Beatriz began interrogating Corita.

"*Quien Corita*? Who? What stranger?" asked Beatriz.

"*El viejo!*" said Corita, with self-importance.

"*Que viejo?*"

"The guy! The mean man who takes kids away," answered Corita, matter-of-factly.

Alma kept apologizing and reassuring Beatriz that Corita didn't know what she was talking about. The poor child had been threatened all her life by stories of the *viejo* who took disobedient children, so she had no other explanation for Mia's disappearance but the *viejo*. In her imagination, the *viejo* had finally materialized and taken someone away.

Embarrassed, Alma told her that Corita didn't mean anything. But Candy had heard Corita and immediately dissolved into a river of tears.

⁓

Another hour had passed and Mateo jumped into his truck and went back to the school. He had already been there once, but felt maybe he would get lucky the second time around.

◡◣

Shaken and unable to imagine a life without her granddaughter, Beatriz picked up the phone to call Isa. She had waited long enough and it was time to escalate the search. Up to now, she had been optimistic, waiting to see some car pull up in front of the driveway, letting Mia off. It was almost eight and already dark outside when Beatriz dialed Isa's number and took a deep breath.

When the phone rang for the third time, Beatriz was debating whether or not to leave a message, when she heard a vehicle pull up. She dropped the phone on the floor and rushed outside, praying it was some parent dropping Mia off. When she noticed that it was just Mateo, her heart sunk, until she heard the other door opening. It was Mia and her backpack. Mia was back. Safe and sound. Candy ran up to her and hugged her sister.

"*Mija, hija de me vida?* Where were you?"

"*Estaba en su casa,*" said Mateo as he put his large flashlight back into the truck's toolbox.

"*Que?*" asked Beatriz, confused.

"I'm sorry, *Wela*. I took the bus that goes into my old neighborhood, and I didn't mean to stay. I fell asleep on my parents' bed, and the next thing I knew, *Welo* was in the house calling my name."

Beatriz was so happy she didn't care what the child's excuse was; she could have been smoking marijuana with the neighborhood *vagos*, as long as she was home.

Other than the birth of her own children, and then the arrival of her grandchildren, this was one of the happiest moments of Beatriz's life. Her mind had gone off to the worst possible places, and now that she was a hundred percent sure that her granddaughter wasn't lying in a ditch, she made a *promesa*. Right there, holding Mia, she promised *la Virgen Maria* to get rid of all of her material possessions—well, almost all of them. She was going to take the advice that Cristina had given her before she died; she was going to purge both the house and the yard of every item she hadn't used in years, unless it was something of nostalgic importance. She had begged God and *la Virgen Maria* to bring Mia back, and they had. She may not have been the most religious person, but a *promesa* was a *promesa*. She would let go.

chapter 38–Isa

Seattle, Washington, 2016

The day after Mia returned safely, Isa woke up in her plain, vanilla-colored hotel room feeling tired and lonely. She had, for the first time since the funeral, seen Cristina in a dream. Desperately, Isa tried to cling to the vision, to the feeling that she had been experiencing less than thirty seconds ago. She didn't want that connection to go away. She wanted to fall lazily back to sleep and keep dreaming of her little sister. She wanted to tell her how much she loved and missed her. She wanted to beg for forgiveness.

Cristina in the dream was ten, not the adult sister with whom Isa had had a troubled and distant relationship. Isa had been dreaming of her childhood with Cristina. They were young, excited about some random discovery in the backyard. Isa felt sapped of all of her strength, not well rested. Wearily she dragged herself to the bathroom. The face in the mirror looked haggard, her eyes rimmed with shadows. She had been on frenzied autopilot, going down a steady list of to-dos, but now, all she felt was depleted. Bereft of energy. She was missing Evie so much right now.

Cristina was gone, and the finality of her life was only now hitting her. The bond she'd had with Cristina had lain dormant when she was stubborn, when she refused to budge. She had thought she had all the time in the world to disrupt both Cristina and Mia, to storm right into their lives and shock them with the truth. Her sadness came from remembering, recalling all their happy times in the past, their shared childhood memories. How they had laid their new school clothes out on their twin beds the day before the first day of school. How they had organized and reorganized their Halloween candy and had drawn up Christmas lists together on fresh sheets of loose-leaf paper.

Isa now cried for Cristina, for Leo, for Candy, for Mia. Isa cried for herself. And she cried for Evie. She would never feel that bond with her sister again, never be able to give or receive support from her sister.

Isa tried to think of the last time she had spoken to her baby sister. It was a couple of hours before her death. Cristina had walked into their parents' house with big rollers in her hair and wearing one of Leo's button-down shirts, for easy dressing later. Cristina had taken care of the majority of the details for the party, and all Isa had to do was to show up three days before to help out.

Over the years, Isa and Cristina had practically perfected the delicate balance required of them—by their parents, relatives, even by each other—to appear like normal siblings, people who remained emotionally connected. They had agreed that some events were non-negotiable; some events you went to, no matter where you were on the mood spectrum. Holidays, birthdays, reunions, and other milestones were to be respected—if only to maintain a façade that made everybody's lives easier. They carried on with the regular norms of the socialization process. Cristina was always complimenting some aspect of Isa's wardrobe, her custom-made jackets or Italian leather pumps that usually matched her purse. As part and parcel of her professional ambitions, Isa had quickly discovered that she had to attend to a myriad of beautification routines, the kind that were visible to people who didn't even know her.

People who hadn't seen Isa since her Rio Chico days were always surprised at her transformation. She had become one of the women of whom others were jealous, tall and lean, with naturally high cheekbones and a full head of thick hair. Evie had always joked that age had turned Isa into a late-in-life narcissist. As part of her professional polish, Isa had perfected a beauty routine over the years that required hundreds of dollars spent on hair and skin care. There was nothing like having a stylist who knew the perfect haircut for you and who could recommend the perfect foundation and other makeup essentials.

While Cristina had remained a natural and classic beauty, Isa had grown into an attractive woman. She would never receive the compliments Cristina did, but acquaintances had no qualms about making unsolicited and awkward comments such as, "You weren't much to look at when you were younger, but now look at you." These remarks were always followed by the requisite, "So, why aren't you married yet?"

The day before the anniversary party, Isa had taken everyone out to dinner. And over coffee and dessert, Cristina had said something about how Mia was going to need Isa's beauty advice soon. Isa knew it was an olive branch, but like all efforts at peace offerings, the stubborn resentment in Isa's heart made her pull away. Isa had answered politely, but at the same time there was something withheld and unfinished in her response, as if she were teasing Cristina and saying, "Maybe, it depends."

⚓

That was then and this was now.

It was time to go home. Looking around her hotel room, Isa suddenly could care less about her job, the house, or anything that had seemed the least bit pressing yesterday. She knew what she had to do.

And Isa was going to start by visiting Cristina and Leo's graves, to ask for their blessing, and then to tell her parents and Mia.

Through cathartic fits of sobbing and a river of tears, Isa stuffed clothing in her suitcases. She would notify work via e-mail. She would live off her savings in Rio Chico until she figured things out. The only thing that mattered was that she was going home because something was becoming very clear to her: problems, whatever their source, will not disappear; they will just follow you wherever you go. She was moving to Rio Chico, and so was Evie.

chapter 39–Mia

Rio Chico, Texas, 2016

Mia felt the weight of her grandmother's body on her bed. Startled, she sat up. She had slept in, like she did every Saturday, but Beatriz was shoving a phone in her face.

"*Habla con tu Tía Isa.*"

"What?" said Mia groggily, as she sat up and watched Beatriz walk out of the room and shut the door behind her.

"Mia?"

"*Tía* Isa?"

"Sweetie? Are you okay? What happened? What's wrong?"

"*Tía* Isa, nothing is wrong. Everything is okay."

"You were not where you were supposed to be. Now, you're not in trouble, I just want you to talk to me about it. What happened?"

"I just took a bus home. I needed to see our house; everyone has kept us away from it."

"Oh, Mia, I feel so bad. *Ama* didn't think that it was a good idea for you to go back. She thought that it was just too hard for you."

"You guys could have asked."

"You should have asked us, too, sweetie."

"*Tía* Isa, no one talks about the accident. We don't talk about it because we're afraid to upset the *welos*."

"Oh, Mia," said Isa, "it's not supposed to be like this."

"*Tía* Isa, I don't know what to do."

"Well, before you say another word, I want you to know something that even *Ama* or *Apa* don't know—yet. I'm coming home, Mia. I'm done with Seattle. I'm moving to Rio Chico. I do need to warn you, we will be living with your grandparents for a while, while I figure out where to work. Later we'll all look for a new home."

"Really?" asked Mia, disbelievingly.

"Really."

"But *Tía*, I didn't mean to cause all of this—"

"Trust me, you didn't. I made this decision on my own, and I have made the right decision."

"Okay."

"Will you do me a favor? I just made an appointment for you and Candy to see the therapist today. Mom and Dad are driving you."

"Oh, no, please, I hate that lady."

"Mia, please, please. Just hear her out. I plan to resign first thing Monday morning, pack some essential belongings, and drive home."

"You're going to drive? By yourself? All the way? What about your house?"

"Yes, Mia, just for you and your sister. Meanwhile, just talk to Dr. Calderon. Let's just see what she has to say, okay?"

"Okay."

⌣✦

Dr. Calderon was down the hall making them both a cup of tea. Meanwhile, Mia stared blankly out the large picture window that overlooked the street. Her gaze was fixed on a tall pecan tree, a tree unusually big for South Texas. She was wondering what life would be like if South Texas were full of tall, lush trees. She was in the therapist's office against her own will. She didn't need therapy. She would be just fine if she could sleep all day. A knock and the click of the doorknob interrupted her thoughts, and she repositioned herself on the large couch. She was ready for the doctor's stupid questions. Therapy was just like she had seen on TV: senseless and predictable.

"So," uttered the soft-spoken Dr. Calderon, "where were we?"

"I don't remember."

"Mia, I know that you would rather not be here, but it really does help to talk about things."

"My parents are dead. Talking about it won't bring them back."

"Why did you run away?"

"I didn't run away. I already told you that. No one was supposed to find out. I was going to get a ride home, but I fell asleep and then everyone made a big deal about it. I said I was sorry."

"What were you doing at home?"

"Seriously?"

"What did you hope to find?"

"I just wanted to go home, to see my old home again. Is that a crime?"

"Tell me about your new home. What's it like?"

"It's okay. My *abuela* and my *tía* are . . . well, they are really there for us."

Sitting crossed-legged, tugging at the hem of her jeans, Mia felt a jolt of anticipation. *Tía* Isa was coming home. And she couldn't wait.

chapter 40–Beatriz

Rio Chico, Texas, 2016

Had she heard her daughter correctly? Isa was coming home? For good? It was so unexpected. Beatriz thought that it would take months, maybe even a year, for Isa to get her affairs in order. Equal parts excited and nervous, Beatriz asked Mateo if they should discourage her.

"*Porque*? She's a grown woman, and she was coming home anyway."

"But she's quitting. Just like that, her *trabajo*! Of so many years."

"Mujer, she has savings. She's the only one in the family who has it together."

"But where will she work?"

"Beatriz, listen to yourself. This is Rio Chico, not the moon. Isa is a lawyer, she can work anywhere she wants."

"I just can't picture her here. I worry that she is doing this just to help us, and that she will not be happy. No one will want to marry her if she has someone else's children."

"You know, woman, sometimes you just aren't very observant. Have you not noticed the way that Isa's eyes light up when she is with the girls? Maybe it wasn't in her life's plans to have her own children. Maybe the husband will come later, but if there is one thing I know, maybe even two, is that she wants to take care of the girls, and she wants to do it sooner than later. And any man who wouldn't want my daughter and my two grandchildren is no man at all."

"So, I shouldn't be worried?"

"Absolutely not. You should be happy. What you need to do is start making some room for her."

Beatriz stood and straightened out her neck. She pursed her lips together and looked like she was deep in thought.

"What are you thinking about, woman?"

"Well, it's about the *promesa*. What are you doing today?"

"Well, if you're going to ask what I think you're going to ask, I guess I'll be hauling junk off to the landfill."

Beatriz smiled and almost hugged her husband. They had spoken about the *promesa*. He had not been too happy when she'd told him, but a *promesa* was a *promesa*. It was time for all of the junk to go.

~

Over the years, the back room had turned into a dumping ground for all things unwanted or, in Isa's own words, "appliance limbo." Today that limbo was being picked apart and hauled away. Gone was Cristina's old washing machine, the clothes dryer that had been passed on to Mateo from a co-worker, and the dishwashing machine missing all its knobs that had been a roadside find that Mateo had promised to revitalize someday. Onto the pickup truck went an old, broken-down freezer that had been filled with crushed aluminum cans, a dozen wooden pallets, iron bed frames with missing wheels, milk crates, a rickety, faux-brass bed, two mildewed mattresses, and countless other items too innumerable to mention. The next day, Mateo recruited two of his nephews and they had three trucks hauling stuff off to the *basurero*. All afternoon, they hoisted scraps of metal, weathered appliances, and years of accumulated detritus onto the trucks and away to the county dumpster.

At four in the afternoon, every surface still looked like it was covered with something. Neighbors had volunteered and people were piling bags and bags of stuff into pickups, but as soon as one mound of debris was taken care of, they had to start attacking what was inside the closets, under the beds, in the cupboards, and along the edges of the long, dimly lit hallway. By six o'clock, everything heavy had been hauled away, but the inside of Beatriz and Mateo's house looked like it had been hit by a tornado and litter from all fifty states had ended up in one house.

"We will continue tomorrow," Beatriz announced.

"When does *Tía* Isa get here, *Wela*?" asked Candy.

"Well honey, it's only Saturday. Your *Tía* Isa might be here by Tuesday."

"Is that when I'm at school day or home day?"

"You will be at school, honey, but we have a lot of work to do."

For the rest of the day, Beatriz, feeling manically electrified and totally driven by adrenaline, directed Candy, Dora, and Mia to fill bags and bags of clothing that hadn't been used in years. She gave Candy instructions to go around putting all wedding, *quinceñera*, baptism, and baby shower memorabilia into a trash bag. Candy ripped old invites from the corners of vanity mirrors, and tossed chipped porcelain baby bottles from baby showers in the early nineties and plastic flower arrangements from two-decades-old wedding table arrangements. Dora was helping Beatriz go through all of the closets and drawers.

"*Comadre*, only what you fit into, the rest, get rid of it!"

"But I can't throw it."

"Don't throw it, give it to Perla, she'll sell it at the *pulga*, but don't keep it."

"What about these?" said Beatriz as she held up some old sheets.

"Give them to Perla."

Mia had been assigned the kitchen, where she had been ordered to throw away everything that had so much as a rust stain and any old margarine tubs that were doubling as Tupperware. There were, most importantly, four junk drawers that Mia was dying to get ahold of. She knew that if she didn't get to them before her *abuela* or Candy did, most of the items would remain in the "maybe keep" pile. There were too many nooks and crannies where, despite her grandmother's "spring cleanings," the house remained full of objects undesignated, untouched, and undiscovered. If she got to them first and made the stuff disappear, Beatriz wouldn't feel compelled to save it.

⚜

On the last evening of the great home overhaul, Dora invited the whole family over to her house for dinner. They feasted on tacos, rice, beans, and potato salad. Beatriz gave her husband three Motrin tablets before going to bed, and she urged the girls to go to sleep early. No sooner had they bathed and were propped up watching television in their room, their weary bodies succumbed to sleep.

Beatriz walked into their bedroom, looked at the girls, their pillows damp from their wet hair, and turned off the television. After Mateo went to sleep, she grabbed her trusty broom and began to sweep every square inch of her home, with the exception of the two bedrooms where people were sleeping. By one o'clock in the morning, she had filled fifteen tall kitchen bags, half with trash and half going to Perla's *pulga* enterprise. The more surfaces she cleared, the better she felt. She no longer felt attached to any of the stuff that had once dotted the landscape of her humble home. When she was ready to shower and crawl into her bed, she was amazed at how clean all the surfaces now looked. There was room on the breakfast bar, the window sills, and even her dressers.

Her home actually resembled the tidy little house she had once moved into. She looked at the walls and realized they hadn't been painted since the girls were in high school. How many times had Cristina encouraged her to repaint and even offered to help her? In the shower that night, Beatriz wept for her daughter and Leo, the life that they left behind.

She knew that they would be pleased with the changes. It was time for a new chapter to be written and the slate was clean, again.

chapter 41–Isa

Seattle, Washington, 2016

On Saturday, after waiting for two hours on the porch for Evie, Isa realized Evie wasn't coming home. She was about to leave when the nosy neighbor's car pulled in and she rushed up to Isa. "I have something for you, wait, wait here."

The woman ran inside and came out with a letter, then smiled and went back inside. Evie had written about how much she still loved her, but how important it had been for her to get away. She needed Isa to know what life without her would feel like. Evie had flown down to South Carolina to spend a couple of weeks with a sister whom she hadn't spoken to in years. Isa smiled and shed tears of gratitude after reading the last line. Evie had signed the note: "I still love you. Take your time; I'll be back in two weeks. We can talk then."

In her heart, Isa was going to do everything that needed to be done to make things right, starting with going home and telling the truth. The rest would all follow.

❦

When Isa had announced she would be leaving the firm, not one of her colleagues was shocked. Attrition at the company was high, and the people with whom she had really bonded had already moved on. Despite this, Isa smiled, not at all surprised, but feeling lighter with every move she was making. On the drive south, Isa felt like everything was possible. She would drive until she couldn't keep her eyes open and then check into a motel for a good five hours.

The fresh air felt good, so whenever she could, Isa drove with the windows down. She entertained her mind with the ever-changing landscapes around her—at least what she could see from the lonely interstate highways. Sometimes it was miles of nothing but the occasional farmhouse or the back of new suburban developments. What she liked best was driving past the small towns and getting a glimpse of other people's lives. She drove past houses with lawns so neat they looked like they had been magically grown, but what made her nostalgic were the ones that reminded her of the *colonia*: trampolines with the fabric ripped, old cars with sun-bleached tarps over them, and the random child's bike that had been left on the side of a driveway or out in the middle of the yard.

She wanted desperately to be able to see a future with the girls and with Evie, but she couldn't picture the bustle of a non-traditional household without thinking of what her parents would say or, worse yet, the position she would be putting her parents in. On some level, Isa entertained the idea that her parents would eventually come around. But the idea of her parents having to explain her living arrangement to relatives and neighbors—well, that's where her optimism ended. Whichever way she looked at it, nothing felt complete. If she left Evie, she could keep her parents and life as it was, but she would lose the love of her life. If she kept Evie, she lost her parents, and both her normalcy and theirs.

chapter 42–Mia

Rio Chico, Texas, 2016

During lunch, Mia sat with Tere. If there were any hard feelings on Tere's part she didn't seem to show them, but she secretly smiled when Mia chose to sit with her and not the group. Taking a bite of her sandwich, Mia excitedly talked about her grandparents' home.

"My *Tía* Isa will not recognize the place. The yard feels so big now and the house—we're talking about painting it."

Tere's eyes were bright as she nodded enthusiastically while shoving fries into her mouth. She liked to see Mia taking such an interest in her grandparents' house. Mia bemoaned the fact that she hadn't taken before and after photos.

"Seriously, it's all gone. It's like we live in a new place."

"You really should have taken pictures."

"People in the neighborhood think we're moving or something."

"Maybe you are moving. I mean, your aunt's not going to live there forever, right?"

"Not forever, but when I talked to her, she said we would live there for a while."

"How long is a while?"

"I don't know, until she finds a new job?"

"Mia, what if you guys move, like, to Seattle?"

"No, *Tía* Isa said it would kill my grandparents, but we'll find a nice place someday."

"Dude, do you think that the new house will have a pool?"

"She'd need to find a job first."

Over in the next table, a gaggle of girls burst out laughing, and both Tere and Mia turned toward their old table.

"Do you want to be over there?"

"I don't care."

"Are you sure?"

"I'm sure. I realized, you know, when you were mad at me, that I've just gone through too much to sweat the petty stuff, you know?"

"Yeah, I know what you mean, Mia."

"I mean, I've known those girls my whole life, but you feel like more of a true friend."

"Well, don't feel that you can't talk to them on my account."

"No, seriously, I don't care. I mean, I'll say hi. It's not like I won't ever talk to them, but it's just good to know that I don't need them, you know?"

"Yeah, I know. So? She gets here tomorrow?"

"Yeah, like she'll be here by the time Candy and I get home."

"You know, she's going to be like your new mother. Is that, like, totally weird?"

"Yeah, sort of, but I don't see it that way at all. I see *Tía* Isa like an older sister who will be my great friend."

"That's good."

"I just don't know what she's going to do, you know?"

"Duh, she's going to look for a job."

"I guess."

⚓

The next day, by the time Mia got off the bus that afternoon, her grandparents' porch was full of people. Her grandfather was unloading her *Tía* Isa's suitcases from her car and her grandmother was serving lemonade and *pan dulce* to Isa and a handful of visitors on the front porch. Dora was there, and so were Alma and Corita. *Tía* Isa had been sitting on a chair with Candy on her lap when the bus pulled up. Not truly able to explain why, Mia ran off the bus and into Isa's arms. She didn't even realize until she pulled back, but she was crying. And her crying made *Tía* Isa cry, which led to all of the women on the porch crying. Isa embraced both of the girls and surveyed the new landscape.

"It's unbelievable!"

"All the clutter is gone," announced Dora.

"It looks amazing!"

"Wait until you see the inside," shouted Candy.

"Okay, we're going to leave you guys alone for a while," announced Alma, as she escorted Corita off the porch.

"I better get going too," said Dora, "but I'll be back. Glad you're home, Isa."

Inside, Candy held her Aunt Isa's hand while Mia and Beatriz spoke of the "process." "So much stuff!" Beatriz announced. Isa could not believe she was inside the same home that she had left not two months earlier.

"Guess what we're doing next?" Isa said. "If *Welo* and *Wela* are okay with it? We're painting! What do you think? *Ama*? *Apa*?"

"Sounds good to me. Cristina always wanted us to paint."

At the sound of her daughter's name, Beatriz asked to sit down. Everyone in the room stopped talking and Mia went and sat by her *abuela*. She took Beatriz's hand in hers, leaned against her shoulder, and gently assured her that it was okay. Beatriz cried, and Mia, Isa, and Candy all hugged her and cried with her. Mateo quietly walked out of the room and disappeared, reluctant to lose his own composure in front of the women. Mia knew how hard it was for her grandmother to mention her mother's name. Cristina. And maybe it was Isa's presence, but Mia felt safe and strong. She wiped away the tears on her grandmother's face and said, "They are gone. Mom and Dad. But we have you and you have us. And *Tía* Isa's here."

ــه

After the grand tour of the newly de-cluttered house and settling in, Isa asked the girls to get their homework done, because she was going to go get some groceries that the *abuelos* needed. Candy begged to go to McDonald's and Mia suggested that they all go to Applebee's.

"*Tía* Isa," called Mia as she poked her head out of her room, "can I go with you to pick up the groceries? I don't have that much homework."

"And I don't have homework at all!" chimed in Candy.

"Sure, why not! Let me just change out of these pants."

Isa walked into her old childhood room, which felt, after the purging of years of accumulation, quite cavernous. For now, this would be home. She felt strange, but pleased. It was as if everything were right in the world. And nothing could go wrong. Beatriz walked in, carrying Isa's laptop bag, and after putting it down, she leaned on the doorframe and gazed at her eldest daughter.

"*Ama?*"

"*Sí?*"

"*Tengo muchas cosas que contarte.*"

"*Cuéntame.* Tell me."

Isa grabbed her mother's hand and motioned for her to sit.

"*Dios*, what is it? Should I be worried?"

"Will you still love me, *Ama?*"

"Will I still love you, what kind of question is that?"

"*Ama* . . ."

"*Me tienes en ascuas hija*, what is it?"

"*Ama*, I'm never going to get married . . . to a man."

"*Hija*—"

Before her mother could continue, Isa burst into tears. Beatriz leaned in to hug her daughter and stroked her hair.

"Okay, so you have a *novia*. Having a girlfriend is not the end of the world."

"You're not mad?"

"*Hija*, you are a grown woman, I can't tell you who to be or not to be. Who to love or not."

"Did you already know?"

"Well, Dora suggested it, but I told her that I wouldn't believe it until I heard it from my own daughter."

"What about Dad?"

"What about him?"

Isa hugged Beatriz and felt like a small child again. "*Ama*, there is something else."

Beatriz said, "Well, I don't know what you could possibly tell me that is more dramatic than that."

"Mia is not Cristina and Leo's daughter."

"What? What are you talking about?"

"Cristina did not give birth to Mia—"

Before Isa could say anything else, she heard something. The paper towel dispenser had come crashing down on the kitchen floor. Mia had been right outside the bedroom door. Isa ran out of the house after Mia, who was already halfway down the street, cutting through someone's backyard and heading for the main road.

꩜

Had she heard them right? Was it really true? Who was her mother? Who was her father? So many questions ran through

Mia's mind as she took off running. She thought that she heard *Abuela* and *Tía* Isa calling out for her, but she was not about to stop. She had to get away.

Panting, Mia turned back to see if *Tía* Isa was behind her. She ducked into a neighbor's tool shed, caught her breath, and waited. Isa ran right past her and turned onto the next street, so Mia ran in the opposite direction toward the main road. She didn't want to be seen, so she ran across a couple of open yards. Hot tears streaked down her cheeks, and that darn knot in her throat had come to visit—and stay. Hurting her, reminding her that it was all so hopeless. No wonder she looked nothing like her parents. Where had she come from? Why wasn't she ever told that she was adopted? Who were her real parents?

Up ahead, Mia saw that if she cut through the Martinez's yard, she could walk along the feeder road that led directly into town and towards her old house. Because that was where she wanted to be. She just wanted to run into her parents' room and curl up in their closet. She didn't even care if they were not her real parents. They were the people she wanted to run to right now. Maybe she would have confronted them, had they been alive, but she couldn't now. Her mother, her father. The aching was so fierce that she didn't know what to do with it all. What was her place in this world if the only people who anchored her to it were gone?

Someone had given her up, and her parents had been the only takers. Now she was an orphan for the second time. Why couldn't they have told her sooner? Is this why *Tía* Isa was moving back? Out of breath, running along a busy road, Mia started to slow down and realized that they could be looking for her and driving up behind her, so she decided to get off the side road and hide in the tall grass. There was an old barbed wire fence that separated the feeder road from some fallow farmland. The grass was really high here, and she figured that she could crouch down and see if *Abuelo*'s truck went past. It was starting to get dark, but not dark enough that she wouldn't be spotted jogging along a busy road. She figured that if she hid in the tall grass and let them pass, then she could cross the busy highway and walk or run the five miles to her old house. They wouldn't look there, and if they did, she would hide until they left.

In her haste, as Mia ducked and tried to get through the barbed wire fence, she caught her jeans and upper thigh on the barbs. A sharp piercing pain struck her and she howled. Once on the other side, she saw that the big gash in her jeans was bleeding, and when she tore at the fabric to look at it, she could see the white deep gash in her flesh, with layers of fat and muscle. Her head started to spin and she tried not to pass out.

Meanwhile, Isa had been up and down all the streets of the *colonia*.

Exhausted, her slacks full of dust, Isa headed back home. This was not the way she wanted her daughter to find out that she wasn't who she thought she was.

"You didn't see her?" asked Beatriz and Mateo.

"No, I was hoping she'd be here."

"Did you check the *tiendita*? Maybe she is in there drinking a soda or something."

"*Ama*, what if she left the *colonia*?"

"To go where?"

"Home?"

"No, she wouldn't go back there. Not if she doesn't want to be found."

"*Hija*, take my truck. Maybe she is walking alongside the highway," said Mateo with a sense of urgency.

"Where's Candy?" asked Isa.

"She's inside watching cartoons."

"I'm going to go and look for her. If I don't find her in an hour, I'm calling the police."

⚓

Mia sat up, straightened her leg, and felt her skin pull against her damp jeans. The blood and skin were stuck to the denim, and it hurt every time she moved. The pain was excruciating, but her intention was still to head home. And if her leg got infected and she died, even better. The knot in her throat came back as she realized something awful. Who would miss her if she died? Her parents were dead.

As soon as she stood up, she noticed a section of the fence where the barbed wire had been pushed all the way to the ground. Why hadn't she seen that before? She crossed over it and she started running. Her leg hurt like hell, but she didn't care. She ran for about two minutes before she realized she had to cross the main highway because the sidewalk was ending.

The cars were coming fast in both directions, and she kept turning her head and waiting for a space where she could cross. When the cars started to thin out, and Mia saw her chance, she bolted out onto the road, only noticing at the halfway mark the headlights coming towards her. The car started braking, but Mia was frozen in place. Her mind was telling her to move, but she was immobilized, her leg in searing pain. She did what came naturally and shut her eyes. It was over. It was all over.

chapter 43–Isa

Rio Chico, Texas 2016

Isa drove on the shoulder for what seemed like an eternity. In the distance, she could see a figure walking along the road. Her heart leapt to her throat. Mia! The closer she came to the figure, the sooner it became apparent that it was not Mia; it was not even a child. Then it hit her: had he seen Mia? Oh my God, could he have harmed Mia? Isa pulled onto the shoulder, almost hitting the man.

"Can I get a ride?" the man asked, as if he were going to come over to sit on the passenger seat. Isa jumped out of the truck.

"No, I'm not giving you a ride. Did you see a young girl walking down the street?"

"On the highway?" answered the confused man.

"Yes, what other main road do you see?"

"No, can I can ride in the back? I just need a ride to the nearest—"

But Isa didn't stay to hear the rest. She jumped back into the truck, turned it around, and started speeding towards Cristina and Leo's old house. She was more frightened than ever now; what if that man had seen her? No, she couldn't go there. Then she saw the ambulance and the familiar halting and stopping pattern of rubbernecking drivers trying to get a look at what had happened. Terrified, she raced toward the scene. The state trooper, who was blocking the far right lane, ran toward her screaming, "Are you trying to kill someone? What's your damn problem, lady?"

She ran past the trooper and straight towards the ambulance. She didn't see any wreckage and soon started to feel relief . . . there was no way Mia could have made it this far, she was just being paranoid. Then she saw the gurney with a white sheet pulled all the way to the top.

"Who is that?" Isa screamed, "Who is that?"

"A girl, she ran into the street, but she's—"

"Noooooooo! Mia! Mia!"

ہے

Did I hear someone calling my name? Everyone was gawking at Mia. The car had stopped a good six feet from her, but she was mortified. Her jeans were covered in blood. The lady driver couldn't answer any questions because she was in shock. Mia pulled the sheet off her face and tried to sit up just as one of the paramedics was restraining Isa.

"*Tía* Isa," cried Mia.

"Oh my God! Mia, are you hurt?"

"No, I was just trying to cross the street, but then I stopped."

"What's wrong with your leg?"

Isa turned to the paramedics and said, "I'm riding with her, let's get going."

"*Tía* Isa, I'm sorry. I just heard you tell *Wela* . . ."

But before Mia could say any more, Isa put her hand over Mia's hand, looked into her eyes, and as her own filled with tears, she said, "I'm your mother."

"You?"

"I'm sorry about everything . . . except having you. You are the best thing that has ever happened to me."

Mia was quietly taking it all in as Isa stroked her daughter's hair and slowly started to tell her some of the details. They were small nuggets of the truth.

"My leg hurts so much," Mia said, tears welling in her eyes.

"We'll get you help real soon, you have quite a cut there. We will get you all stitched up, okay?"

Isa had so much explaining to do, and she was fully aware of the challenges that lay ahead, but she was ready to move forward. The hardest part was over.

THE END

epilogue

Things moved pretty quickly after the revelation. There was a lot of crying, and I know that *Tía* Isa spent many nights at the kitchen table with the *abuelos*. I don't know when or how it was decided—because adults don't tell us everything—but during the time that Candy and I finished up the school year, *Tía* Isa and Evie found jobs. Well *Tía* Isa found a job with a local law firm, but Evie, *Tía* Evie—that's what she wants to be called—started her own chiropractic practice out of our new house.

Tía Isa said the new house is for making memories—not that she is suggesting that we forget the past, but that we start our new lives in a new place. We live about an hour east of Rio Chico. *Tía* Isa works late—but she works really hard at trying to be home by six o'clock three nights a week—while *Tía* Evie is home. *Tía* Isa drops us off at school, and *Tía* Evie picks us up in the afternoon.

We have all settled into a new kind of rhythm. I am still seeing Dr. Calderon, as is Candy, and she tells me to see all of these new moves as brand-new chapters in our life.

I love our new house, and I'm getting used to my new school. It's private, so it comes with a whole new set of good and bad. I can't say that I miss Rio Chico, either, only Tere. We drive there every other weekend to see the *abuelos,* and when we go out to eat, we sometimes pick up Tere.

So far we are the only kids with "two moms" at our school, but *Tía* Evie said that will probably change. *Tía* Evie is as nice a person as they come. Sometimes it's really weird, because it seems like the four of us have been together forever.

I'm not going to say that learning all of *Tía* Isa's secrets were easy. I'd always suspected that she was a lesbian; I'd even asked my parents about it. What I never imagined was that she would be my mom—well, my biological mother—because she knows that my real mother and father will never be replaced. Candy might feel differently some day, but I am too old to ever forget them.

My grandparents don't say much about *Tía* Isa and *Tía* Evie's "arrangement." They treat *Tía* Evie kindly, and that's that, but you can tell that they respect her. The only person who asks *Tía* Isa impertinent questions is *Abuela*'s best friend, Dora. Her questions make *Tía* Isa laugh, but she still won't tell me what they are.

I know the biggest question on your mind is, what's it like between *Tía* Isa and me? It's regular, I guess. I mean, now that I know, I can see how much we look alike, but that doesn't mean I am going to start calling her Mommy, or crawling onto her lap like Candy does. She is still my cool aunt. She helps me with my work and drives me over to my friends' houses, the library, and the mall. She is like a really good friend, but one who doesn't let me stay up past 9:30 on a school night or drink diet soda. *Tía* Evie is a total health nut, and Candy and I eat so "cleanly" that I feel a little queasy when we eat honey buns at Grandma's.

Candy sneaks into my room at least three times a week, and I will admit that it's our sister time. I hold her close, and I tell her stories about our parents that she's too young to remember.

I tell her everything I can remember, so she doesn't forget, and so I don't forget. We have matching lockets with a picture of our parents, and every time we see *Abuela*, she asks to see them. We don't know why, because *Abuela* always starts crying when she sees one. And she always says the same thing: "It's okay, *hija*, crying is good, it means that you have not forgotten." And she's right, we have not forgotten.

acknowledgments

Peter Krumbiegel, you are my sun, my moon, and all of my stars. Thank you for accepting my past, supporting my present, and always encouraging my future. Every love story is beautiful, but ours is my favorite.

Xochitl and Annika, so proud to call you my children. In the words of Toni Morrison, "I would love you even if you weren't my own." Even though you have seen me do nothing but hustle, always striving to be better and do better, you, my children, are my true masterpieces.

Olga y Eliazar Garcia, mis padres maravillosos. Este libro no existiría sin su apoyo. Mi pasión por vivir y escribir se los debo a ustedes dos. Gracias desde el fondo de mi corazón.

Miriam, Olga, Eliamar, and Norma, my sisters. George Burns says that happiness is having a large, loving, caring, close-knit family in another city. I agree. That said, your absence only sharpens the love that I have for your beautiful souls, and your presence only strengthens it.

This novel, like all novels, has been through so many drafts and sets of eyes . . . so, in addition to everyone mentioned above (and another hundred that I am logistically not able to list), thank you to my dear friends who have read drafts and accompanied me on this journey: Gabriela Gomez-Carcamo, Mary Schwingen, Ute Kraidy, Jaqueline Maruca, Donna N.,

Sam Allingham, Phyllis Hurwitz, Kelly Sarabyn, Amy Hawes, Mary Sullivan, Tabitha Lord, Kirstin Jacobson, Kate Newton and everyone who has made our wonderful Book Club Babble what it is today. Shout-out to my ladies in WACPAC, Main Line Writer's Group, and The Bridge Writer's Club, as well as the trailblazers and industry game-changers at She Writes (Brooke Warner) and SparkPoint Studio (Samantha Strom). I would also like to thank my publicist, Jay Nachman, my little social media guru, Grace Lewis, and Julie Metz for such amazing cover art—what an honor!

And finally, thank you, adversity.

For knocking me down so many times that sometimes I just didn't know when to stand back up again and for teaching me to, as the saying goes, hustle until I no longer have to introduce myself.

about the author

Maribel Garcia is a Mexican-born, naturalized American citizen who is known for addressing bicultural themes that deal with the immigration experience of Mexicans crossing over to the United States. Her stories concentrate on the ways that race, class, gender, and sexuality intersect with family relationships, loss, forgiveness, and self-discovery. Her writing has been featured in academic publications and on the book review site Book Club Babble, which she cofounded and where she serves as managing editor. The inspiration for *Profound and Perfect Things* comes from her own experiences as both a native of the South Texas Latino/a community and from her anthropological fieldwork studying Mexican American women living on the US/Mexico border. Garcia completed her PhD and MA degrees in the anthropology department at the University of Texas, Austin, and taught in the women's studies department at California State San Marcos University for five years before settling down to write seriously.

SELECTED TITLES
FROM SHE WRITES PRESS

She Writes Press is an independent publishing
company founded to serve women writers everywhere.
Visit us at www.shewritespress.com.

American Family by Catherine Marshall-Smith. $16.95, 978-1631521638. Partners Richard and Michael, recovering alcoholics, struggle to gain custody of their Richard's biological daughter from her grandparents after her mother's death only to discover they—and she—are fundamentalist Christians.

The Rooms Are Filled by Jessica Null Vealitzek. $16.95, 978-1-938314-58-2. The coming-of-age story of two outcasts—a nine-year-old boy who just lost his father, and a closeted young woman—brought together by circumstance.

Appetite by Sheila Grinell. $16.95, 978-1-63152-022-8. When twenty-five-year-old Jenn Adler brings home a guru fiancé from Bangalore, her parents must come to grips with the impending marriage—and its effect on their own relationship.

What is Found, What is Lost by Anne Leigh Parrish. $16.95, 978-1-938314-95-7. After her husband passes away, a series of family crises forces Freddie, a woman raised on religion, to confront long-held questions about her faith.

Again and Again by Ellen Bravo. $16.95, 978-1-63152-939-9. When the man who raped her roommate in college becomes a Senate candidate, women's rights leader Deborah Borenstein must make a choice—one that could determine control of the Senate, the course of a friendship, and the fate of a marriage.

Faint Promise of Rain by Anjali Mitter Duva. $16.95, 978-1-938314-97-1. Adhira, a young girl born to a family of Hindu temple dancers, is raised to be dutiful—but ultimately, as the world around her changes, it is her own bold choice that will determine the fate of her family and of their tradition.